FAKE CROWN

Bellerive Royals Book 1

W Million

Stomill Books

To my brother
For all the wonderful memories of pools, swimming, and swim meets that we made together.

Proofread: Red Adept Editing
Cover Design: Najla Qamber Designs

CONTENTS

Posey

The professor at the front of the lecture hall closes her presentation to take questions from the students around me. Since she's one of the foremost interior designers in the state, I should be paying attention. A career like hers is exactly what I want to have when I return to Bellerive. Instead, I've passed my phone to my newest friend, Monica, so she can add her details to my contacts. It's a long list. My sister, Julia, calls me a friend collector.

"I'll add you to the group chat." Monica tucks her dark hair behind her ear with her thumb and forefinger. "I've never met anyone from Bellerive island before. Is it as pretty in person as the photos make it seem?" She returns my phone to my outstretched palm, and then she turns her computer screen toward me. On her screen is an aerial view of the island, spreading across the ocean, a mix of sand, lush greenery, and visible coral. An answering ache extends across my chest.

Home.

"Prettier," I say. "The best place in the world." Though it annoys me how people always call it Bellerive Island as though the 'island' is necessary for understanding. Like Barbados, Bermuda, the Bahamas, and almost every other island, it's just Bellerive. I drop my phone into my bag, and my pale skin makes me cringe. Living in Michigan has caused me to lose my island glow. But just the sight of the photo on her screen has caused a trickle of homesickness to leak into my consciousness. Some days it amazes me I've made it almost four years in America at Northern University.

"Jensen," Monica muses. "Are you related to Secretary Jensen? It says here she works for the king."

"The former is my mother, and the secretary in training is my sister." I wink. "Yes, I know the Bellerive Brothers." That's the hashtag everyone uses for the three Bellerive royal heirs.

Each one is a thirst trap for a different reason. Brice, the youngest, is my favorite now, but Nick, the middle son, used to be. That was back when he and my sister were best friends. Their friendship ended years ago, and now, he's a man-whore. Julia calls the women who flock to him Crown Bunnies. They exist on campus too—people who want to get close to me to get noticed by them. I've learned to suss out those people quickly.

"I'd totally bang Brice." Monica shuts her computer and shoves it into the bag at her feet.

An acceptable response. Anyone who goes for Alex, the future king, is a gold-digger and cannot be trusted. While Alex is just as hot as his brothers, he's more aloof on social media. Much more guarded. Women who pinpoint him are after a title and position, not the man himself. I 'lose' the numbers of those women. Prince Alexander does not suffer fools, and I don't intend to be on his foolish list. At least not in regards to the friends I make.

"Brice is totally shaggable." To everyone else but me. I can appreciate them without wanting to have sex with them. Too much like brothers since we all grew up together. Each one annoys me in his own unique way.

When I was younger, Nick had the most crush potential. His friendship with my sister was the stuff teenage fantasies are built on. They rarely speak, but once in a while, I catch him staring at Julia with naked longing. As though he wishes for something he can no longer have. The one time I tried to bring up their past friendship, Jules shut me down by saying Nick wasn't who he used to be. Apart from all the sex, he still seems like the same guy to me. What do I know?

Monica walks me out of the lecture hall. "Any plans for the long weekend?"

"Probably just sticking around here. All my family is out of Bellerive on various adventures. A couple of my friends from home were talking about coming but never booked their flights." November isn't an ideal time to visit Michigan. Not cold enough for snow to stick and not warm enough for other outdoor adventures.

"I'd invite you home with me, but I'm going to my boyfriend's place. I'll send you the link to another chat I'm in," Monica says. "There are always people making last minute plans in it on a long weekend."

"Awesome," I say. "My extroverted heart will love it."

"Sit together next week?" Monica holds the door open as we exit the concrete building into the crisp late-fall air.

A chill rushes through me, and I zip my jacket. "I usually sit with Destiny, but she went home early for the weekend. We can all sit together," I say. "I'll introduce you."

"Perfect," she says. "Maybe this class won't be so boring anymore." A horn beeps ahead of us, and Monica waves at a Black guy driving toward us. "That's my boyfriend." She rolls her eyes when he sticks his head out the window to yell something incoherent. "Do you have a boyfriend?"

3

"God, no." I laugh. "Men are best in bite-sized pieces." I give her a wicked grin. "Sinful and delicious."

"Oh, you're trouble, Posey Jensen." She wags her finger at me as she walks backward. "My boyfriend isn't going to like me hanging around you."

Reason number one why I don't have a boyfriend. Who wants to be on a leash? "Maybe you need a new boyfriend." I waggle my brows when the horn honks again.

Monica throws the middle finger over her shoulder and grimaces. "I'll dump him when Sebastian Swan comes calling."

"The football player? The one involved in the big scandal last year?"

"He wasn't part of that. He dates the girl's roommate. Natalie, I think?" She crosses her fingers. "Is it wrong to wish for someone else's breakup?"

We reach her boyfriend's car, and Monica circles to the passenger side.

"Need a ride?" the boyfriend asks, leaning out the window. "We can drop you somewhere on our way outta town?" He's skinnier than I expected given Monica's fixation on a football player, but his grin is infectious.

"I don't live far from campus, but thanks. Have a good weekend." I wave to them both and head across the street to the eastern campus exit, which isn't the closest to my apartment, but it's the route past the Olympic-size swimming pool.

As I walk, I scroll through my various social media accounts on the hunt for my own thirst trap. Brent Faulkner is a legend on campus and in Bellerive. He's chasing Michael Phelps's medal count at the next Olympics. While his mother was born in Bellerive, her family left the country when she was young. She married an American, and her eldest child, Brent, has chosen to swim for America, instead of Bellerive, in the Olympics. I guess he feels more

4

attached to the good ole U.S. of A. than his mother's birthplace.

Do I know far too much about a man I've never met? Yes, yes, I do.

It's not really my fault, though. His girlfriend constantly posts envy-inducing photos of Brent's finely tuned physique. He's catnip, and I'm the cat.

Like Monica, a tiny part of me might be wishing Brent would suddenly find himself single too. His girlfriend appears completely and utterly gone over him, so I can't see a breakup happening anytime soon.

I scan her accounts and the hashtags she uses. Weird. Silence today, and she's normally posted something by now. Not a single word or photo. I click through to his accounts, and I don't find anything there either. He rarely posts.

Maybe they've both returned home for the weekend too? Thanksgiving isn't a holiday in Bellerive, and my parents and sister are away on work-related travel. In hindsight, I should have said yes to any of the offers I got before now. A part of me held out hope Julia, my sister, might surprise me by turning up on my doorstep. She did that my first year at Northern University when she was still working in California. After she took over as the king's secretary, her free time became almost non-existent.

Instead of dwelling on what a boring long weekend I might have ahead of me, I click on the group chat Monica sent to me. With my thumb, I scroll to the newest posts. Lots of people hosting parties, looking for Thanksgiving dinner dates, a few requests for someone to come home with them and pretend to be their significant other. The various claims made in those posts make me laugh, and by the time I reach the apartment I share with Destiny and Nadiya, I'm feeling lighter.

The silence of our second-floor apartment closes in around me, and I collapse into the couch to check all my other group chats. Everyone is wishing everyone else a happy long weekend, chatting about the ways they're returning home, and who they're bringing with them.

Maybe I should have gone home anyway. An empty house in Bellerive would at least have a better view from the window and warmer weather outside.

My phone chimes in my hand with a text from Monica.

Check the group chat I sent you. A sweet weekend away.

Opening the chat, I scroll to the post from a BF with a Captain America avatar. Inside I release an *ugh* before I read the post.

Weekend wedding in Bermuda. Flight leaves at 10 pm. Back Monday at noon. Looking for my +1. Those with drama need not apply. Pay own flight. Hotel is all inclusive.

Instead of texting Monica back, I hit call and press the phone to my ear. She'll be in the car with her boyfriend, but I'm not replying to this post. The guy sounds like an idiot.

"Do it," Monica says when she answers.

"Two initials and a Captain America avatar? He's going to be the worst. A sleazy, misogynistic jerk."

Monica cackles over the phone. "You're judging that hard over initials and an avatar?"

"'Those with drama need not apply,'" I say. "He might as well scrawl 'I've got issues' at the end of his post."

"Oh, I see what it's like," Monica says. "You're all talk."

"What?" I sit up straighter on the couch.

"In class you were all 'I seek adventure' and 'my extravert-loving heart,' but when an opportunity drops in your lap, you're *not* taking it?" She tsks. "Something better than a trip to Bermuda come up?"

"I have to pay for my flight."

"That's a bonus—you can leave early if he really is a sleazy jerk." She hums over the phone. "Never mind. Someone else replied. I gotta go. Devon doesn't like it when

I talk on the phone when he's driving. He wants his tunes cranked."

"Have a good weekend," I say again before hanging up.

I click into the chat and stare at the exchange of messages. Shared hotel room, but separate beds.

They're still hashing out details.

I'll come.

I send the response before I can second-guess myself.

The bubbles pop up under my response.

DM'd you.

In my private messages, I find a picture of flight details and a link to purchase. *Other girl was wasting my time. If you're serious, book this and screenshot as a reply.*

Once I'm on the airline page, I grab the credit card that my parents still pay out of my wallet. There have to be some perks to being abandoned on a long weekend. I don't allow my brain to engage as I type in all my details and press on the *pay now* button. While the payment processes, a brief shot of panic spikes in me. This guy could be anyone, and not in a good way.

A boarding pass appears on my screen and a thank you for my payment.

God, that was expensive. It's a good thing he's paying for everything else. At least I can justify it to my parents that way.

I screenshot the transaction and send it to BF in our private chat. He sends me another picture of the hotel name and location. Immediately, I save it to my phone, and then I text it to Monica.

In case he's a murderer. This is where I'm supposed to be for the weekend.

Monica responds immediately with an LOL and heart eyes. One of us is a bad influence, and I'm starting to think it's not me.

When I click back over to the chat with BF, he's left another message.

I'll text you at the airport. Glad you're a dude. So tired of the drama!

I frown at the message. He thinks I'm a dude? Why would he think I'm a guy? On my chat profile, the other shoe drops. My avatar is a J in Bellerive blue, and the only name visible is my last one: Jensen.

My fingers hover over my keyboard. I've already paid for my flight. Do I tell him I'm a drama-rama girl or leave him to be surprised at the airport?

My lips twist into a smile.

See you tonight!

BRENT

Valentina falls into step beside me as soon as I exit the locker room. "Brent, I know you weren't in the mood earlier," she says, "but I haven't posted anything today."

Lately I've been wondering whether her interest in me is directly tied to the influencer status she's building off my abs. Last week she told me about another brand who'd reached out to her for a deal...as long as I was willing to participate. When I told her no, we got into a giant fight. Seems to be the pattern. She oversteps. I tell her no. She flies to Mars on the strength of her anger.

Don't get me wrong. She has a banging body, and the make-up sex is next level. We used to have fun together, but I'm not sure we've ever wanted the same things.

"Not today, Val." I sigh. "And not tomorrow or anytime this weekend either."

"Oh please. We're going to Bermuda for Trev's wedding. Of course I'm going to be taking photos. People are dying for them."

"But they're not *dying* for them, are they?" I shove my swim bag higher onto my shoulder. "Trev already asked for a social media ban on the wedding." I glare at her. "For everyone. That means you too."

"Fine. I'll just post them when we get back."

I whirl on her in the courtyard outside the athletic center. "You're missing the point." I run a frustrated hand through my hair. "This isn't working anymore." The words are out of my mouth before I can consider them. But they're true. I've been frustrated and angry with her more than I've been happy for months. We've broken up before, and I've let us slide back together. My swim schedule has allowed me to ignore my feelings for the most part, but the thought of an entire weekend with her isn't a joy.

"If I don't post every day, the algorithm penalizes me." She's staring at her phone, flicking through various apps.

Her dismissive attitude hardens my resolve. "*We* aren't working anymore."

She snaps to attention, and she slides her phone into the pocket of her winter coat. Her dark eyes blaze when she meets my gaze, and she tosses her jet-black hair over her shoulder.

Here comes the onslaught, and I'm done with the dramatics. With her, it never ends.

"I'm building your brand. You're not going to be an Olympic athlete forever. We have to think about the future. Beyond all this." She makes a sweeping gesture to the athletics' facility behind us.

"I never asked you to do that." In fact, I don't want it. My master's degree at Northern University is my exit strategy. Business management is pretty fucking versatile. Pimping my body on social media isn't on my to-do list when this is over.

"You don't need to, baby. I'm building everything for us."

"Except it's starting to feel like you're doing it for *you*. The latest brand that wanted to leech onto me sells high-end makeup. I looked it up, Val. Why would they want *me* in their ad campaign?"

"Brent—"

"We're done. Seriously. D. O. N. E. I'm out."

"We both know you don't mean it. You'll be back." Her jaw tightens, and she glares at me. "I'm getting really tired of you starting fights and breaking up with me over nothing."

"Which is exactly why we're always fighting. You're not *listening* to me. I really need you to hear me when I say we're over. I'm breaking the cycle." I slice a hand through the air between us. While a permanent break has been coming for a while, I didn't expect to do it before our long weekend away. The reality of what this weekend would look like should have hit me earlier. She's obsessed with updating her socials and wedging me into a future I don't want. This weekend would have been more of the same. Fighting and fucking.

"We're going away together," she scoffs. "You can't break up with me right before we leave. Talk about awkward."

She's not upset. Shouldn't that tell her something? "I can. That's what I'm doing. Right now." I take my phone out of my pocket. "I'm cancelling your flight even as we speak."

"You'll lose your money."

"I paid the extra for cancellation. I'll be fine."

"You can't be serious!"

I close my phone and slide it into my pocket. "I *am* serious. *I* can't believe you're happy with the endless fights. Who'd want that?"

"We fight a bit. Big deal. People argue. I want you."

"Nah. You want what I can give you. There's a difference, and I've ignored it, but I can't pretend anymore."

"God, Brent," she huffs out. "You're so fucking cold and emotionless. You're dumping me before we go to your best friend's wedding in Bermuda? You're unbelievable." She sticks her hands on her hips and whips her hair around. "Good luck finding someone who puts up with your shit like I did." Val gives me the finger and storms away.

I'm cold and emotionless? Her rebuttal to me breaking it off was the cost of an airline ticket. No declarations of love (there haven't been any on either side, but still...), and no commitment to changing her attitude.

The whole way back to my apartment, I replay our conversation with better comebacks and increased frustration. By the time I reach the building, I'm over-the-top angry. I shove my key into the lock and open the door.

"Hey, man," Jaxon calls from his bedroom. "What time's your flight? Is Val coming here or...?"

"We broke up!" I carry my bag to the bathroom and start tossing my wet clothes onto drying racks.

"What? Again?" Jaxon pops his blond head out of the door. "You trying to escalate the make-up sex to the next level for your weekend or what?"

I release a dark chuckle, and I meet him in the hallway. "Nah, we're done. I'm serious this time."

"We'll see. Being around her is some kinda chemical reaction for you. No way you're giving that up."

"Just did." I raise my fist. "I am man. Hear me roar."

Jaxon beats his chest in mock solidarity. "Whatever. The two of you will be back together after this weekend. Hell, I wouldn't put it past her to show up at the airport. She's still got a spot in your hotel room and a ticket to Bermuda?"

"Not the ticket," I say. "I cancelled that in front of her."

Jaxon barks out a laugh. "You're such an ass. I love it. She'll show up at the airport, guaranteed. She's the biggest cling-on I've ever met."

I rock back on my heels and frown. "You don't like her."

"Dude, none of us *like* her. But you seem to enjoy her." He shrugs. "You need a rebound to take to Bermuda or Valentina is going to crash that wedding hard."

I'm stuck on the notion that none of my friends liked her. Other than her hot body, what did I like about her? Am I shallow? I think I might be shallow.

Jaxon chuckles. "Your brain is in overdrive. I'd go with you and help you keep your dick in your pants, but I promised my mom I'd be home this Thanksgiving. I've missed the last two."

"Nah, it's fine. I'll text some people. Someone will be up for it." I scroll through my contacts and start texting women I used to screw around with before I let Valentina suck me into her orbit.

"Thanksgiving weekend might be a tough sell, even if it is Bermuda." He takes out his phone. "I'm in this campus group chat. People on there are always looking for a last-minute co-signer to their adventures. Throw up a message."

"A complete stranger?" I raise my eyebrows.

"It's a weekend. What's the harm?" Jaxon shrugs.

My phone pings with a message from him with a link to the chat, and then it pings with three more responses to my 'what's up' text message. So far, they've all got weekend plans and questions about my status with Valentina.

"Maybe I don't need to take someone," I hedge.

He slips his phone into his front pocket. "She'll show up, get on her knees, and your naked bod will be all over her socials by the end of the weekend. I'll even put money on that. Big money. How much you want to bet?"

Without too much trouble, I can imagine his scenario playing out. When another rejection arrives in my text messages, I open Jaxon's link.

"Group chat it is," I say. "Should I make a point of saying I don't want any drama?" I bite my lip.

"You using your real name in there?" Jaxon peers over my shoulder.

"Initials."

"Use the drama line. It's a good one." Jaxon slaps me on the back and heads into his room to finish packing for the weekend.

The first woman I chat with already seems high maintenance. I couldn't have spelled out *no drama* any clearer. I frown at my phone for a beat when someone named Jensen jumps in.

"Jax, do you know a Jensen on campus?"

"Jensen." He leans against his bedroom door and stares up at the ceiling. "Only Jensen I know is a last name. It's a first name?"

"Seems like."

"Gotta be a dude. Maybe it's Jensen Ackles."

"Gonna go out and slay some demons in Bermuda." I chuckle, and I mull it over for a beat. A bros weekend wouldn't be so bad. Whoever it is can be a buffer between me and Valentina if she really does turn up. Jaxon is right—my ex is a wild card. I write back, and while I wait for him to get back to me, I field a few other questions from random people.

"He's in. Sent me his flight details already." I scan the screenshot for a name, but there's a black box over his payment details. Smart, actually.

"Sweet. It's a dick party." Jaxon grins. "He can be your wingman for your rebound hookup at the wedding. Any of the bridesmaids single?"

I let out a sigh, and for the first time since I left the athletics' complex, a twinge of sadness sneaks in. While Valentina might not have been my ideal girlfriend, she put up with my hectic training and travel schedule as long as I let her take an excessive number of photos when I was around. Most girls are not cool with being ignored, and I am laser focused on my next set of Olympic medals.

Instead of seeking a lackluster relationship, I should be looking for short-term hookups. No commitment. No chance of hurt feelings. No one gets let down. My focus can stay on hunting down Michael Phelps's records one race at a time.

"I don't know if any of them are single," I say. "But I guess Jensen and I will be finding out this weekend."

Jaxon gives me a high five and heads back into his room. I follow his lead and go into my bedroom to pack for the weekend.

Fingers crossed this Jensen dude is up for some fun.

Posey

Most people would probably be nervous or scared about meeting a stranger at the airport for a weekend getaway. Not me. I'm excited to see the look on Mr. No-Drama-rama's face when he realizes Jensen is Posey Jensen, and I don't just stumble into drama, I thrive on it. Give me all the nonsense, and I'll give it right back.

When I get to the terminal, I head to the check-in. He messaged me to say we'd meet up on the other side of security for a beer before boarding. Just thinking about our exchanges makes me chuckle. Rather than fessing up, I poured more half-truths down the chat lines. Hair brown, eyes brown, average build, beer drinker (any alcohol, who am I kidding?), sports enthusiast (I enjoy men's assets)—all true. Not quite who he'll be scanning the crowd for. In for a penny, in for a pound.

Once I'm checked in and on the other side of security, I sashay through the terminal with my short skirt and high heels. Rather than my usual low-maintenance makeup application, I went full face. There's something about any man implying women are difficult and saddled with drama that gets my back up. Lots of women aren't like that at all. Sometimes I'm one of them, and sometimes I'm not. I hate the idea of being slotted into some jerky guy's preconceived notions of what a woman should and shouldn't be.

Enjoy your weekend, asshole.

When I'm near the pub, I shoot a message into the chat app to let him know I'm here. He messages back that he's in a booth near the rear of the pub wearing a Northern University baseball cap. My heels click across the faux wooden floor on my way to the scattered tables and booths. In a far corner is a broad-shouldered man staring at his phone with a baseball cap concealing his face. I bet he's one of those types that lives in the gym and stares at himself in the mirror.

A hint of a grin twists my lips as I approach. I cannot wait to see his face.

"BF?" I ask when I'm standing beside his table.

He glances up, and my heart stops. *Holy fucking shit.* Heat rushes through my body, followed by a jolt of ice cold.

It's Brent Faulkner. My mouth drops open. He's not the one who has been obsessively staring at his body. I am.

"Jensen?" He frowns and sits straighter in the booth.

"Brent Faulkner?" I'd recognize those golden-brown eyes, that angular face, and the jet-black hair anywhere.

"Your name is *Jensen*?"

"Posey. Posey Jensen." I slide into the booth across from him. "*You* have a girlfriend."

"*You're* supposed to be a dude." His lips twist in distaste. "I said no drama. Does this situation seem drama-free to you?"

I cross my arms and slump into the booth. Of course my thirst-trap secret crush would turn out to be Mr. No-Drama-rama judgmental jerk face. It annoys me to no end that I can't stop scanning his features and comparing them to the hundreds of photos I've drooled over.

"Okay, so technically I never told you I was a dude. You assumed, I guess, based on my name."

"I would have been less shocked if Jensen Ackles showed up here."

"Yeah, sure. You and Jensen, slaying demons in Bermuda." I roll my eyes. "Total bros weekend."

A hint of a smile curls his lips, and he glances away while sweeping a hand over his face. When he meets my gaze again, all trace of humor is gone. "Am I going to regret this, Jensen?"

"Regret inviting me? Probably." I lean across the table toward him and try to decide whether his attitude is a turnoff or a turn-on in person. The fact that he's chiseled like a Greek god is definitely softening my rock-hard resolve to make his weekend hell. "To assume all women are filled with drama and trouble is—quite frankly—*not* a good look."

"You misled me. You *invited* the drama."

"You have a girlfriend. Why are you on a campus chat looking for some rando date to your friend's wedding? She's supposed to be going with you."

His gaze narrows. "How the hell do you know all that?"

My cheeks heat, and I break eye contact. "I follow her." I follow him, too, but he clearly doesn't realize that. She has thousands of followers. He has millions. I've never liked or commented on any posts. But I have viewed and read them all. So. Many. Times.

"Why would you follow Val? Do you know her? Everything she's posted since we met is about..." He cocks his head at something in my expression. "Ahh." He sits back in his seat and drums his hands on the top of the table. "Do I need to call security? Are you some kind of stalker?"

"Stalker?" I gasp.

"You follow my ex-girlfriend on social media. You knew she was coming with me. You responded to my chat in the group."

"Yes. Your initials of BF along with your stupid Captain America avatar gave your identity away."

"Captain America is not stupid."

"Grown men don't use superhero avatars in a campus-wide chat group."

"All my friends do."

I raise my eyebrows and say nothing.

A hint of a smile peeks out of one corner of his lips. "Did you know it was me?"

"Of course I didn't know I was meeting Brent Faulkner at the airport."

"Really?" He gestures to my outfit.

"Really." My cheeks are on fire again. "I dressed like this because you seemed like a misogynistic asshole, and I was prepared to put you in your place all weekend."

He lets out a startled laugh. "You were prepared to spend a weekend in Bermuda with a misogynistic asshole? Seriously? That's kinda fucked up."

"Those with drama need not apply? I applied anyway." I give him a saccharine smile, and then I realize the waitress is hovering a few feet from our table.

"Can I—can I get either of you a drink?" she asks.

"You paying?" I stare at Brent.

"No," he scoffs.

"All inclusive."

"When we get there. Until we land, you pay your own way."

I turn to the waitress. "Just water, thank you." Could I afford my own beer? Sure. But I'm not in the mood to drink with him. Brent Faulkner is not the guy I built in my mind. Not even close.

He lets out a snort. "A pint of your house beer."

We sit in silence for a beat after the waitress leaves.

"You and Val broke up?" Curiosity is not my friend.

"We did." His jaw tics.

"Today?"

He gives me a withering glare.

I can't help a grin. "She didn't post about you today. But yesterday, you were a total thirst trap." There was something about the way he mentioned Val's social media account that made me think he wasn't a fan of her posts. When he scowls at me, I realize my instinct is correct.

"We won't be talking about her," he says. He leans across the table. "You're okay with objectifying me, but if I did the same to you, I bet you wouldn't like it."

"There's a long history of women being objectified and their worth being dictated by the size of their boobs instead of their brains. Once that reality is a bit more balanced, I'll be happy to have you objectify me." I flutter my fake eyelashes at him.

"But not before that?" His gaze travels over my fitted T-shirt. "Your choice of outfit says otherwise."

"These are my travel clothes. Most comfortable items I own."

"Bullshit. You already admitted you dressed like that to make my weekend hell."

I raise my eyebrows and close the distance across the table. "How would my choice of clothing do that?"

"Look but don't touch, I'm assuming."

He's got me there. Now that I realize he's Brent Faulkner, I'm reconsidering my no-touching stance. I shouldn't, though. Turns out Brent Faulkner is an asshole. A smoking-hot body only gets anyone so far.

Before I can respond, the waitress returns with our drinks. Brent takes a large gulp of his beer and lets the silence sit between us.

"Whose wedding is it?"

"My best friend from high school, Trevor. He's marrying a girl from Bermuda. Sebastian Swan's cousin, if you've heard of him. You said you were into sports."

I scrunch up my face.

"Another lie?" He swigs his beer. "I'm tempted to call this whole thing off."

If he did, I'd get my own hotel room, make some new friends, and have a blast. I paid for my own flight, so it's not like he can stop me.

But in life, sometimes you only get one chance at something, and I've spent enough time staring at his photos that I want to be sure I'm rejecting a jerk and not some guy who's screwed up from a bad breakup.

"I scrunched up my face because of what happened last year to the girlfriend of Johnny McDade, the star quarterback. I don't want to get into school or sport politics, but the whole situation with the football team was unacceptable. Star athletes shouldn't get special treatment when they're shitty people."

His gaze sharpens. "I don't disagree."

"Does this mean we *agree* on something?" I cock my head.

"Basic human rights and integrity. I'd be *very* worried if we didn't."

My mind is ticking through the new pieces of information that have landed now that I realize who he is and why he's going to the wedding. "If he's one of your best friends from high school, you didn't need a plus-one, did you?"

"Val and I have broken up before." He clears his throat. "A few times, actually."

This is news to me. All her posts are loved-up adoration for Brent, who wore the swimming world's crown at the last Olympics. He's on track to do it again in another two years.

"Is she coming to the wedding?" If so, I have walked into something hella awkward.

"Possibly?" He runs a finger down his frosted glass. "It would be like her to turn up. Other times when we've broken up, she's been persistent, and I've been..."

"Indifferent?" The word rises to my tongue and shoots out of my mouth before my brain has a chance to catch up. While her socials are dedicated to him, he's never posted about her. The realization hits me like a ton of bricks. I never noticed before, but it makes so much sense now.

He winces. "When you say it out loud it sounds—"

"Terrible?" I pick up my water. "A toast."

His gaze narrows, but he raises his glass.

"To guys who lead with their dicks." I take a big sip of my water and try not to sputter at the outrage on his face. "Oh, come on. If you're not in love with her and you've got this massive break-up/make-up cycle going, the *only* thing working in your relationship is the sex. That's it."

A muscle in his jaw tightens, but he doesn't contradict me.

"If she does show up, how do you want to play this? I'm assuming you went with a plus-one to act as a buffer between your dick and her vagina?"

He runs a hand down his face and groans. "Are you always this blunt?"

"Yes." I smile. Not really, but his discomfort is amusing so I'm laying it on thicker than normal. Reading a room is my specialty. It's how I collect friends. But it also means I'm capable of turning my skills in the opposite direction too. Annoy. Annoy. Annoy.

"Yeah," he admits. "I need a buffer. Are you willing?"

Placing my body between his and his ex's? It's a hell yes. There's just one thing that makes me a little reluctant. "Is she in love with you? It certainly seemed like it."

"If she is, she's never said it." He shrugs.

I bite my lip. "If she turns up, and if *I* get the vibe she's in love with you, I won't be deliberately mean or cruel.

That's my line."

"Fair enough." He finishes the rest of his beer. "I just don't want to be sucked back into Val's orbit."

I almost spit out my sip of water, and I sputter on a laugh. "I take it there's been a lot of *sucking* in the past?"

"You went there."

"Oh, I *always* go there."

"You're going to take some getting used to." He gives me a wry smile.

"Good news, my newest buddy." I grin. "You've got all weekend."

BRENT

We didn't sit together on the plane, and by the time we're waiting in line for a taxi at the airport, she's exchanged numbers with the three people who sat near her. Friday night drinks at the Hamilton Princess is a must, apparently. Good thing that's our hotel and today is Thursday. We've got all day tomorrow to spend in Bermuda, and I'm suddenly wondering why I thought this stranger date thing was a good idea. What am I going to do with her before the wedding on Saturday?

While I listen to her talk to her newest pals, I realize she hasn't given me the version of herself she's offering to other people. There's nothing combative or blunt in her exchanges with them. She's light and funny, and she practically glows under their adoring attention. For the first time since she turned up beside my table in the terminal, the complete Posey Jensen package is attractive. *Highly* attractive.

I must rub her in all the wrong ways.

I have to admit as I size up her willowy frame and wide smile that I'd be okay with rubbing her in all the *right* ways too.

She might have a point about me leading with my dick. But if my vow to forget relationships and focus on my training is going to stick, I can't change my superficial ways. Until I'm done with my Olympic appearances, I'm married to my sport, and everyone else comes second. At least Valentina understood she couldn't and wouldn't come first.

When it's our turn to grab a cab, she waves to her newest friends before slipping into the back seat. She lets me and the cab driver get her bag without a second glance. Even that feels contrived for maximum annoyance, as though she realizes the diva behavior will cause me to grit my teeth.

I fold myself into the cab beside her, and she glances in my direction. Probably expecting a comment about her prissy attitude.

As the cab swings away from the curb, I take a look out the back window. "Man, I would have thought you'd want your bag. Do they still call the bomb squad for abandoned stuff at the airport?"

She doesn't look behind us. "You know, if you want me to play games when Val shows up, you might have to be just a little bit nice to me." She presents her index and thumb with the tiniest space between them.

"Me? You tricked me into believing you were a guy."

"You assumed. That's not on me."

"But you rode that assumption hard."

She gives me a once over from head to toe. "I enjoy a good, *hard* ride."

Jesus. I've met women who were upfront with what they wanted before, but there's something about Posey's brand of wickedness that's landing exactly where she intends. Her outfit and her attitude have me standing at attention. I shift in my seat and break eye contact.

"You're unbelievable."

"I'm definitely the type of girl who will blow...your mind." She stifles a laugh.

This time my answering chuckle is genuine and colored with a hint of embarrassment. The cab driver is listening. The sexual innuendos pile on top of each other with this girl. "There's a time and place."

"The time is now. The place is here. Your point?"

I huff out a breath. "You can cut the act. I know this isn't how you are around other people. I saw you with your seatmates at the airport."

"This is exactly how I am with people I'm not sure I like."

"You don't know me. What's not to like?" This time I'm the one who drags my gaze from her dangling heel to her wavy hair. "I know you enjoy the look of me."

"Because I'm not blind." She crosses her arms. "You're not what I expected. Too shallow."

She's got to be kidding me. "Says the girl who follows my ex for photos of my half-naked body."

"Sometimes it was more like three quarters. She knew how to work an angle."

"Posey, you sound insane right now. Do you get that?"

The cab driver eases through the pillars in the circular front entrance and brings the car to a stop. "Hamilton Princess." He jumps out to retrieve our bags from the trunk.

Behind the car, I take out my wallet and pass him the fare with a substantial tip. A porter offers to take our bags, but both of us have duffels. Without Posey asking, I shift her bag into the same hand as mine. At least she packed light.

At our check-in, I request a switch from a king-size-bed suite to a two-bed one. The receptionist clicks through and confirms she can make the switch. I breathe a sigh of relief. Posey is off to the side with both our bags at her feet. She's texting someone, and I need to remember to tell her about the social media ban on the wedding.

The whole time I'm answering and asking questions with the receptionist, Posey's comment about me not being who she expected pierces my consciousness like sharp pinpricks. *I'm* shallow? In the elevator, she's quiet as we ride to our floor. Somehow her silence grates on me even more.

"You know," I say as soon as we're in the door to our room. "You thought you were spending a weekend with a misogynistic jerk, so the fact that I'm not what you thought I'd be should be an *improvement*."

She purses her lips as she riffles through the pamphlets and brochures left on top of the table. "Agreed. It really should be."

I throw up my hands. "Whatever." My temptation is to ignore her, but when she goes to the window to stare out at the view of the harbor, I'm enticed by her lonely silhouette. My arm brushes against hers when I sidle next to her.

She glances up at me, and I'm caught off guard when the air in the room electrifies. She might not like me, but she definitely wants me.

"It's a nice view," she says.

"I can't complain." I scan her face, trying to figure out whether giving into the vibe between us is the right thing to do. She appears to hate me.

"I don't want you to kiss me," she murmurs, but her gaze strays to my lips.

"Feels like you do."

Her head shakes a fraction. "Not until you see me as more than a pair of tits."

"You have a nice ass, too, if that helps." We make eye contact, and I'm startled by how deep and rich her brown eyes are. "Is this your criteria for all your flings? Or are you a relationship girl? I'm not cut out for that a second time."

"You're not, and neither am I." A hint of a smile touches her lips.

"So why do you care how I see you?" I tilt her chin with my finger and inch closer to her lips.

"You should value a woman for more than her body pieces."

"You think it's possible for me to *value* you in a weekend?" I raise my eyebrows and withdraw my hand.

"Spend the day with me tomorrow, and I bet you'll understand my worth by the time we're sipping Rum Swizzles on the terrace of the hotel." A sly smile rises.

"I do like a woman with confidence." That had been what drew me to Valentina in the first place. The woman oozed a *don't mess with me* vibe, and she pursued me with relentless determination.

"I've got it in spades." Her phone buzzes on the table. "Is that a yes?"

"You haven't told anyone you're with me, have you?" Despite what I let Valentina do on social media, my natural inclination is toward privacy. I'd also prefer Val doesn't find out I brought Posey to the wedding. If she turns up with her invitation revoked, that's one thing. Flaunting my single status is another. Seeing a photo of me or reading a post about the wedding would be enough to cause her to jump on a plane if she hasn't already.

"Not a soul. Texted my sister and a friend the hotel information just in case you were a psycho murderer."

I chuckle.

"I'm not a social media maven." She shrugs. "I read other peoples' stuff, but I rarely post anything myself."

I checked her socials on the plane. Lots of photos of Bellerive, a place I've never been even though my mother was born there. "There's a social media ban on the wedding."

"Your friend thinks he's a big shot?" Posey smirks.

"He kind of is?" I shrug. "He's in a movie with Ellie Cooper and Wyatt Burgess that's coming out next year. His profile is supposed to skyrocket after that. They're guests at the wedding. Can you be cool with famous people or are you going to be weird?" A bit late to be asking.

When she meets my gaze, her eyes dance with an amusement I don't understand. "I've had lots of practice keeping secrets, and I'm good with famous people. No worries." She ignores her phone on the table and picks up one of the brochures instead. "Tomorrow? You in or out?"

"Is this a challenge?" A fire lights in me, and I follow her to the table. "You don't think I'm capable of valuing a woman?"

"I hope you prove me wrong." Posey rises on her toes, and her lips graze the sensitive skin by my ear. "I'd love to find out whether you're what I expected in other ways." Her voice is breathy.

I close my eyes and clench my jaw. It takes everything in me not to pick her up and toss her on the bed. I'd follow her down with my mouth and my hands, and I'd show her that, at least in some ways, I'm better than she expected.

There's a knock on the door, and I'm grateful for the interruption. "Must be my suit," I murmur, and I step around her to grab the door.

Posey

While Brent answers the door and grabs his suit from the hotel employee there, I fan myself. There's a five-alarm fire in my panties, and I'm pretty sure I'm not going to get enough privacy this weekend to douse the flames myself.

Will I be able to last until tomorrow night before I sleep with him? I've got no idea. While I don't do relationships, I've also made it a policy not to sleep with men I don't even like. Brent is making me reconsider my stance on that. He's my fantasy man, even if he can't live up to it.

For him to spend a year with his girlfriend, for her to make all these loved-up proclamations, and for him to be indifferent about their breakup is not the grand romance I pictured in my head. Social media is often fake, but I have to admit, Val got me. I bought what she was selling. Does he realize the things she used to post about them? I scrolled through a bunch of it on the plane, trying to reconcile the information he served me with what I've been devouring on her socials. Fast food versus a five-course meal.

"You're in the wedding party?" I ask while he hangs the suit bag in the closet.

"One of the groomsmen."

"What are your commitments this weekend? There must be things you're expected to do. Do you want me to go to them or keep myself scarce unless Val shows up?" I perch on the edge of the bed closest to the window and cross my legs.

He turns and shoves his hands into the pockets of his jeans. His triceps pop, and I die a little inside. "You're being very agreeable."

"Am I supposed to be difficult?" Truthfully, I can't get an impression of him to stick either. One minute I dislike him intensely, the next, I suspect I *could* like him, and in both scenarios, I want to rip his clothes off.

"I cannot get a beat on you," he admits. "You're like this mishmash of a bunch of people."

"Everyone wears more than one face." I circle my makeup-heavy one. "This is mine today. You'll get a different one tomorrow, I promise." I wink.

He picks the pen off the nightstand and twirls it across his fingers. "Nothing planned for tonight. I have practice at the Saltus Pool tomorrow morning. Then I'm free the rest of the day until the wedding party has drinks on the terrace tomorrow night. Saturday, the wedding starts at four, followed by dinner and the reception. Sunday, I have a practice again mid-morning, and then we fly out Monday morning."

"Do you practice every day?"

"Usually doubles, plus weights. This is basically a vacation for me." He chuckles. "Which I wouldn't have been able to take if we weren't two years out from the next Olympics."

"You wouldn't have come if the Olympics were closer?"

"I would have, yeah. We've been friends since we were kids. But my spare time would have been taken up with training. Wouldn't have been drinking." He shrugs. "More discipline. Less freedom. The rewards are worth it."

The timbre of his voice when he talks about his training causes a warm sensation to sprout in my chest. There's something about the declaration of hard work and sacrifice as 'worth it' that makes him less of a lost cause.

"What's your thing?" He takes a seat on the other bed across from me. "What makes Posey Jensen tick?"

"I'm taking interior design, but my real claim to fame is probably face-to-face networking. Put me in a room, and I can leave with ten new contacts, easy."

"You're a people person."

"An extreme extrovert, yeah. I love talking to people."

"I'm kinda in the middle." He leans back on his hands, and his T-shirt rides up. "I think I'm naturally more introverted, but this whole swimming thing has forced me to be more extroverted."

"Media?" I've watched some of his interviews. He comes across well. Of course, it's easy to be gracious when you're winning every race.

"Media, camps or tutorials, fans on the street." A hint of a smile tugs at one corner of his lips. "Women who pretend to be someone else to get close to me."

His tone is teasing, so I take it as he intends. "Damn dramatic women."

He chuckles, and a heavy silence stretches between us. "I didn't mean to offend you—or anyone—with my phrasing. Val and I had just broken up, and I was angry. I asked Jaxon if I should use that line, and he said yes."

"Jaxon Parish?" Explains a lot.

"You know him?" Brent raises his eyebrows. "He's my roommate."

"We had a class together freshman year. His decision-making skills are...questionable. But he's a lot of fun." He was in my group for an actual escape room for our psychology class, and every idea he had to get us out was hilarious and terrible. Back then I liked him because he reminded me of Prince Brice. We haven't run into each other much since that class.

"You're saying I shouldn't have listened to him?"

"There are two guy staples I hate." I raise a finger. "One: the implication that any ex-girlfriend must be or is 'crazy' for a variety of reasons that often say more about the guy than the girl. Two: the idea that any and all drama in a relationship—platonic or otherwise—comes from the female part of the equation."

Brent shifts so he's stretched out on the bed across from me. I mirror his pose, and I tug on the hem of my skirt to keep it covering my bits.

He smirks, but when our gazes connect, the room electrifies, the same way it did by the window. As though the oxygen is being suctioned out of the room. I've wanted guys before, but I've never experienced this level of instant love-hate chemistry.

"Speaking from experience?" he asks.

"Not sure there's a man alive who'd refer to me as an ex-girlfriend. I enjoy my free agent status."

"A series of one-night stands?" There's no judgement in his tone.

"Not really?" I take a minute to decide how best to answer. "Casual hookups with like-minded people. Relationships are confining and restrictive. When I'm done with college, I'm going back to Bellerive. No point in getting attached to someone who can't follow me there. The immigration laws are ridiculous."

"That's where you're from?"

A slow smile spreads across my face. He didn't search my name on the plane? Monica discovered my mother and sister worked for the royal family within minutes of us talking. Most people do since Bellerive and royalty are intrinsically linked. I'm a short internet hop from the royal family with all my close ties to the Summersets.

"It is." Before he can tell me something I already know, I continue, "Your mom is from there, right?"

"Yeah, she is." He sighs. "I've never been. My grandparents were there working, and she happened to be born in Bellerive. She has citizenship, but no one else in the family does."

"Not even you?" When he became a swimming superstar, Bellerive ran an article about how he *could* swim under our flag or the American one.

"You must already know the answer." He swings his legs around to land on the floor. "Dinner?"

"You're inviting me to dinner?" I press my palm to my chest in mock surprise.

"Are you coming?"

"Just give me a sec to change into shorts." I wiggle myself around to get my legs on the floor. This skirt was a poor choice. "I wouldn't want to lead you into temptation." I crouch to grab shorts from my bag, and I head for the bathroom.

"I can keep my dick in my pants," he grumbles.

I stick my head out the door. "Does Val know that?" An adorable blush creeps up his neck, and a slight twinge of regret surfaces. Maybe I shouldn't tease him.

"May come as a shock to her." He gives me a wry grin. "Get changed. I'm starving. I've normally had about ten snacks by now."

Train a lot. Eat a lot. Makes sense. I change in the bathroom, and when I tug the door open, I find Brent is also in cooler clothes.

He has a sheet of paper in his hands. "The all-inclusive part might not have been completely accurate." He glances at me. "We've got a list of places we can eat for dinner that's included in our package through Trev's travel agent. I just

34

show this letter or something. Or we can eat somewhere else."

I hold out my hand, and he passes me the paper. I skim the details. "The Mad Hatter." With my phone in my other hand, I get directions. "A fifteen-minute walk."

"Did you bring other shoes?" He stares at my heels.

"Did I bring other shoes?" I scoff and peel open my duffel to reveal my expertly packed closet. "Actually, that reminds me I should get out my dress for the wedding." I slide my teal outfit out of the bag and hang it in the closet.

"You only brought one option?" He frowns and peers into my bag.

His bafflement is cute. "I'm a decisive person."

He gives me an appraising look, and there's a new softness around his eyes. "I'm starting to see that." Brent rubs his stomach and then pats his abs. "Let's feed the beast."

Brent

November isn't prime tourist weather, and the air is thick with the promise of rain when we leave the hotel. I can't remember why Trevor said their wedding had to be this weekend—knowing him it's because the venue was cheaper. Nothing in Bermuda is cheap.

A low concrete wall frames every property we pass, and most of them have a metal gate or some other way to get into their enclosed gardens. The stucco houses are painted blue, yellow, white, or pink. A tropical paradise, and I wonder whether any of it reminds Posey of home.

"Give me your worst memory," Posey says as we stroll along the sidewalk to the restaurant.

"You're going for the jugular?" I stuff my hands into my pockets. Deeply personal is not happening tonight. "Is this what Bellerive is like?"

"Since you're keen to discuss my favorite place in the world, I will let you sidestep my very important question."

I snort. She doesn't need my worst memory. I've had a pretty good life, and that memory isn't going to tell her much the world doesn't already know.

"Bellerive is magical."

She says it without an ounce of insincerity. "Like fairies and shit?"

"Fairies and shit." She pretends to think. "I'm sure there's shit. It's a natural by-product of living things. As for the fairies, really, Brent? Really?"

I chuckle. "All right. What makes it so magical then?"

"It's the perfect blend of modern and old-world. My limited experience of Bermuda, which includes my internet searches on the plane, tells me that this island is an infant compared to Bellerive."

"Oh really? An infant. Bold statement."

She eyes me with a sly smile. "Bold is the only way to go, baby." Her voice is husky with fake desire. She can turn it on and off like a faucet.

I shake my head at her audaciousness. One thing I can say about Posey already—life with her would never be boring. "How old is Bellerive?"

"We go all the way back." She winks. "Monarchy records start in the 1100s after a brief war for power. We weren't discovered, so much as evolved. We're one of the few countries that didn't have multiple external power exchanges. Our monarchy, when other countries came knocking, was strong enough to maintain control. We're also small, and not particularly useful in terms of war or trade."

"Does everyone on the island know so much about royal history?"

"Um." Posey's gaze darts away as though she's unsure how to answer.

"Hard question?" I smirk. "It's not like I asked for your worst memory."

"Would you like to know my worst memory?" She squares her shoulders.

"Feels like a trap." I check the map on my phone, and then I glance at her.

"My worst memory involves my sister, Julia Jensen." She tries to smother her grin and fails.

The name rings a bell for some reason. I frown and indicate the street ahead of us. "We turn here. What makes it so bad?"

"Her best friend, Nick, was in a motorcycle accident, and he refused to see her." Posey's expression turns far away. "She was so hurt. So, so hurt. Unrequited love is the worst."

"She was in love with him?" I place my palm on the small of her back to steer her toward the restaurant's entrance, and the contact warms more than my hand. "Sounds like a disaster."

"She was. It was." She sighs. "Still is. Love is nothing but trouble."

"That why you don't do boyfriends?"

"I—I don't know." She frowns.

"If your worst memory is your sister having her heart broken, that's quite an impact. Bound to make you cautious." Did Val and I ever talk about anything important? Most of our time together was spent with me balls deep in one of her orifices or with her posing me for thirst-inducing photos. Soul searching questions like my worst memory never came up.

"I'm probably about one hundred paces away from cautious... Is there a phobia of relationships? That might be me."

I open the door to the restaurant, and I consider Posey's claim. "Sounds hyperbolic."

"Oh yeah. Totally is." She laughs. "I have a healthy fear of relationships."

A slow smile spreads across my face, and as a waiter approaches, I whisper in her ear, "Sounds like an oxymoron."

"For two?" the waiter asks.

"You sound like an English major." Posey beams at the guy. "Yes, for two."

"Business major." I follow the two of them to a small table in a corner. The restaurant is tiny, with maybe fifteen or twenty tables in total. On coat hangers, hung from the ceiling, and around the perimeter of the restaurant are hats on hooks, so many hats.

"Ah, big business." Posey smirks.

"Alliteration," I say while I take in the deluge of hats. Odd, but I suppose that's how they sell the Mad Hatter image without infringing on *Alice in Wonderland*.

"Well done. You've become my senior English class in a slightly more attractive package."

"Slightly more attractive?" I scoff. "I bet the hearts on my ex-girlfriend's portfolio of photos say otherwise."

"I don't give away my hearts to just anyone." Posey tucks in her chair and then flaps out her napkin.

"I think you might be emotionally stunted."

"Says the guy who dated his girlfriend for a year and doesn't know whether she's in love with him. Your armchair diagnosis is unreliable." She opens the menu. "Besides, I freely shared my worst memory. No hesitation." She eyes me over the top. "You, on the other hand..."

"I didn't share it because it's common knowledge for super fans."

"The only thing I'm a super fan of is your body."

"Slightly." I mock her claim about how attractive she finds me while the waiter fills our water glasses.

"Perhaps more than slightly." She holds up a finger. "I never acknowledge any of her photos or yours. Not that you post much."

"Maybe not with your finger on the button." I lift my water for a drink. I've fallen behind on my hydration.

"Oh, there have been some fingers involved." She gives me a naughty grin. "Two?" She shows me her index and middle finger squeezed together. "They just press a different button to demonstrate their approval."

I choke on my sip of water. Did she just admit to masturbating to my photos? She could be lying to get a rise out of me, but I'm not convinced in either direction. Hot as hell, though. I could get used to these overshares—true or not. "I hope it was a satisfying experience for you."

"To be honest, I hope other experiences prove to be more satisfying this weekend." Her gaze travels over me.

"Than your own hand?" I tease.

"If your hand satisfies you more than someone else's, they're doing it wrong." She doesn't bother to meet my gaze as she peruses the menu. "I hope that's not an indication of what I'll be getting because..." She makes a thumbs down motion.

"Nice to see you're capable of more than rotating your fingers in a circular motion around me."

"Yep!" She purses her lips and peers over the menu again. "And if you see either happening while we're together, you're not winning any points."

"Oh, there's a points system?" I lean forward. "I do appreciate a challenge."

"Ooh. You enjoy being treated like a child? Would you like me to create a chart? Maybe buy some stickers for it?"

The waiter appears at our table before I can say anything, not that I had much of a retort. Replies seem to drip from Posey's tongue as though she has her witty autoreply engaged.

"Have you decided?" the waiter asks.

"We have a food voucher from a friend's wedding," Posey says, and she motions for me to get it out.

I pass it to the waiter.

He nods. "Ah, okay." He rattles off the menu for starters, mains, and desserts.

"Ladies first," I say to Posey when the waiter is done. She orders the mixed greens and rock fish. "Make it two. And a bottle of your house—" I gesture for Posey to fill in the blank.

"White."

"Very good. I'll bring your soup out shortly." He takes the menus and disappears behind the serving doors.

The restaurant is quiet, and we sit sipping our water for a beat. When Posey isn't talking, it feels like a punishment, as though she's withholding her chatter. I've never been around a woman where I couldn't wait to hear what she'd say next.

While I'm sure she can't always be switched on, her witty banter amuses me. I'm somewhat surprised to admit it, but I'm enjoying myself. A few hours ago I met a complete stranger at the airport, and she already feels like a friend.

A slightly combative friend.

"My worst memory?" I suggest.

She wiggles in her chair and sets down her water. "Ooo. Yes. Give it to me."

"I'll give it to you all right." I grin.

Her eyes light up with delight in response. She places her elbows on the table and angles herself toward me as though I'm about to tell the best story. "Go deep. I want you all the way in."

Christ, my pants are uncomfortably tight. It's a good thing we've got multiple courses before I need to leave this table.

"You really don't know the story?" I ask.

"No." She shifts away from the table. "I'm this shallow. Your hot body was the extent of my investigation."

"At fourteen I missed making the Olympics by .001. The loss was terrible. Absolutely terrible. I gave up so much to be in that pool in that moment. Felt like I choked, even though it was a best time. Zero perspective. Then I was a complete dick to my coach on camera. You must've seen that?"

She shrugs her shoulders. "I think it's probably wrong for me to say you were cute even at fourteen? Is that wrong? I would have been fourteen too. Maybe not so wrong."

"As I am sure you can imagine, the backlash wasn't pretty." I rub my face. "Learned a lot in that experience. Never played the 'poor me' card again. No need for the world to know my true feelings. Just get on with it. Ignore it all and keep pushing forward."

Posey tips her fork from side to side on the table, and the waiter returns with the wine to pour us each a glass. He sets the bottle in the middle of the table.

Before the waiter can leave, Posey sits up straight in her chair. "Excuse me? The hats around the restaurant. Are we able to try some on?"

The waiter nods. "Of course." He disappears into the kitchen.

Posey stares at me expectantly.

"No." I take in the vast array of apparel, but no part of me is tempted to indulge. "I'm not putting some lice factory on my head."

"If lice are the worst thing you catch in your life, that's not so bad." She rises from her chair. "I've spotted yours."

"That's not a valid argument," I call to her.

"Pick one for me or forfeit your chance."

I leave the table to snatch up the one with a bunch of snakes sprouting out of it. When she comes back to the table, she's got a psychedelic squid. I didn't go ugly enough with my choice. She pushes the hat onto my head with a satisfied smirk.

I pass her the abundance of snakes.

"Medusa." Her lips twitch. "I mean, there is a piece of you I'd gladly turn as hard as stone."

I run my hands down my face, and Posey laughs.

"Everything that comes out of your mouth is a giant sexual innuendo."

"Giant. Mouth. Putting those two things in a sentence is just asking for trouble." She bats her eyes at me. "I already have certain expectations. I have seen you in a very tight, very little swimsuit."

"I'll make a sign when we get back to the hotel to slap over top of my underwear."

The waiter slides a bowl of soup in front of each of us.

Once he's out of earshot, Posey says, "Out of curiosity, what would the sign say?" She raises the spoon brimming with hot liquid to her lips.

With my hand, I get ready to space out the three words in the air. "Not as advertised."

She sputters out a laugh and drops the soup into the bowl again. She points her spoon at me. "We're going to have a fun weekend."

There's no doubt in my mind either. She's not at all who I expected, but she might be exactly who I need.

Posey

Last night was a lot better than I anticipated. After I cracked the ice with the first goofy hat and we got into the second bottle of wine, Brent loosened up. Soon, we'd tried on and taken multiple stupid hat selfies.

For a sports-obsessed jock, he was good for a laugh, and surprisingly honest.

But his worst memory turned out to be more intimate than I bargained for. I didn't even know what to say afterward. A lot of times people play off my request or give half the truth. Having seen the videos and the reaction to Brent's meltdown, I can appreciate how truthful he was. True to his word, I've never seen him behave poorly again on camera, and his social media is largely absent of anything personal.

Obviously I lied to him last night about how much I knew. Telling your crush when he's sitting across the table from you, weird squid hat or not, that you've been obsessed with him for years just isn't done.

Besides, I didn't really know him then. What attracted me initially was his pretty face and hot body. My claim to only be interested in his body wasn't a lie, exactly.

I peer at my makeup in the mirror. Much lighter than yesterday, but I'm not going barefaced. With a sigh, I flip my compact closed. Brent left for the pool at the butt crack of dawn, but he was so quiet I didn't even wake up. I can respect a man who knows when to let a sleeping bear get some shut-eye. A morning person, I am not.

When we got back from the restaurant, we were both a little tipsy, and I stumbled on my way to the bathroom. Brent with his cat-like reflexes managed to grab my elbow in time to steady me. Then our gazes locked for a beat too long, and the air hummed again, a sound I'm becoming familiar with when he's around.

"What if I already value you?" he whispered.

I laughed and asked him when little Brent learned ventriloquism. For some reason, big Brent didn't find that funny. His tolerance for my teasing only goes so far.

With one last glance in the mirror, I grab my bag for the day ahead and shut the hotel door behind me. I've got a twenty-minute walk to the pool where Brent is practicing, and then we're going to rent scooters to sightsee around the island for the day.

The wind whips through the trees, messing with my hair, but the ocean air is so refreshing and familiar, I reach the pool early. At the perimeter fence below the high school, Brent's voice booms out above the buzz of the kids getting ready to enter the school building. I tilt my head and move closer. Instead of in the water practicing, which is what I expected, he's working with a small group of kids on front crawl on deck. Although I might not be headed to the Olympics, growing up on an island meant a lot time in and around the ocean. My mother was adamant about swimming proficiency for me and my sister.

While I wait for the practice to finish, I watch Brent's unending patience with one of the boys who is struggling to master his breathing. By the time the head coach blows his whistle, Brent must have explained the technique five different ways, and not once did his tone slip into frustration.

He'll be a good dad one day.

The thought appears out of nowhere. Brent glances over as though he's read my mind. Our gazes lock across the pool, and then he holds up his finger while he tries once more with the boy in the pool. The last time, whatever Brent says to him when he leans down, works. Brent lets out a whoop of triumph when the boy surfaces at the wall.

The boy hoists himself out, and Brent high fives him, then he speaks to the coach before grabbing his bag and meeting me at the pool gate.

Warmth floods my body at the realization Brent Faulkner is spending the day with me.

A dangerous sensation.

He's not supposed to be winning me over, he's supposed to be learning how to value a woman for more than her tits and ass. I take a deep, steadying breath just as he reaches me.

From his bag, he takes out a power bar and unwraps it. "Want some?"

"You probably need it more than me," I say. "I had something at the hotel. You didn't swim?"

"Oh, no. I swam. Here from five to seven with the coach. Kids showed up at seven, and I spent the last two hours coaching with him. My coach set the whole thing up so I could get my workouts in. Trading favors." He shrugs and bites off a large piece of his bar. "Happens all over the world if I ever want to leave campus."

"Really?" I take out my phone and punch in the address for the scooter rental place. A twenty-minute walk.

"They changed their practice times to accommodate me today. I won medals in freestyle, fly, and backstroke at the last games. I'm a hot commodity. Everyone who is serious about the sport wants a piece of me." He smirks around his bar and eyes me. "Even some people who aren't into the sport."

"You really believe you can beat Phelps's medal count?" I've read the articles, and while it's theoretically possible for Brent to do it given his performances at the Olympics when he was 18 and 22, the next one at 26 will tell the tale. In four Olympic appearances, Phelps won twenty-eight medals in total, including relays.

"If I didn't believe it, I wouldn't have announced my intention." He adjusts his backpack to both shoulders. "If you want something, you go after it. You don't think about failure; you focus on success."

"You sound like a motivational poster. I bet your bedroom is plastered with them. '"You miss one hundred percent of the shots you don't take.' Wayne Gretzky.'" I eye him. "My favorite is by Maya Angelou. 'People will forget what you said. People will forget what you did. But people will never forget how you made them feel.'" I make a leaping motion with my hand. "Then, much like at the end of a fortune cookie, you have to add 'in bed.'"

"Sounds like you need to get laid." Brent shoves the last of his bar into his mouth.

"From your lips to..." I hold up both hands with crossed fingers.

He runs his hand over his mouth to wipe away any crumbs. "The rest of that is 'god's ears,' right?"

"Yes, but god isn't the one I need to be listening right now." I give him a pointed look.

"From my lips to my own ears? I told you last night I value you."

I sigh as we approach the front-facing desk of the scooter rental place. "I'll know when the right part of you perks up and takes notice."

Brent digs the scooter voucher out of his back pocket and passes it to the man behind the counter.

"One scooter? Who's the driver?" the rental agent asks.

I raise my hand at the same time as Brent says, "Me."

"Oh, no." I frown. "I grew up driving these things around Bellerive. I'm not trusting an amateur with my health and safety."

"I'm bigger than you." He scans me. "Much bigger than you. Makes sense for me to be driving."

"Actually—" The attendant holds up a finger.

"That's bullshit. I'm not accepting any patriarchal 'I am man, hear me roar' arguments." I put my hands on my hips. "The best driver should be on the agreement."

"I'm not having you drive me around." Brent mirrors my stance.

"You can rent a second bike," the attendant says. "Or I can put you both on the rental for ten dollars."

Brent fishes his wallet out of his bag and throws a ten on the counter. "We can both be on it."

We hand over our licenses, and I grab a helmet off the rack. Brent tries on three before he finds one that fits. *Amateur.*

The guy brings out the scooter, one with enough power for the two of us, and he takes Brent through the basics. I stuff my bag under the seat, and I take Brent's and use the bungee cord to secure it in the carrier at the back.

"I'll drive first," Brent says.

"Whatever," I say. Unless he's well versed in driving on the opposite side of the road to North America and familiar with Bermuda's traffic laws, it'll be a short ride before I take over.

He climbs on, and I get on behind him. Instead of keeping my space, I wrap myself around him as close as I can get.

"Is that necessary?" Brent asks over his shoulder.

I wink at the attendant who is standing beside us. "Very necessary."

The attendant smothers his grin. "Have fun!"

"We will," I say. "Come on, Brent. Hit the throttle."

He turns his wrist, and we fly forward with a jerk. Turns out holding on this tight *was* very necessary.

"Whoa," Brent says with a chuckle.

"Whenever you want me to drive," I call out in an overly sweet voice.

"I got this," Brent says. "I got this."

We inch up to the exit from the rental place where the parking lot connects with the first main road. It's a busy one, and I wonder whether I should have been more stubborn about driving. Despite Brent's bravado, I have zero confidence in his driving skills.

When we sit at the intersection of the road and the parking lot while three perfectly good openings to merge into traffic pass us by, I tap his shoulder.

"I grew up driving roads like these. There's zero shame in letting me drive."

"We won't crash?" Brent asks.

"With you? Yes. With me? Not a chance."

He releases a long-suffering sigh. "All right. Fine." He fumbles for the kickstand, so I climb off the bike and help him.

I pat him on the shoulder. "Know your strengths, Faulkner. I'll let you save me from drowning later at the beach." I waggle my eyebrows at him and trail a finger down his chest. "Might even let you do a little mouth-to-mouth before I'm revived."

"Sounds like a fair trade. My manhood for some mouth-to-mouth action." His lips quirk up.

I resist the obvious verbal setup. Manhood. Mouth. Too easy. Gotta keep him on his toes.

Once I'm secured on the scooter, he climbs on behind me. With no hesitation, I take the first opening to merge, and we're off on our adventure.

Brent collapses onto my thin blanket and sets the pizza between us. "You're impressing me, Jensen."

"Was there ever any doubt?" I pop open the box from Upper Crust and grab my slice. We have the same taste in toppings—everything but the kitchen sink—and I couldn't be happier.

"You drive a bike like a boss. You've got excellent taste in pizza. And you somehow had and packed this miraculously large blanket-towel thing, so we don't end up sandy." He fingers the yellow material.

"No pinching." I slap his hand. "I've had this since I was thirteen, and I don't need your careless fingers wrecking it."

He grabs the largest slice, and he takes a substantial bite. While he chews, he stares out at the gentle waves.

We laughed all the way to the beach from the pizza place as Brent tried to hold onto the pizza and maintain his balance on the scooter. He didn't trust me that the safest place for the box was between my feet.

Scooter rookie.

There's a light breeze, and the sun is shining, but it's not warm enough to swim. There won't be any mouth-to-mouth action due to a pretend drowning. A good chance I'll let his mouth encounter mine later. He's been surprisingly good company.

"Is Bellerive like this?" He turns onto his side to face me, and he squints against the glare of the sun.

"Better," I say, and I adjust my sunglasses. "More history. Bermuda feels like a tropical island, but Bellerive is a slice of the United Kingdom that got lost. We found the better weather, though. King George would hate that comparison." I laugh. "Similar architecture to the UK. Similar street design—and by that, I mean narrow and chaotic."

"Maybe I'll have to visit someday."

I flip up my sunglasses to meet his gaze. "Maybe I'll let you."

"Like you could stop me." He laughs.

Stopping him would be easy enough. A word in the ear of the king's secretary, my sister, would be enough to halt his approval upon arrival. He hasn't asked me any questions about my family and apparently sucks at search engines.

I slide another slice of pizza out of the box. An amused smile tugs at the edges of my lips. "Eat up," I say. "I need enough time at the hotel to glam myself up to meet your friends."

He takes two pieces of pizza and turns them into a sandwich. It's a good thing we got the extra-large box. "I don't need to be told twice." He grins at me between bites.

While he chews, I examine his profile, and a tiny flutter rises in my stomach. I clutch my abdomen in horror. Did I just...? Was that a butterfly?

"Are you okay?" Brent's light-brown gaze examines me.

"Fine." I let out a strangled laugh. "Totally fine. Nothing to see here." But whatever I just felt better not come back.

Sex I can do, but feelings? Those have disaster written all over them. He's on a hardcore rebound, and I don't do relationships.

I stare out at the ocean, my palm on my belly button.

One flutter means nothing. Nothing at all.

BRENT

When we get to the terrace for drinks, there's a buzz circulating through the crowd. After Posey and I grab rum swizzles, we step down into the crowd near the waist-high white wall meant to ward off the harbor beyond. Lights from across the inlet are barely visible as dusk approaches.

Beside Trevor and his fiancée, Imani, are Wyatt Burgess and Ellie Cooper. The two of them ooze Hollywood glamor despite the fact they have a house on the island. Wyatt's in what must be a custom-made suit, which emphasizes his tall, broad frame. His black hair is a stark contrast to his bright blue-green eyes. Where he's sharp edges, Ellie is rounded corners in a flowing floral dress that screams money. Her hair is in loose waves that fit the beachy island vibe.

While I don't have all the details on the movie they're in together—a thriller of some sort—it's hard to believe being so close to so much star power won't seep into Trevor too. They're both Oscar nominated, and Wyatt actually won a few years ago. Trevor classes working with them as his big break, and I can appreciate those stakes.

As we approach, I lean toward Posey. "Be cool."

"As cool as ice," Posey says, and when she glances up at me, she winks.

This girl, man. I can't remember the last time I had so much fun with a member of the opposite sex. We spent the entire day laughing and one-upping each other with sexual innuendoes. The tightness in my pants only eased long enough for another sexually tense conversation. She hasn't even touched me, and I've got blue balls.

Her lack of filter makes me slightly terrified for her to meet any of my friends, and especially the two celebrities beside Trevor. Bringing an unknown woman to his wedding who embarrassed him would haunt me for the rest of my life.

Surely, she'll understand what's appropriate?

When we get to them, Wyatt glances in our direction and does a double take.

"Posey Jensen?" he says before Trevor has a chance to introduce either of us. "Aren't you on the wrong island paradise?"

Beside me, Posey beams. "Did Haven and Cooper come? Or did you leave them at the house?" She pretends to search for them.

Wyatt chuckles, and he nudges Ellie, who is speaking to someone on her other side. When she spots Posey, her face lights up with recognition.

"So good to see you," Ellie says, and she leans forward to envelop Posey in a half-hug.

"Uh," I say, completely caught on the back foot.

"You all know each other?" Trevor asks. "I haven't even met Brent's date."

My chuckle is unsteady. How the hell does Posey know Wyatt Burgess and Ellie Cooper?

"We go way back." Ellie's broad grin is infectious. "Wyatt shot a movie in Tucker's Town a long, long time ago, and he's been invited to King George's birthday party every year since. Last year, Posey graciously amused Haven and Cooper. Which is no mean feat—a teenager and a toddler."

"You know the king of Bellerive?" The words come out slow, and I probably sound like an idiot. She's my date, and I don't have a fucking clue.

Wyatt's gaze zips between me and Posey. "Her mother has been the king's secretary for years, and did I hear your sister just assumed the position?"

"Yeah," Posey says, and there's a hint of pink in her cheeks. "She's training right now to fill the gap until they've selected someone else. Mother was ready to retire."

"Tell Julia and your mother I said congratulations." Then he turns to me, sizing me up. "And you must be Brent Faulkner." Wyatt is sweeping Trevor's job aside one introduction at a time. He extends his hand. "Ellie and I watched a few of your Olympic races at home earlier. Amazing stuff."

Always a bit surreal to realize people who are a thousand times more famous than me have taken the time to watch me race. I accept his handshake. "Thanks," I say, and I sneak a peek at Posey, who is glowing as though my accomplishment is her own. She's a whole new level of adorable.

Posey drags her hand across my waist while she steps around me to get closer to Ellie. Her dress swirls around her thighs, and my mind drifts to what it'll be like later to draw the dress up her legs, run my hands along her bare skin. I shift on my feet, trying to subtly adjust myself. I've been attracted to women before, but never quite like this.

Ellie and Posey have fallen into an animated conversation. Stunning to realize how little Posey told me about herself.

Trevor appears beside me, and he taps his glass to mine. "Seems like you've dug up a winner."

"And I didn't even know it," I say.

Except I did, didn't I? All day, she's amazed me. She hasn't name-checked any of the royals, and she's had many opportunities. My "be cool" and "can you handle famous people" comments must have had her in internal stitches. Now that I think about it, was the Nick she mentioned earlier Prince Nicholas?

I'm such an idiot. Why haven't I asked her any questions? She's pried out my life story.

"She's slotted herself in," Trevor says. "She's even got Imani talking, and my fiancée is shyer than most."

Sure enough, when I glance at Posey, she's facilitating some sort of conversation between Ellie, Imani, and four other women. A marvel.

"She's an extreme extrovert," I say.

"Not so extreme," Trevor says with the hint of a smile. "She's fully dressed."

"I didn't say exhibitionist." Truthfully, she could be that too. She appears to have no barriers, but now I'm wondering if that's a distraction to keep people from *really* knowing her.

Other people appear to shake Trevor's hand and congratulate him on his wedding while passing by. The interactions feel a little like they're trying to drink in Ellie and Wyatt's aura. I'm familiar with that sort of stargazing, but it must be surreal to experience it everywhere. Most of the time, I'm only recognized in swimming circles.

"What happened to Val?" Trevor asks once we're alone again.

"We broke up."

"Again?"

"This time, it's going to stick."

Trevor observes Posey with me. "I hope it does stick. This girl suits you." He tips his glass in Posey's direction. "With Val, you were always tense. Tight. As though the two of you were one wrong word away from World War III. Watching you walk over here from the drinks tent, you were loose. Light."

"Meeting someone new is easy. No baggage." I shrug off his observation as though it didn't cause warmth to spread across my chest.

"Meeting someone new is *hard*. All that negotiating to figure out whether your true self is compatible with their true self. How often do you sink into a connection like it's always existed?"

Daily, for Posey. I'm convinced she's never met a stranger. The shopkeeper, the guy at the pizza place, the attendant at the lighthouse, she charmed them all. The ease I've experienced around her is a testament to how good she is at networking, and it's got nothing to do with some airy-fairy *connection*.

"Yeah, I can't do another relationship," I say. "I have two more Olympic appearances if I can stay healthy, keep improving. Six years is a long time for anyone to wait to be put first."

Trevor sips his drink and surveys the crowd. "Same as anyone else seeking a work-life balance. Some aspects of life are glass. Commitments that cannot be broken. Other aspects of life are rubber. You can drop them, and they'll bounce back."

The ocean breeze catches a wisp of Posey's hair, and it whips across her face. When she tucks it behind her ear, she catches me staring at her. Her smile widens, and she winks.

"You get too many glass balls, and you're bound to break one," I say.

"True," Trevor says. "But it doesn't mean you can only have one. Swimming isn't going to fulfill you forever." He waves his hand. "This is me being happy and in love and trying to talk everyone else into being happy and in love."

"How'd you know?" I stir my swizzle with my straw.

"That Imani was the one?" Trevor frowns. "All I got is clichés, man. The reason no one can ever tell you how they know is because it's an intangible. There's just something *right* about the other person. They fit in a way no one else ever has, in a way you can't imagine anyone else ever fitting."

I'm certainly keen to see which parts of me fit with Posey, but that's not some sort of *rightness*, that's just sexual attraction. She's gorgeous, and I've got eyes in my head.

"How'd you two meet, anyway? Didn't seem like you realized she was royal adjacent."

"Campus chat server," I admit. "I was looking for a buffer in case Val shows up."

"Val was your guest," Trevor says. "I can't see her crashing the wedding."

"One of the few things I can say I genuinely admire about Val is her persistence." I sip my swizzle. "When she wants something, she doesn't let you or me or anyone else get in her way. She'll trample the lot of us."

"Trust you to admire someone who annihilates everyone else."

Posey extracts herself from the group of women who have gravitated to her. As she picks her way through the crowd, there's a tingle of anticipation in my stomach.

"You'll be happy to hear I'm learning to admire a few new qualities," I say just as Posey reaches us.

She gives Trevor her winning smile and extends her hand. "In all the catching up earlier, I didn't get a chance to introduce myself. Though I've met your soon-to-be wife, and she's a riot." Her glass is empty, and I take it from her. "I'm Posey."

"Trevor." He clasps her hand.

While they strike up a conversation, I go to the bar to get us more drinks. When I return, Posey loops me into the conversation they're having about my high school years with Trev. For the rest of the evening, Posey wanders from my side and into different groups of people. She weaves herself effortlessly into my friends, Trev's family, Imani's family, and his work colleagues.

At last call, most of the wedding guests take their leave, citing their need for rest before tomorrow night's party. As the dust clears from people exiting the Hamilton Princess or going to their rooms, I spot Posey by the harbor staring out.

"Make you miss home?" I ask when I sidle up next to her.

She releases a deep sigh. "Yeah, kinda."

"Back to our room, or have you got other plans?"

She leans against the low wall when she rotates to face me. "You're in the wedding party tomorrow, so I shouldn't tire you out too much." She snags the edge of my suit jacket, but she doesn't close the distance between us.

I step between her feet and stare down at her. Her brown eyes, which have sparkled with mischief all day, look soulful in the dim light cast by the hotel. "I'm not too tired yet," I say.

Her lips twitch, and she cocks her head. "No?" She straightens, and we're so close that rum and pineapple juice lingers in the air between us.

"What do you want me to say?" I ask, and I ease the strands of her hair caught by the wind back behind her ear.

"Oh, Brent," she murmurs. "You disappoint me."

"I value you," I try.

A wide grin spreads across her face, but it's followed by a tiny headshake. "No."

Her insistence on something real causes a twinge of discomfort to lodge in my stomach, but I brush it aside. I suspect everyone values Posey for the easy reason—she can work a crowd like no one I've ever met. She doesn't want the easy answer, and it's not the one I want to give.

"Your scooter skills are unparalleled," I say, and I use the voice we've been teasing each other with all day. Husky, turned on, as though I can't wait to rip her clothes off.

"That's why you value me?" She lets out a giggle.

"I think you're underestimating how much I enjoy being alive." I scan her amused face. "How much I enjoy feeling alive with you." My stomach flips at how honest my admission is.

Surprise enters her dark eyes, and she sucks in a sharp breath. "This isn't..." She takes a deep breath. "Whatever happens this weekend between us ends on Monday. No need for you to get the wrong idea."

Instead of letting her obvious unease bother me, I loop a strand of her long hair around my finger. "I don't form romantic attachments easily. No need to assume that'll change."

"Ground rules." She gives me a sly smile, and she runs her fingertip along my chin. "This ends Monday. No romantic attachments. Anything else is fair game."

I slide my hand into her hair. "We've got a deal." Then I dip down and capture her lips with mine.

Posey

First kisses have never been my favorite. Too much tongue. Not enough tongue. Hard lips. Limp lips. Kisses where there's enough slobber to bathe a dog. And teeth. The clash of teeth is the worst. Most of my first kisses don't lead to a second.

Brent is none of those. From the moment his lips touch mine, we're in sync. Tasting, teasing, an exquisite amount of pressure, as though we've spent weeks practicing with each other. It's the sort of immediate compatibility romance novels are written about. The thought makes me giggle, and I draw back on a laugh.

"Gotta say," Brent mutters. "That wasn't the impression I was hoping for."

"No, no." I wave him off and weave his fingers with mine while I tug him toward the hotel entrance. "I'll tell you when we get to the hotel room, but I swear on Bellerive, it was a good thought."

"A thought that inspires laughter in the middle of—" he sets his free hand over his heart while he lets me drag him through the lobby to the elevators "—what I considered to be a very good kiss."

"Only very good?" I cock an eyebrow while we wait for the elevator to appear.

The elevator stops in front of us, and it's empty. I tug him into the metal box, and I shove him against the wall.

"Only very good?" I ask again before I dig my hands into his hair and meet his lips for another kiss.

That's when I find out I was wrong on the terrace. First kisses, no matter how good, are no match for the second. Whether my laughter causes it, or our innate sexual chemistry, we devour each other. As though someone in security isn't watching us make out through the pinhole camera in the corner. We're hands and lips and murmured nonsensical words.

I shove his jacket off his shoulders, and it falls to the ground with a thud. His fingers find the zipper on the back of my dress, and he draws it down, leaving my back exposed to the air conditioning.

When the elevator signals our floor, Brent snatches up his jacket, and then he scoops me into his arms as though I weigh nothing.

"Tell me why you were laughing," he says.

"You're going to think it's dumb."

"Nothing you've ever said to me has been dumb," he says while he tries to wave his key across the lock without dropping me.

I cling to his neck, and the door pops open.

He carries me to the bed, and he tosses me into the center of the mattress. I laugh, and he hovers over me, an arm braced on either side of my head.

"Tell me," he says, and his gaze is narrowed.

Honest or honest adjacent? "That was the best first kiss I've ever had."

"Ever?" He puffs out his chest. "And the second kiss?"

"Best second kiss too."

"Jesus." He lets out a low whistle. "I'm really setting myself up here."

"Can you score the trifecta?" I tease.

"I'm on board with the scoring part," he says. "In this instance, I'm playing the long game. By the end of the weekend, I'll be the best you've ever had. See if I can mount a perfect score."

"Ooo," I moan. "I do enjoy being mounted, but the dismount is critical. Can you stick the landing?" I do my best to make it sound as dirty as possible.

"I'm excellent under pressure, but if you keep making those noises and using that tone, I'll also be the fastest you've ever had."

"I have heard you're quick off the blocks." I laugh.

"The quickest," he says. His teasing air fades, and he searches my face. "You sure? There's no expectation—"

I drag him down so his lips are a hair's breadth from mine. "Just fuck me already."

He chuckles against my lips, but his laughter fades when he deepens the kiss. He slides his hand from my ankle to my thigh. "God, your skin is so soft. I've wanted to touch you like this all day."

"Yeah? All day?" This time the huskiness in my voice isn't faked. Just the thought of being with him is enough to make my core throb with need. No need to worry about the dismount. I could probably dismount myself right now.

He kisses a trail from my collarbone to my earlobe, and his teeth graze the sensitive skin. With his fingers, he draws the sleeve of my dress down my arm.

Part of me expected him to rush through this first time. We've been teasing each other all day, but there's so much reverence in how he's touching me, as though he can't believe he gets to. His attitude is causing an unexpected warmth to course through me that has nothing to do with sex. I shake my head to clear my thoughts.

Concern enters his expression, and he backs off. "You okay?"

"You're wearing too many clothes," I say.

"Easy to solve." His shirt is already partially unbuttoned, and he yanks his shirt over his head, then he stands to let his suit pants pool to the floor at his ankles.

In just his boxer briefs, the guy is breathtaking. So many well-defined muscles everywhere. He's a chiseled masterpiece. How did none of Val's photos do him justice?

"Wow," I murmur.

"You haven't even seen the best part." He tugs on my hand, so I come to stand beside him.

"During the main event, I'll try to come up with something better than wow."

"As a suggestion, 'it's so big' is always a welcome comment." He suppresses his smile.

I run my fingertips over the outline of his erection, and then I meet his gaze. "It's so big and hard." Not a lie. "I can't wait to feel you inside me." Also not a lie.

He groans. "I'm going to last about five seconds."

"Please let it be ten," I say, and I raise my other hand with fingers crossed.

He chuckles, and then he reaches around to undo the rest of my dress. He gives it a gentle push, and it falls off my shoulders to a heap on the floor.

For a beat, his humor fades as he brushes aside strands of my hair that have fallen across my cheeks. Then he's kissing me again, and I bend into him. My bra hits the floor, and my panties follow in short order. I stick my hands in the back of his boxer briefs to grip his ass, and then I tug down the fabric.

His hand slips between my legs, and when he skims my folds, he groans. "You're so wet."

"Just for you." I'm breathless. Not a lie. I'm not sure I've ever been this turned on by so little contact.

He eases me back on the bed, and he trails kisses down my body until he reaches my core. There, he parts my legs, and he flicks his tongue across my clit. I grip the sheets and tilt my hips.

"More," I gasp.

He grips my thighs while his tongue works magic on my most sensitive parts. So many guys fumble in uncertainty when faced with female pleasure, but Brent seems to be enjoying himself as much as I am. Such a turn on.

"You taste so good," he mutters.

I dig my fingers into his hair. "Protection?" There's some in my bag, but I didn't think to get it out earlier. The urge to feel him inside me is more than I can take.

He backs off me and opens the nightstand drawer to remove a foil package. He's more prepared than me. I take it from him, and then I grip his shaft. Before putting on the condom, I give him a few leisurely strokes, and then I lean forward to tease the tip with my tongue. A taste. A taunt.

He sucks in a sharp breath, and I can't resist. I ease him completely into my mouth, and his hands slide into my hair.

"Fuck," he hisses. "God, Posey."

Hearing my name said with such guttural need ratchets up my own desire. It's not going to take much for me to hit all the high notes today.

I draw away from him, and I tear open the condom. As I roll it down, greedy for him, he tips my chin, so we make eye contact.

"How do you want it?" His voice is hoarse.

"From behind. Hand on my clit."

"I like a woman that knows what she likes." He flips me over, and he traces the line of my spine with his palm. "You're fucking gorgeous."

When he enters me, we both let out low moans of pleasure. He reaches around, and his fingers find my clit. The pace he sets is slow and steady. I'm both dying for him to go a little faster and enjoying the climb. Each thrust of his pelvis and swirl of his fingers inches me closer.

With one hand, I grip the sheets, and with the other, I squeeze his hand on my hip. "I'm so close."

"How close?" Brent asks, and the raw desire in his voice makes me think he might be barely holding on too.

"A little faster," I gasp. My body is strung tight.

He picks up the pace, and I cry out with the force of my orgasm. While I soak in the waves of our spent sexual tension, Brent follows me over the cliff.

"Wow," he mutters against my neck.

I let out an unsteady laugh. "It's a good word."

"I didn't misread that did I? You're good?" He kisses my neck.

"Didn't misread a thing. I am sooo good." I glance at him over my shoulder while he withdraws, and then I collapse into the bedding. "Full dismount achieved."

Brent disappears into the bathroom. When he comes out, he hesitates for only a minute before climbing into my bed.

"You can kick me out whenever you want," he says, and he slides his hand across my waist.

"Hot guys in my bed are always acceptable," I say, and I kiss his shoulder.

"Just how many hot guys are usually in your bed?" His tone is teasing.

"Oh, you—you didn't see the line outside the door?" I feign confusion and eye the closed door.

"Impressive," he says.

"Is it? Guys can be weird about that stuff."

"What stuff?"

"Sexual history. Other guys. Jealous. Possessive. Or whatever." All my casual flings go sideways for those reasons.

He turns to lie on his stomach, and he rests his head on his arms. I mirror his pose, so we're side by side.

"You've gone quiet on me," I whisper.

"Thinking about what you said. Trying to figure out where I fall." He bites his lip. "As long as the sexual history was consensual and something you wanted, I don't see why any other guy would need or care to know about it. But if there was something in there that might help me understand how to treat you better, I'd want to know."

"That's a very mature response." His sincerity takes me by surprise.

"Did I nail it?" His lips twitch.

"Oh, it was nailed," I purr. "Bang, bang, bang, baby."

"Three bangs," Brent says. "I nailed it good."

I laugh and turn onto my side to face him.

"To be clear, I'm not asking you to be my girlfriend, and I'm not angling to have you become my girlfriend. I'm too busy for that shit, anyway. But what's holding you back?"

"What makes you think anything is holding me back? You just said you don't want another girlfriend. How is it inconceivable that I don't want a boyfriend?"

"Just tell me." Brent sighs. "I'm chasing an insane Olympic medal count. What are you chasing?"

I trace a line from his shoulder to his hip. Even his back has visible muscles. "When I'm done with my degree, I want to go back home."

"And a boyfriend would stop you?"

"Might make me reconsider, and I think I'd be miserable eventually."

"A boyfriend could just move to Bellerive," he says.

"It's not that simple. The immigration laws are ridiculous. Any visa is good for two years, and then someone either has to be on the track to becoming a permanent resident, or they have to be in the process of marrying a native Bellerivian."

"Okay, so if that's your excuse for why you're single in college, what about high school?"

"Did you have high school girlfriends?" I ask.

"Sure, if you want to call them that."

"Did *they* call themselves that?" I laugh.

"Honestly?" He purses his lips. "I've been focused on swimming since I realized I might be able to do the impossible, and the rest of my life has always felt like excessive noise."

"Well, that's...honest."

"I sound like an asshole, right?" He grimaces. "It's not that I'm incapable of maintaining relationships. Tomorrow, I'm in my high school friend's wedding party. It's just..." He frowns. "I've never been willing to invest in a romantic relationship." He gives a dark chuckle. "A functional one, at least." He nudges my arm. "You didn't answer *my* question."

How many years have I fluffed off people's prying questions? Friends, casual hookups, guys who wanted more, none of them have gotten to the heart of the matter. But there's something about Brent's honesty that's making me bold.

"One boyfriend. When I was fifteen."

"And what was that like?" Brent asks.

"Claustrophobic." I let out a little laugh, but the memory isn't funny. "Smothering."

"Ah." He strokes my cheek. "So, not a good one."

"Maybe." I hesitate to say the word, but in my heart, I understand it's true. "Abusive?" Julia labeled it that when we were younger, and I was aware enough of how I was eroding to break up with him. Not everyone is that lucky.

He skims his hand along my back, and it comes to rest on my hip. "Would make anyone wary."

"Or scared," I admit. "It might make someone scared too."

He kisses my temple, and I close my eyes at the contact.

The tenderness between us is unnerving, and when he draws away, I snag his lips with mine. "How's your recovery time?" I slip my hand between us to caress him, and he hardens on contact.

"Recovery time?" Brent asks, and the gentleness morphs into a cockiness I'm more comfortable with. "Recovery time is for wimps. I can race to the finish over and over again."

"Oh yeah?" I press my body to his. "Prove it."

In one swift motion, he rolls me onto my back, and our lips start the now familiar dance. Sex and mutual pleasure, I can do. No one needs to root around in my emotional baggage. The only things I'll be unpacking from my luggage are more condoms.

Brent

Listening to Posey talk about her high school boyfriend last night was a punch to the gut. The notion of anyone treating her poorly stirs an unexpected protectiveness in me. Probably an emotion she wouldn't welcome, but it's there whether either of us are okay with it.

I adjust my tie in the mirror, and I hope the humidity comes down a notch before the ceremony. Otherwise I'll be shedding my suit jacket the minute the reverend allows Trev and Imani to kiss.

"Christ, I'm nervous," Trevor says from beside the window.

"About?" I haven't called the stirring in the pit of my stomach nerves for years. Anticipation. The thrill of the chase. At the end of a race, I've either done it or I haven't. Nerves have no place.

"Why did we invite so many people?" He stares at the gathering crowd.

We're in a suite on the top floor of the hotel. Imani and her bridesmaids are getting ready in another room. It's go

69

time in three minutes.

Earlier, I left Posey by the pool, and I realized for the thousandth time I got lucky when she replied to my chat. She's slotted herself into my weekend, into my life, as though she belongs. I don't need to worry she'll be bored or lonely. Wherever Posey goes, a crowd follows.

I catch a glimpse of her teal dress in the crush of guests. She's talking to Wyatt and Ellie, and it looks like she's managed to introduce herself to Sebastian Swan and his girlfriend Natalie. I've met them a handful of times at campus sporting events. The school likes to parade their stars at regular intervals, and while the football team might be tarnished, odds are Sebastian's going pro.

"Just focus on Imani," I say. It's good advice. I can barely tear my eyes away from Posey below. "Treat it like a stage performance."

"I much prefer acting in movies," Trevor mutters.

"All right," the wedding planner appears at the door, and the five of us in the room straighten. "We're going down. Imani is prepped and ready to go. Let's get married!"

Trevor tugs at his tie, and I pat him on the shoulder. "All those people down there are here because they like you."

"Or they're related to me or Imani."

Fair point. Can't choose family.

The wedding planner leads us through the hotel to the front of the neat rows of white chairs. The harbor is behind us, and I'm the last man in the row of best men. Just made the cut.

Despite what I said to Posey last night, I haven't been great at keeping up with my friends either. Some, like Trevor, are understanding because their lives are busy too. But it isn't just romantic relationships that have fallen by the wayside while I chase Olympic glory.

While we wait for Imani and her bridesmaids to appear, I scan the crowd. Posey is sitting beside Natalie, and the two of them are deep in conversation about who knows what. My gaze lingers on her for a beat before I check to see who else is here. Most of the people I saw last night on the terrace, but long dark hair on the opposite side of the aisle stops my heart cold. She's twisted around speaking to someone behind her, but I'd recognize her anywhere.

What the fuck is Val doing here?

The music starts for Imani to come down the aisle, but instead of watching the wedding, I'm trying to figure out how Val wrangled an invitation or if she's truly crashing. When the crowd rises for the bride, the guy Val is sitting beside clicks in my mind. Trevor's sleazy cousin. Her talons are wrapped around his forearm as she watches Imani.

That's a new low. Even for her.

The whole ceremony, I can barely focus. Val's here, and instead of being happy Posey is present to run interference, I'd prefer they didn't meet. They're as different as two people can be.

Their only similarity is a lack of filter. Where Posey's boldness tends to be playful; Val is vicious. A wildcat cornered. I've seen her take down more than one woman who expressed too much interest in me. While I have no doubt Posey is quick enough to hold her own, she shouldn't have to.

The vows conclude, and Trevor and Imani file down the aisle. I'm jittery waiting for my turn to take the arm of the bridesmaid who's my partner. Somehow, I manage to make it to the cocktail area to grab a drink.

Do I rush to warn Posey, or do I avoid her to keep Val off the scent? Earlier I was patting myself on the back for taking a risk on the chat server, and now I'm sweating bullets at the idea of the two women meeting.

The decision is snatched from me when I catch sight of Posey approaching from the right while Val zeroes in on me from the left. I close my eyes and send up a prayer to a higher power.

Val reaches me first, and I cringe inside. I shoot a quick glance in Posey's direction, and I hope she somehow realizes I don't want her to come over right now. Her pace slows, and a frown sits between her brows.

Yep, it's Val. Stay away, Posey.

Val has dragged Stephen, Trevor's cousin, along with her. Her nails are half-moons in his arm, but he's either too drunk or too high to care. Where did she dig him up?

"No date?" Val asks, and she peers around me with false innocence. She turns to Stephen, and she cups his cheek. "Stephen heard you and I broke up, and he swooped in to rescue me from heartbreak."

"A woman on the rebound is not something you turn down," Stephen says, and his drink sloshes over the edge of his cup. "Am I right?"

"Lucky you," I say. Turn down, huh? Sounds like someone swooped, but it wasn't him. She probably sent him a DM and invited herself. Her attractiveness is a weapon she wields with ease. "When did you two arrive?"

Val glares at me. She wants me to respond like I normally would. Consumed by jealousy, I'd cart her off for a *conversation* that would turn into a hot reunion against the side of a building.

"This morning," Stephen says, and he takes another gulp of his drink.

"That's right." Val straightens. "We watched them set up the chairs for the wedding from our room. We have a great view."

"Sure do." Stephen stares at the cleavage spilling out of her dress.

His focus is clear. Get drunk. Get laid.

A twinge of something stirs in my gut. Not jealousy, but I can't pinpoint the emotion.

Her focus is also obvious. Make me jealous. Knowing her, she'll do whatever it takes to provoke a reaction. We've done this pattern before. Dysfunctional to the nth degree. Trevor was right last night. Val and I are always one wrong word away from breaking apart. Even if we'd loved each other, there was no longevity there.

I'm in for a long, uncomfortable evening filled with excessive PDA between her and Stephen through drinks, dinner, and the after party. While I might have come to my senses about us, she hasn't.

She's after me, whether I want her to be or not.

"I hope you two have a good night," I say, and I try to extract myself from the conversation.

"I need to speak to you privately for a minute." Val grabs my arm before I can get past her.

"Brent," Posey says from a few feet away. "I've been looking for you."

The tightness in my shoulders eases at the sound of her voice, but a stone of dread drops into my stomach at Posey and Val meeting.

Val's expression rotates from seductive to suspicious. "Who's that?" she spits out.

Posey arrives, and she wraps herself around me. She extends her hand to Val and gives her a wide grin.

"Posey Jensen," she says. "I'm Brent's wedding date. And you are?"

Guess she decided Val doesn't love me after all. As an opening move, that's a shot across the bow.

Posey

I pick my way through the crowd to Brent, and I'm almost there when I catch a glimpse of a familiar brunette beauty making a beeline for him, dragging a guy who appears either stoned or drunk. She crashed the wedding with a date?

"That Brent's ex?" Natalie Chapman, Sebastian Swan's girlfriend, appears at my side.

"Yeah," I say. "But I can't figure out what's going on." Instead of continuing to Brent, I'm caught between assessing the situation and barging in.

Natalie nods toward the man on Valentina's arm. "That's Trevor's cousin. I heard Imani and the wedding planner talking earlier about how he never sent in his RSVP and then showed up with a date. They were scrambling to figure out food and table settings."

While Natalie and I chat, I search Val's expression for any hint of longing or love. She's doing her best to make Brent jealous, and her date is ogling her chest like it's his job, but there's no heartbreak there. Is that because she doesn't believe they'll stay broken up, or is Brent right and she doesn't love him?

"Would she really put all this effort into finding a date and crashing the wedding if she didn't love him?" I ask.

While we waited for the ceremony, Natalie and I became fast friends. She's the kind of person I genuinely like. No pretense. No bullshit.

Natalie's shoulder-length dark hair falls across her cheek, and she sweeps it back. "She's been making a lot of money off her socials because of him, right?"

"Yeah. Influencer status. Without him, she's got no platform. The only reason I followed her was to stare at him."

"Does he know?" Natalie's brown eyes light with amusement.

"Yep. I have no shame." I give her a helpless look. "I'm a sucker for a hot body."

"I can sympathize." Her lips twitch.

"What impression are you getting?" I ask.

"From here?" She tips her head from side to side. "Possessive, maybe? She doesn't look heartbroken or...you know, that feeling you get when you're desperate for someone? I don't see it. You can't hide that. Leaks out of you. The *worst* kind of misery."

My sister Julia's expression after her friendship with Nick blew apart pops into my mind. *Misery.* That's definitely what glazed over my sister like an oil spill. Sticky. Impossible to ignore. Thank god I've never been that desperate for anyone's company.

Natalie's assessment matches mine. Val wants him back, but it doesn't have anything to do with love.

"All right," I say with a nod. "I'm going in."

"Get your armor on," Natalie says. "Money is a powerful motivator, and she'll think you've highjacked her gravy train."

"I definitely took a ride last night." I give her a sly smile.

"I wouldn't lead with that." She laughs and swirls the drink in her hand.

"In about two minutes, Brent will be shouting 'shots fired' in the 'holy shit' voice guys use when they're impressed and terrified." Val latches onto Brent's arm, and that's my cue to intervene. "Listen for it."

"He's not going to say that!"

I half-turn back to her. "I guarantee he'll be thinking it. My pussy...cat is coming out to play."

"Posey!" Natalie's expression is part scandalized and part amused.

"Brent," I call to give him a heads-up that I'm entering the fray. "I've been looking all over for you." When I reach him, I ignore Val and loop my arms around his waist. He relaxes against me, and I cuddle in tight for a quick squeeze to let him know he doesn't have to deal with her alone.

"Posey Jensen," I say, and I extend my hand to Val. Whether or not she takes it will dictate how nasty this is going to get. The fury in her dark gaze is a clear indication she doesn't see me as a nuisance but as a threat. Girl-on-girl hate is my least favorite, but I learned a long time ago to stand my ground. Being super social isn't always a blessing. "I'm Brent's wedding date. And you are?"

Above me, Brent releases a strangled noise. *Yeah, Brent. I fired the first shot.*

Valentina's eyebrows get lost in her bangs, and her gaze narrows. "Valentina," she says, and she ignores my hand. "I'm Brent's girlfriend."

"Ex," Brent and Trevor's cousin say at the same time. They give each other startled glances that morph into silent 'I got your back' head tips.

Valentina tunes out the two men, and her calculating gaze never wavers from mine. "If I searched my followers, would I find your name?"

She's got me there. "I'm a big fan of Brent's *body* of work." I run my hand along his chest.

"Brent." Valentina tears her gaze from mine to glare at him. "You brought an obsessive swim fan to Trev's wedding? She could be unhinged, a stalker."

"Can you imagine?" I let out a delighted laugh. "We could be on one of those true crime programs." Escalation is the best defense. Call me a stalker? I can go one further than that. "'Wedding date gone wrong' would be a great hook."

"You're dating fangirls now?" Valentina keeps focused on Brent. "Is that what this is?"

"To be fair," I say, "he didn't realize I was a fangirl until I met him at the airport." I gaze up at Brent before meeting Valentina's rage head-on. "But who wouldn't be a fan of him? Am I right?" I give her a beaming smile.

She doesn't respond to me. Instead, she whirls on Brent again. "You could catch something from her. Anything. Girls who meet random men at the airport can't be trusted."

"Syphilis, chlamydia, gonorrhea, herpes, pubic lice..." Amazing how often jealous women make this particular argument. "But what you're really concerned about is that he might catch feelings."

"Oh, sweetheart." Valentina crosses her arms. "The STDs are far more likely. You're not his type."

"Val," Brent says.

I rotate to Trevor's cousin, who has been sipping his drink and gawking at Val's assets. "I'm Posey. And you are?"

"Stephen," he says, and he shakes my hand.

"When did you and Val meet?" I ask.

"She slid into my DMs with a few pics." He grins. "Be crazy to turn that down, even if I had to attend this thing." He waves his drink around. "Fucking rich, stuck-up family."

"Oh," I say, and I stare at Val as I ask the next question. "Did you two meet in person for the first time at the airport?"

"Don't answer that," Val says.

My logic isn't lost on her. People in glass airports shouldn't throw stones. If I can't be trusted, she can't either.

"I think we're done here," Brent says.

"We're not done." Val's hand snakes out to grab his arm.

"We are," Brent says, and his hand is firm on the small of my back. "I'm one of the groomsmen, and I'm not doing my job while I'm here talking to you. Enjoy your weekend. Stephen, it was nice to meet you."

"You too, man." Stephen lifts his drink in salute while Brent steers me away from them into the crowd.

"Jesus, Posey, I'm sorry," Brent says. "But you were brilliant."

"Not my first time at the jealous girlfriend rodeo," I say as he leads us to the bar.

"No?"

"I talk a lot." I shrug. "Sometimes I talk to the wrong people. My sexual innuendos get wasted."

He laughs and squeezes my hip. "A crime." He orders us swizzles, and once we have them, he glances in Val's direction.

"Were you tempted?" From a distance, he didn't appear to be struggling.

"She lured Trevor's cousin into bringing her. I'm not sure what to do with that. I suspected she might crash the reception, but the whole thing? I bet she even paid for their flights, possibly the hotel."

"She has enough money for that?"

"Her family is very wealthy, but she says she hates using their money. She wanted to make her own fortune."

"Except she's been creating it off the back of your fame and hard work," I say. "Out of the frying pan and into the fire on that one."

Brent sips his drink. "That's basically the crux of the problem between me and Val. She's willing to put up with my lack of attention, but in exchange, she requires my body to be at her disposal. I'm not sure she's ever cared about who I am, but she *loves* what I represent."

"Have you never read any of her posts?" She painted them as a couple madly in love to her followers. The photos she's taken of him are intimate, and honestly, beautiful. Her gushing, supportive captions alongside her images framed their relationship as aspirational for me and thousands of others.

"Skimmed a few. All bullshit." He shrugs. "I know the truth. So does she. Best not to engage."

"You just let her lie to people?" I'm not sure what I expected him to say, but his indifference to her misrepresentation is surprising.

A hint of color enters his cheeks, and he shifts on his feet.

Other wedding guests mill around us getting drinks, and I scan the crowd for someone else to talk to. Brent's easy dismissal of Valentina's deception irks me. Or maybe it's how she fooled me when I consider myself savvy about social media.

"With Val," Brent says, "her method of negotiation, during arguments or when I wouldn't give in to her, was very persuasive."

I roll my eyes. "Repeat after me: the sex was good, and I didn't know how to find my balls."

"Should I tell you where they kept ending up?" One corner of his mouth tips upward.

"Eww. No." But I can't help laughing. "You understand how dysfunctional that is?"

"Yep." He angles his drink at me. "Hence you, here. Buffer, remember?"

"Right. Right. The sacrificial vagina."

Brent sputters out his drink. "That's not—"

"Relax. I'm kidding. Mostly. It's not much of a sacrifice." I smirk. "I get that you think you're too busy for a real relationship, and this isn't me vying for the role, but you deserve someone who values who you are, and not what you can do for them." I hesitate. "Or maybe they can value that, too, but it shouldn't be the *only* thing they value."

He gazes at me, and the intensity of it causes my stomach to flip. Like so many others, I've viewed him from afar, but I didn't know him. To realize the guy I've been lusting after is standing in front of me, looking at me as though I'm the most interesting person in a crowd of people, is a heady sensation.

"I'm beginning to appreciate the value in a few things myself," he says.

"Oh yeah?" The words tumble out just as another butterfly bursts out of its cocoon in my stomach.

"I'm glad you responded to my chat."

"Why's that?" I shouldn't be pressing him. Confessions won't help me keep some distance between us. We get this weekend together, and then I'm out.

A hint of a smile tugs at the corner of his lips. "Turns out a witty woman with a heart of stone might be just what I need in my life."

Another slew of butterflies breaks free, and heat rushes to my cheeks. "This weekend. What you need *this* weekend."

"You didn't even balk at my heart of stone comment."

"Of course not. I'm allergic to commitment, and I enjoy my status as a nutcracker."

"That imagery, Jensen." He covers his fly with his hand.

When I grin in response, he loops his arm around my neck and drags me to him to kiss my temple. I settle against him, more content than I'd ever admit out loud.

"Brent," a male voice calls from behind us. "I have some people for you to meet."

With a sigh, Brent lets me go, and then he grabs my hand. "You up for socializing with more new people?"

"Always." I let him lead me through the wedding guests, and the warmth from his hand travels straight to my heart.

BRENT

If Posey wasn't beside me through the cocktail hour and while dinner progressed, I may have done something stupid. Valentina's hands and lips were all over Stephen each time I happened to glance in her direction. The emotion welling up in me isn't jealousy; it's anger. So many people at the wedding understand who she was to me just last week. For her to behave like this with Trevor's asshole cousin is a kick in the teeth.

Given our pattern, my anger would have led me to get her alone, and she'd have broken my will with her lips or her hands or some other body part she offered up. Somewhere on this property, I would have fucked her, or she'd have had my dick in her mouth or grasped in her hand. There isn't a doubt it would have gone exactly as my roommate Jaxon said. We're not good for each other, but I've been incapable of saying no in the past.

Posey runs her hand along my thigh and leans close. "You doing okay? She's putting on quite a show."

"Fine, yeah." I take a large sip of the wine in my glass. Trevor and Imani made their own, and I've either become a lightweight or the alcohol content in this is higher than normal. Drunk decision-making will get me into trouble too.

All the groomsmen and their dates are at one table, and the bridesmaids and their dates are at another. Unlike some weddings, the head dinner table is made up of family—siblings, parents, grandparents. The caterers are circulating, gathering up the last of the dessert plates, and all the speeches are done.

"If that changes, let me know. I'm very good at revenge PDA." She gives me a sly smile before taking a sip from her glass.

"So humble too."

"Humble is overrated. Know your strengths and play to them. No shame in that." She turns in her chair and throws her arm over the back. "Of all the people to play the humble card, I didn't have you pegged for that."

"You don't think I'm humble?"

"Do *you* think you're humble?"

"You say play to your strengths. I say play to your audience. People don't like cocky, even if you are."

"People don't like cocky?" Her brow furrows, and she feigns confusion. "What kind of world do you live in?"

"One where your brand of cockiness is cute, and mine is less so."

"You can rub your cock-iness all over me whenever you want."

I sputter on my sip of wine. She seems to enjoy catching me mid-drink. On impulse, I give her a quick kiss.

Posey glances in Val's direction, but I didn't do that for Val's benefit. There's something about Posey that hits me differently than any other girl ever has. Her company is truly enjoyable, and while she might experience that with every person in this room, I don't.

One of the catering employees appears at our table to invite us to get a drink from the bar while they set up the dance floor.

"Bathroom," I say to Posey as we rise.

"I'll meet you at the bar," she says, and she waves to Natalie before heading to her and Sebastian, who are gathering their things from a table near the back of the room.

My wine-addled brain takes a moment to remember where the bathrooms are. When I come out, Val is standing against the opposite wall with her arms crossed.

"We need to talk," she says.

"No," I say. "No, we do not."

"Brent, we were together for more than a year. You owe me a little more explanation than what you gave me outside the athletics complex."

Do I? It's hard to believe she enjoyed the pattern we developed. The break up—hot sex—make up can't be her version of a good relationship.

"Five minutes," I agree.

She grabs my arm and hauls me out another door to a part of the terrace that's empty. The laughter and joy from the wedding floats out open doors and windows, but it's windy out here, and Val's hair gets caught by the wind. She grabs the bulk of her black hair in her fist and gives me the wounded puppy expression I've only seen a handful of times. That's not going to win me over. I won't let it.

"We can make this work," Val says. "I'll stop posting so much, and I won't ask you to be part of stupid products and sponsorships. Only ones that genuinely fit you." Her wounded expression morphs into a glare for a beat before she seems to remember she's not supposed to be pissed at me right now.

The quick flash of emotion almost makes me chuckle. She'll say anything to get me to agree to whatever plans she's probably already made in the background. This is what happened last time. She agreed to cut back, and she did, but only until the next big offer came knocking.

Jealousy hasn't worked the way she expected, so now she's turned to bargaining. The order of her manipulation is slightly different, and she's going to be shocked when the outcome is too. We're not getting back together.

"This isn't a healthy relationship," I say.

"Fuck healthy. We're young. Who cares? We get what we need from each other."

"Do we?" I got a lot of sex in all sorts of forms, but I can't remember the last conversation we had that didn't revolve around orgasms and algorithms.

"You don't want a real girlfriend." She huffs out a breath. "Come on, Brent. You're too busy. I ask for some photos and a bit of your time. I don't distract you from your goal. Do you really think someone like Posey Jensen is going to be a good fit for you? She won't be okay with being ignored. Brushed aside. Dropped at the last minute for a swim meet, an extra practice, a meeting with your coach, an amazing interview opportunity. The excuses for breaking a date with me have been endless."

Hearing her list all my boyfriend shortfalls isn't aiding her argument. "Why do you want to be with me if I'm such a shitty boyfriend?"

Val holds up a finger. "You're good in bed." She bites her lip. "You're good for my brand."

"Which is?"

"Doting girlfriend."

"Your *brand* is being my girlfriend? That's not sustainable. People really buy that shit?"

"I can sell anything I want to my followers. I bet your little wedding date thought we were the perfect couple. Was she shocked we'd broken up?"

"Whatever Posey thought doesn't matter. You and I know the truth. We're not well-suited to each other. Great sex doesn't make for a good relationship."

Maybe I don't have time for the right relationship, but I should probably stop making time for the wrong ones too. Romantic relationships like the one I have with Val are the only type I've ever experienced—convenient, easy to pick up and discard. Someone who wants a partner who cares about their satisfaction in bed, and other than orgasms, they don't expect much else.

"Why would you want to give up great sex when so little is asked of you in return?" Val closes the distance between us.

"The little you ask, is a little too much." If I wanted to be an Instagram model, I could get a hell of a lot more from it than just great sex.

"I said I'd cut back." She rises on her toes, and her lips graze my ear while her fingers work my zipper.

My body didn't get the *hell no* memo, and it's responding to her like it always does. Her long nails skim over my length, and she lets out a throaty moan.

"You're already hard for me." Her breasts are against my chest. "I'll get us a hotel room, and you can fuck me any way you want."

"You came with someone else." I manage to keep my voice firm, but she's got the other firm part of me in her hand. With a superhuman effort, I step back from her, and I zip up my pants. "No."

"You want me. Take what I'm offering."

"No." I roll my shoulders. While my body might be responding to her proximity and the familiarity of what she promises, the logical parts of me don't want to go down this path again. It's madness to keep repeating this pattern and never learning.

"If you don't want me, I know someone else who does," she says.

"I hope he enjoys getting naked and having his photo taken. Maybe you can become his doting girlfriend." I run a frustrated hand through my hair.

"I won't ever ask for more of your time than you're prepared to give." Val grabs her wind-swept hair into her hand again. "Once you've had time to think about this, you'll know I'm right. Sure, maybe we're not a forever couple, but we're good for now. We are. We get what we want and what we need from each other. Don't be a fool."

I'm tempted to tell her that maybe I've decided I want something deeper than our shallow relationship, but I don't even believe myself. Spending time with Posey has been nice this weekend, but I'm on vacation. My limits and time commitments change as soon as we're back on campus. Swimming has to come first.

"Enjoy your weekend, Val."

"Fuck you, Brent. I'll come see you this week, and we'll work this out. Once you're back at home, you'll realize I'm right."

I wave to her over my head as I make my way along the terrace. Ahead, leaning against the moon gate, is a figure in teal. Posey. Jesus, I hope she didn't see or hear any of that.

When I get to her, she passes me a drink. Her rum swizzle is cradled in her other hand.

"What are you doing out here? Shouldn't you be inside in the center of the action?" I ask.

"Even extreme extroverts sometimes need a five-minute recharge. Plus, being out here reminds me a bit of home. The smell of the ocean, the lights glinting off the water, the breeze whipping through my hair."

I lean against the other side of the stone arch and stare out at the ocean with her. "You want me to leave you alone with your thoughts?"

"Not really." She glances over her shoulder toward where the music drifts out.

"Why'd you come to America for college if you miss home so much?" I ask.

"The only college on Bellerive is a trades school. If I wanted to be a carpenter, a plumber, an electrician, or a host of other practical professions, I could have stayed. But I wanted to be an interior designer."

"Making the world prettier."

"One color palette at a time." The wind catches a few tendrils of her hair, and she lets them fly, untouched. "They'll be starting the first dances soon."

There's something about being close to Posey in front of all those people that feels too much like a performance when I'd prefer it to be real. She's probably right about the timing, since the music gets louder as the next slow song starts.

I tip up the rest of my drink and set the cup on the ground. With a flourish, I hold out my hand. "All your favorite things are out here. Dance with me."

"Seems a bit too romantic." She takes a sip of her drink and eyes me.

"I promise to talk about my ex-girlfriend the entire time we dance."

"You've got yourself a deal." She drains the rest of her rum swizzle and grasps my hand.

When she enters my embrace, I rest my other hand against the warm, bare skin of her back. Despite my vow to talk about Val, I let silence stretch between us. I'm enjoying the feel of her pressed against me while the wind and the waves serenade us at the same level as the music being carried toward us.

In six years, I'll have either broken Phelps's records, or I'll have sacrificed everything trying. When that's over, I want to remember this moment, how it felt to have a woman like

Posey in my arms. She's making me realize that beyond the medals and swimming glory, eventually I want to chase a real relationship, one that makes everything in me solid and happy instead of angry and volatile.

This weekend is a vacation, though. It's not real life, and in my real life, there's no room for a woman like her. Not yet. But it's fun to play pretend.

Posey

The music drifts out of the hotel, and Brent has me pressed against him as we sway together. While I accused him of being too romantic, I can't deny how much I'm enjoying this moment. The reminders of home in the smell of the ocean, the swirl of the breeze around us, and the solidness of him, are a perfect combination. Things I long for melded with the one I lust after.

He might be turning out to be better than I initially expected, but it's still his body I'm interested in. Nothing more.

"I noticed Val disappeared from the dining room about the same time as you."

"She followed me to the bathroom," he says.

"And?"

"She tried to convince me that our shallow, dysfunctional relationship is actually the best thing for me for the next six years."

I emit a low laugh and graze my fingertips against the nape of my neck. "And?"

"And then she stuck her hand down my pants, and I was, I will admit, a little tempted."

"Little? Brent, you're not giving yourself enough credit. If you were tempted, nothing about that was little."

He spins me around, and I let out a surprised laugh before he dips me low. "When you put it that way..."

"Was it only the big guy tempted, or was Brent tempted too?" The idea of him going back to her sours my stomach, but I don't know why. Whatever happens between us this weekend is temporary. If he wants to resume his shallow relationship with her, that's up to him.

He sets me on my feet, and he picks up our discarded cups from the ground. "She thinks she can convince me. Next week she's going to stop by my place so we can talk again."

"Which body part is she hoping will spring to attention during that conversation?"

"In the past, when she pulled stunts like today, I'd be consumed with jealousy, and we'd get back together. Or if jealousy didn't win out, her persistence to get me back would." He grabs my hand, and he leads us back to the wedding. "I'm not jealous this time, so she'll hit me hard with persistence."

"Why would she want such a superficial relationship for six more years?" I don't want any relationship, and I can't imagine clinging so hard to someone based on sex and profit margins.

"She said we get what we need from each other." We're at the doorway to the banquet hall, and he stares into it. "She seems to enjoy the drama, and I'm just done with it."

"She definitely put a lot of effort into making you jealous tonight." After my boyfriend experience in high school, jealousy is my least favorite trait. Chris was jealous of everyone I spoke to, every person I spent time with who wasn't him. Even now with my casual hookups, as soon as there's a hint of possessiveness, we're done. Brent and Val going back for that over and over again is baffling. "I'm no relationship expert, but from the functional ones I have seen, it's about protecting each other, not possessing the other person."

"I would never claim my relationship with Val was functional or healthy. But it was fun for a while. Easy. Low stress and commitment." He releases a sigh. "Which is exactly why she won't give up when we get back to campus. She's well acquainted with what works for me once I'm in training mode."

The MC announces all the groomsmen and bridesmaids need to come to the floor for a dance. Brent kisses my temple before he takes his leave.

Natalie appears at my side. "Was he talking to her?"

"He was."

"She convince him to take her back?"

"Not yet," I say.

On the other side of the room, Val is running her fingers through Stephen's hair while her gaze is glued to Brent on the dance floor. Her strategy hasn't changed. She's still hoping to make him jealous enough to cave.

"Do you think he will?"

"For his sake, I hope not." There's a funny twinge in my chest at the thought of him going back to her.

"You're not tempted to extend your fling beyond the weekend?"

"Nope," I say. "Boyfriends are overrated. He'd be a terrible one, anyway."

"I used to think Sebastian would be a terrible boyfriend too," Natalie says.

"What changed?" Brent is chatting to the bridesmaid in his arms, and our dance is still at the forefront of my mind. I'd gladly switch places with her.

"To me, he ended up being worth the risk." Across the room, their gazes lock, and Sebastian grins. "No regrets."

Their connection is palpable, even from a distance. The song changes, and on the dance floor, Wyatt and Ellie sway to the music, oblivious to everyone else. Wyatt appears to be singing in Ellie's ear, and her expression is one of absolute contentment.

God, to be loved like that.

"May I have this dance?" Brent asks, appearing in front of me.

"I'm going to snag my own dance partner," Natalie says while Sebastian weaves his way through the crowd to us. "Talk to you later."

"Another dance?" I pretend his request is scandalous. "What will people think?"

He takes my hand and spins me onto the dance floor. I laugh as I twirl into the center of the fray. When we stop, we've carved out our own section of the floor, and Brent draws me close. His warm hand settles over the bare skin on my back, and desire rushes through me. Just like when we were outside, his proximity is enough to make me crave more intimate contact.

"I was thinking," Brent says.

"I don't know you well enough yet to determine if that's a good thing or an 'oh shit, here we go' thing."

"I have a proposition for you."

"Oh," I say, and I bat my eyelashes at him. "I like the sound of this."

"I'm going to be very busy when we get back. My schedule is packed, but Val must have it tattooed on her somewhere. She always knows where I am."

"Want me to guess where she tattooed it?"

"I've checked everywhere," he says. "I've never found it."

I smother my grin. His ability to free flow with my jokes is definitely a plus. "Let's get back to the big P."

"Proposition, not—"

"Penis, right."

His eyes are alight with amusement when he gazes down at me. "Pretend to be my girlfriend when we get back. One week, two tops. I'll give you my schedule—"

"Do I have to tattoo it on me? I don't think that'll work for me. Though I would be okay with you looking for it everywhere." I give him an exaggerated wink.

He frames my face, and he kisses me, soft and deep. His tongue dips into my mouth, but it's prodding, not demanding, as though he's coaxing me to give him more. I rise onto my toes, seeking his heat, his pliable lips. As I've come to learn, his kisses curl my toes and cause my gut to clench with longing. I cling onto his biceps. Whether the kiss is for show or for real doesn't matter to me. I just want more.

"As an incentive," I say when we break apart, "that was a strong move." I slide my arm around his neck, and he clasps my other hand in his so we're dancing again. "You want to fake a relationship? Just for show?"

"For a week or two. At some point, Val will get tired of chasing me. She's got some self-respect."

From what I've seen, and from what I can still see happening on the sidelines, it's very little. Her tongue is in Stephen's mouth, but she keeps glancing our way. I'm trying not to notice her, but her over-the-top public display is making it hard.

"You've told me over and over again she's not what you want. That you're done with the drama. At some point, you need self-control," I say.

"When I get busy with training, I get lazy in other ways." He runs his fingers along my spine. "I don't know that she'll wear me down this time, but I'd rather not take the chance. A couple of buffer weeks is all I'm asking for."

While I might technically be able to pretend to be his girlfriend, I'm not sure it's a good idea. Boyfriends are a no-go for me, even fake ones.

"We don't even have to sleep together if you want to keep it totally for show," he says.

"What?" I rear back. "What would I get out of this if not your hot body?"

"My undying gratitude?" He chuckles.

"I'll take both, thank you very much."

"You're in?"

Unease crawls across my skin at the ruse he's proposing. I've never had any problem playing pretend with a guy before, whether that be role-playing or faking interest to get out of an awkward situation or feigning the big-O to stroke a so-so lover's ego. I'm an expert at emotions that aren't real.

"I'll need to think about it," I say. "I'll tell you on the plane ride home."

"We won't be sitting together."

"That's what makes it exciting," I say. "I get to keep you in suspense."

He's not the only one who'll be in suspense. I have no idea what I'm going to say on Monday. Saying yes is risky, but I'm not sure I'm quite ready to let go of the fantastic sex either. He said he'd be the best I'd ever had by the end of the weekend, and we've still got more than twenty-four hours for him to earn his medal.

"And I," he says, "get to convince you my undying gratitude and my hot body are well worth your time."

When I glance up at him, another butterfly emerges from its cocoon to flutter around my stomach.

My fear is that I already believe he's worth it, and that's terrifying.

BRENT

We're barely in the hotel room before Posey's lips are seeking mine. The door clicks shut behind us, and I press her against the wall while I deepen the kiss. Her lips are an addiction. After I kissed her on the dance floor, I couldn't stop for the rest of the night. She might have assumed the make-out sessions were for Val's benefit, but as far as I was concerned, they were foreplay for this. Her, pressed up against a wall, my erection straining my dress pants, begging to find some way inside her.

I slide my hands under her dress and along her ass to prop her against the wall, and her legs circle my waist. She grinds against me, and I'm about to be the world's worst lover.

"Do you have something?" she says. "I want you to fuck me against the wall."

I brace her with one arm while I root around in my pocket with my other hand. I hold up the condom, and she snatches it from me before ripping it with her teeth.

Holy mother of god. Sexy as fuck.

She reaches between us, and she's got my pants undone and the condom on in record time. When I slide her thong to the side, her wetness is gratifying. I wasn't the only one on the brink of losing it in the ballroom. I ease into her, and I have to hold still for a beat while I collect myself. She feels fucking amazing.

She arches her back and lets out a moan. "This is all I could think about for hours."

"Can you come like this?" I ask while I try to keep a handle on my eagerness.

"A little to the right, and hold me tight, and yeah, I can get there." She kisses me and runs her fingers through my hair.

I make the adjustment, and she lets out a whimper. "Yes?" I ask.

"Yes," she says, and she kisses me deeply. "So much yes."

Everything in me is screaming to go fast, but I've already learned she needs slow and steady for the climb and fast to tip her over. I rock into her while I kiss her neck, and she breathes heavy in my ear. When her breath hitches, I know what's coming next, and before she can say anything, I increase the speed a touch.

"Jesus, you're good," she gasps, and she clutches the back of my head.

I swallow her cries of pleasure with a kiss, and then, as she's still riding her wave, I come hard and fast behind her.

Posey crawls across the bed toward me, still naked from our second round of the sex Olympics—her phrasing, not mine. One of the only places in my life where I'm content to let someone finish ahead of me is in bed.

She collapses on top of me with a sigh. "Tell me about this fake relationship business."

"Two orgasms and I've already convinced you? Geez. You're easy."

"Two orgasms, neither of which I had to fake, is making me contemplate what I *am* willing to pretend. I'm not sold on the relationship product, but I'm now browsing the store."

"You know, it might be an opportunity for you to practice having a boyfriend. A chance to slay those old demons in a situation that doesn't count for much."

"I am now exiting the store because it reeks of desperation. That is not how you convince me."

"You'd be a good girlfriend."

"That's a no-brainer. I'm good at everything."

Her airy response makes me laugh. "It'd probably be a shitty job for you with my schedule. Maybe I haven't thought this through very well."

"You do realize how convincing works, right?" She crosses her arms over my chest and stares at me.

"That's what the orgasms were for. That's my main argument. Incredible sex."

She taps her lips and then purses them. "I think you're confusing main argument with *only* argument."

"You drink coffee, right?"

"Lattes."

"Of course."

"Convincing also doesn't mean mocking my beverage of choice."

"Every morning when my practice is done, I'll deliver a coffee to wherever you are—in class, in bed, wherever you want."

"Now we're getting somewhere." She tucks her hair behind her ear. "If I'm to agree to lattes and orgasms, we'll need some ground rules."

"Sounds like something you'd want."

"It's for your protection."

"You're worried about me? Baby, you've got nothing to worry about. I don't catch feelings. Once I'm in training mode, the only thing on my mind is swimming."

"Social media. I'm not posting anything about our fake relationship. We can trick Val, but I draw the line at sucking anyone I might know into this."

"Suits me. I won't post anything either." Basically my mantra now. I only use my socials if some endorsement or FINA ask me to.

"What exactly do you want from me then?" she asks. "Am I your penis guard? Not a full bodyguard. I'm just hanging around to make sure your appendage doesn't get out of control."

"Right. Yeah. No wayward dicks allowed." I let out a grunt. "Sometimes it detaches itself from my body and runs all over the place. No manners. No sense of what sorts of holes it should be hiding in. Completely disrespectful."

Posey laughs and rolls off me to stare at the ceiling. "Oh my god. The imagery."

I turn onto my stomach and rest my cheek on my crossed arms. "In all seriousness, I need someone to hang out with me during the little downtime I have. That's it. Keep me and my wayward dick on the straight and narrow."

"I'm okay with straight, but I do like a bit of girth."

"Are you so commitment phobic you can't even agree to a fake relationship?"

"Bingo," she says, and she points her finger at me. "I'm breaking out in hives at the thought." She examines her arm.

"You want me to pinky swear I won't catch feelings? Cause I'll do it."

"You're that sure it won't happen?"

"Yes."

"Well, now I'm kind of offended."

I let out a huff, and she laughs. She rotates onto her side to face me, and she traces a line along my back with her fingertip.

"I promise it'll be a fun couple weeks with lots of lattes and orgasms. At the end of it, we'll shake hands and go our separate ways." While I might question whether I can keep my promise when we're lying here next to each other and she's charming my pants off, once we're back on campus, real life will resume. My vow to keep any tricky feelings at bay will be easy then.

Posey scans my face, and there's something brewing behind her brown eyes.

"Have you ever been in love?" she asks.

"No," I say. "You?" There's never been time to get to know someone well enough to love them. My cabinet full of swimming medals and trophies is my first and only love.

"No." She thrusts her pinky finger toward me. "We swear to be heart-of-stone assholes who have great sex and drink a lot of lattes. Heart of *stone*, Faulkner."

"I'm offended you think I'm the soft one here." I grab her pinky finger with mine, and when our gazes connect, warmth spreads across my chest. Her eyes sparkle with mischief, and I'm not sure I've ever seen a prettier sight than Posey Jensen naked in my bed with her pinky finger linked with mine.

Shit.

She's right. I *am* the soft one.

POSEY

Since Brent's practice on Sunday is closer to lunch than breakfast, we sleep in and order room service. While we eat naked in bed, Brent gives me all the Olympic village gossip from his last trip there. It's amazing to hear how much the athletes talk about each other. Though I suppose almost all of them are famous in the village for one reason or another. Some of them are just more famous for their STDs.

"That's the village, and you were eighteen the first time you went. Were you running around getting venereal diseases?" I take a sip from my latte.

"Nope," he says. "I wanted to prove I belonged there in the pool, not in some chick's bed."

"You made it. That doesn't prove it?"

"I was still clinging to the sting of disappointment from when I was fourteen. To be so close and to not make it. Then I trained, and I grew, and I got a lot faster. Close races were mine to win, not lose. That first Olympic appearance wasn't much fun. The pressure to perform was crushing."

"Pressure you put on yourself?" I slop a piece of toast through the egg yolk.

"Me. My coach. The press. My family—my parents and siblings gave up experiences and opportunities they wanted to see me succeed. I was terrified I'd let everyone down."

"But you didn't. Do you worry about the same things now?" The sense of pressure is something I'm familiar with —the Bellerive Royals exist under a similar microscope. Except theirs never ends, whereas Brent's happens every four years.

He spreads peanut butter and jam over a piece of toast. "No. The second Olympic appearance sort of cured me of that. I came home with one less medal than predicted. Fucking fourth in the 400 free." He takes a bite of his toast and chews. "There's only so much I can control, and most of the time, I'm okay with that now."

I set my finished plate back on the trolley and bring Brent his second plate of food. He passes me his empty one, and I set it on top of mine. I've never met a man who could eat this much in one sitting. Once I'm back in bed, I snuggle under the covers while Brent is stretched out beside me eating his mound of fruit. I snatch a strawberry off the plate and pop it into my mouth.

"What do you consider in your control?" I ask.

"How often I practice, how hard I work in practice, the food I eat to fuel me, the amount of sleep I get. None of it's earthshattering. Deviation from any of my routines can impact performance."

"You're still two years away from the next Olympics. Not a criticism, but a question—where's the balance? Is there a balance?"

"You sound like my coach." He turns a piece of cantaloupe around with his fingers.

"There are a lot of things I'd be happy to coach you on." I waggle my eyebrows. "Swimming isn't one of them."

He chews his bite of melon, and his gaze is alight with amusement. "I'm pretty sure that comment should offend me, but I'm gonna let it slide."

"I know why I think you should have some balance, but why does your coach think that?"

"He's worried I'll burn out before I get to Olympic appearance number four."

"You don't think that?"

"I don't know. That's the thing about burnout; you don't always see it coming. Right now, I can't imagine it happening. Who knows how I'll feel six years from now?"

My mother and sister thrive on intense organization, which makes them perfect for keeping the king's life in order. My father and I are twins—spontaneous, quick with a joke, good in a crowd. Even though I'm having a much better weekend than I expected, thinking about them makes me a little sad.

"What's your big goal?" Brent asks.

"Honestly? You won't laugh?" I suck in a deep breath.

He crosses his heart and stares at me.

"I want to run an HGTV-type show in Bellerive about interior design. After I've been there for a few years. Not right away. People need to care about the designs I'm doing."

"You'd be good at that," Brent says. "I can imagine you on TV."

"What do you want to do when swimming is over?"

"Not a clue." He gets off the bed to grab a spoon for the yogurt. "I'm taking a master's in business, but I'm not exactly passionate about spreadsheets and marketing."

"You could be a coach. You were great with that kid yesterday. God, Bellerive's swim team could use someone like you. They're—" Then I realize what I've said, and what I'm implying in even bringing it up.

"Go on. You were saying?" Brent dips his spoon in his yogurt and grins.

"I was saying that Bellerive has a swim team. That was the point of my comment. I live in a country where a swim team exists, and you'd be a great coach. No connection there."

He chuckles and licks his spoon. "Because it sounded like you were trying to convince me to move to Bellerive."

"That is the opposite of something I would do," I say, and I drag the covers to my chin.

"Heart of stone, Jensen. Heart of stone."

"Mine is rock solid. It's been forged in fire."

"Maybe it's time you let that burn heal," he says, and before I can respond, he takes his empty plate to the trolley.

One stupid, thoughtless comment by me, and we've dipped into dangerous territory. Except he doesn't want a girlfriend any more than I want a boyfriend. He shouldn't push me when he doesn't want the job.

"I don't need fixed, you know," I say when he starts getting his things ready for practice.

"Won't mention it again." He shoves a towel in his bag.

"Good, because we're temporary, and I don't want you getting the wrong idea."

"Says the woman who invited me to live in her precious country only a few moments ago."

I grab the pillow from behind my head and whip it at him. He ducks and laughs.

"What are you doing while I'm at practice?" He hitches the shoulder strap higher.

Contemplate why I agreed to be your fake girlfriend and how I can get out of it. "Booked a pedicure."

"Are you upset with me? It feels like you're upset with me."

"No. No. Why would I be upset with you? This is the advantage of a fake relationship. We don't get mad at each other. We get to be assholes, and no one cares."

"Right," he says, dragging out the word. "I'll be back in a few hours."

As soon as the door to the hotel room clicks closed, I sigh and throw another pillow at the wall. After Chris, I never cared about having a boyfriend. Casual hookups. People around me all the time. Those things were enough. I didn't need a specific person; I just needed someone. Brent Faulkner won't be the one to change that. Developing a crush on more than his hot body is a recipe for disaster.

At the spa, they have me change out of my shorts and T-shirt and into a robe and flip-flops. It's standard fare for expensive hotels like this, but I'm impressed by the plushness of their robe. I'm wasting time by examining my eyebrows in the mirror when a familiar voice sounds through the locker room from the exit into the treatment area.

Kill me now. I'm so not in the mood for another encounter with the ex-girlfriend from hell. The fact that she had so little respect for me as Brent's wedding date that she had her hand down his pants last night is more infuriating than I expect. I shouldn't care where his dick was or where her hands were.

She stops at the entrance to the bathroom area, and her gaze sweeps over me. "He's training, is he? No such thing as a day off with him."

Do not engage. Do not engage.

I'll be early for my treatment, but it's better to be out there sitting in an armchair waiting to be served than in here with her smugness.

"He eats, he sleeps, he trains, he fucks. Not much to offer a girl like you who's social all over campus."

The way she says it makes the implication that I'm a slut clear. Instead of getting mean in return, I draw my perkiness from my toes up into my expression. She doesn't need to see how much I dislike her.

"You're right. I am *all over* campus." I grin.

"Whatever is going on between you two this weekend, it'll be over next week. Brent wants a particular type of girl, and I'm able to provide that."

Does she mean a sex doll? I bite down on my lip to keep from letting my mean girl out. No one wants a catfight in the spa bathroom.

"I guess we'll see what next week brings," I say in my perkiest voice. "We already synched our calendars. Maybe he needs more than one woman to provide what he needs."

"You're a weekend fling, and I'm the real deal." Her eyes narrow. "I understand him better than anyone. Brent doesn't do synched calendars and multiple women. Next week you'll be in the rearview mirror, and I'll be back riding shotgun."

I let out a deep sigh, and my perkiness is expelled with it. "Maybe you think you know him. But if you do, then it means you believe the best you can do is a guy who doesn't value you. He sees you as a pair of tits and a nice ass. That's what you want for yourself?"

With that, I push open the spa door and exit into the treatment area. My heart pounds in my chest. I'm not sure whether my little speech will have poked the bear or shot it dead.

As for next week, I'll gladly put myself in harm's way if it means Val can't sink her claws back into Brent. I might not want him to be my boyfriend, but he deserves a hell of a lot better than her.

BRENT

Posey's thighs rest on my shoulders, and she's perched on the tiny ledge in the shower while I eat her for breakfast. We need to catch our plane back to campus soon. Her fingers are digging into my scalp, and she's breathing heavily. Fuck the plane. I want to watch her come. After I brought her a rose I picked on my way back from practice, she gave me the road map to this orgasm last night in bed, and now I'm driving the same route to O-Town this morning.

"Oh my god," she cries and clutches at the wet wall of the shower.

I slip two fingers into her, and while I pump and lick, she comes apart around me. Beside her, she fumbles for the condom, and tugs me up.

"I want you," she says.

The water from the shower pounds onto my shoulder while she rolls on the condom. I lift her off the ledge and grip her ass, pressing her against the wall for leverage. She locks her legs around me, and I enter her.

She lets out a groan of satisfaction. "I don't understand how this just keeps getting better," she says when I adjust so each thrust will drive her to another release.

"You can tell me I'm the best you've ever had," I murmur against her neck. "I can take it."

She lets out a throaty chuckle. "Keep going, and you might earn the medal."

"Not a sticker?"

"Oh, no," she gasps. "This definitely deserves a medal."

When I lift my head out of her neck to meet her gaze, she looks like she's on the verge of losing it again. She grabs my face, and she kisses me deeply. Her forehead falls against mine, and her enthusiastic noises are going to be the death of me.

She squeezes my biceps, and I pick up the pace.

"Holy shit," she breathes. "Oh god. Brent." Her legs tighten around my waist, and as she pulses around me, I meet her orgasm with my own.

We didn't sit together on the plane, so I am once again watching her journey through customs and immigration with all the friends she made. Since we took separate vehicles to get to the airport, I could leave. But instead, I stand by the exit doors waiting for her.

When she reaches me, a grin splits her expressive face. "You waited for me?"

"Do you need a ride back to campus?"

"I took an Uber here."

"I'll take you home." I take her bag and sling it over my shoulder.

"For a fake boyfriend, you're actually not so bad."

"Just wait for your latte and orgasm tomorrow. I'll be climbing the ranks."

"Hopefully I'll be the one climbing something." She bats her eyelashes at me and then laughs.

While we walk to the car, we fall into a comfortable silence, and I marvel at how much can change in a few days. On Thursday night when she appeared at my table, I was sure the weekend would be some version of hell. The way she was dressed to tease and her insistence that I had to be a misogynistic asshole wasn't a great starting place. Somewhere along the line, we morphed from strangers to friends. Friends who take immense pleasure in each other.

"Where do you live?" I ask once we're settled in my car.

"Jane and Clarence." She rubs her hands together and zips her jacket to the top. "I forgot how cold it would be."

I pay the parking fee at the exit and turn the car toward her apartment building.

"Where do you live?" Posey asks.

"Montgomery and Horton." We're on opposite ends of the campus, but the athletics complex is on her side. There's a chance I could run into her by accident. Not that I need to worry about that right now.

"I'm surprised you didn't look for a place on my side. Closer to the pool."

When Jaxon found the apartment, we couldn't find a time to view it together, so I told him to take it. "I don't mind the walk." Except in the bitterly cold winter months, which feels like most of them when it's November and I'm staring them down for another season.

"Do you have practice today?"

I check the clock in the dash. "In about two hours."

"You probably need to get home and unpack."

"I should," I say. There's something in her tone that makes me want to do the opposite. "What did you have in mind?"

"Oh, I was just going to invite you up to meet my roommates and give them the rundown on the fake relationship. Thought it might be easier for us to tell them together so they realize we're not a big deal."

"Who are your roommates?"

"Destiny Carter and Nadiya Manji. Destiny is on the women's basketball team, so you might have seen her around?"

"Yeah," I say. Everyone who's worth anything to the university PR department gets paraded around at regular intervals. Star athletes at Northern bear the brunt of the heavy lifting. "She's likely going to the WNBA, right?"

"The draft is in April, but all signs are pointing to yes right now." Posey pats my knee. "If you don't want to meet them, it's cool."

"No, no. I'll come in." Explaining to her roommates that I'm worried I can't keep my dick in my pants around my ex-girlfriend isn't on my list of top ten things to do, but laying out the circumstances will make the next couple of weeks less awkward. I hope. Please let this conversation be the only awkward one. Val doesn't have roommates, so being vetted by Posey's close friends will be a new experience. Fake or not, I don't want to be a letdown.

I've got Posey's bag in my hand when she opens the door to her apartment. A high-pitched squeal greets us.

"Girl," someone calls. "Was he a trash fire or a total hottie?"

Posey glances at me over her shoulder with a mischievous grin before stepping into the apartment. I hesitate for a second behind her before revealing myself.

Destiny Carter gasps. "Shit. Posey, you need to warn a girl. I'm sorry, I didn't realize—" she stares at me for a beat and then glares at Posey "—that you were Brent fucking Faulkner."

"Technically fucking is not my middle name." I offer her my hand that isn't holding Posey's bag, and she accepts it with a grin. She's the same height as my six-foot frame, and her jet-black hair is in microbraids.

"But he's very good at it," Posey chimes in before collapsing into the couch. "It really should be."

Destiny laughs, and heat creeps into my cheeks. Her boldness should not embarrass me, and yet, here we are.

Posey pats the couch cushion beside her while Destiny slides into the love seat opposite. Netflix is paused on the TV, and Posey glances around. "Where's Nadiya?"

Down the hallway, a door opens. "You back, Posey? Was that the worst experience ever or—" Nadiya stands dumbfounded at the corner where the hallway intersects the open kitchen and living room. "Or your wet dream come true? Holy shit. Brent Faulkner."

The nice part, sometimes, about being semi-famous around campus are moments where I get to do cool things or get to cut a line because I swim fast. Days like today, when I don't need to introduce myself, and her roommates' comments are embarrassing and slightly baffling, I'd love to be Joe Nobody meeting his fake girlfriend's friends for the first time. Obviously, they both have preconceived notions about who I am, and I have no idea if I should be combatting those or sinking into them.

Nadiya glances at Posey before zeroing in on me with narrowed eyes. "I thought you were dating Valentina Consuelos."

"We broke up on Thursday before I went to Bermuda," I say. "A long time coming."

"Wouldn't know it from the girl's social media," Nadiya says.

"And," Posey says, holding up a finger, "Brent and I are now fake dating to throw Val off the reunion scent."

"Fake dating?" Destiny lets out a cackle. "Yeah, right."

"Posey doesn't need to fake date you. Man up and tell Val you're done." Nadiya crosses her arms.

"He did," Posey says. "She's persistent. And actually, not very nice."

Nadiya ignores Posey. "Look, if you want to date our friend, just ask her. She'll tell you no, and then there's no need for this ruse to win her over."

"Whoa, whoa, whoa," I say. "That's not what's going on here. Posey and I have a deal."

"It involves lattes and orgasms in exchange for me giving him some distance from Val. There's no relationship happening." Posey slashes the air. "None."

Her total vehemence is causing a twinge of something I can't identify in my chest. Even after days of her zero filter, her bluntness still surprises me. "It's just a couple weeks," I say.

"Uh-huh." Nadiya eyes me with distrust.

Apparently Posey isn't the only one with guy issues. Awesome. Gonna be a pleasant couple of weeks hanging out here with these two.

"Brent has to go to practice," Posey says, saving my ass from this continued discomfort. "But I just wanted to let you both know that he'll be around delivering lattes and—"

"Orgasms," Destiny says with a shake of her head. "Heard that part, thanks."

In the doorway, I lean toward Posey and give her a quick peck on the lips. "I don't think they like me."

"They don't like any guy I bring home. They'll come around. Maybe. By the time the two weeks is done, probably. You know what? You should bring them lattes too."

"Tomorrow? I don't know your schedule," I say when she tries to shut the door on me.

"Oh right. Yeah. I wrote in all the places I need a latte delivered on my calendar during the flight. In the car on the way here, I synched our schedules. Easy peasy." She winks at me. "See you tomorrow."

Then she shuts the door in my face.

I stand there stunned at the entire encounter. Our schedules are synced? I take my phone out, and sure enough, tomorrow morning at nine is a latte icon and the location of her class.

This girl, man. This girl.

Posey

As soon as the door closes on Brent, Destiny starts laughing. I pray to god Brent hustled his ass out of here after they gave him such a hard time.

"You can't be a little bit supportive of my fake relationship?" I say with a huff.

"Are you trapped in a romantic comedy? Are we being pranked? Are there cameras hidden in here?" Destiny checks our plastic plants and peers behind picture frames.

"I had heard Valentina wasn't very nice, but there is no way you need to be involved in this," Nadiya says.

"It'll be fine. The sex is great. He's easy on the eyes. What's the worst that can happen?" I grab a cup from the cupboard and get myself a glass of water.

"STDs, pregnancy, heartbreak," Nadiya rattles off. "Those are just off the top of my head."

"We pinky swore to no feelings," I say. "We're hanging out for a couple weeks until Val catches on that he's not coming back."

"Oh," Destiny says. "Well, if you pinky swore on it, it must be true."

I hurl a dishrag at her, and it makes a satisfying thwack when it hits her back.

"I don't understand what you get out of this," Nadiya says. "You can get your own coffee, and I know you can get your own orgasms too."

Valid question. Those are nice perks, and if I hadn't run into Val at the spa, I might have backed out of our deal. His comments about trying to restore my faith in boyfriends made me wary. "He needs help, and I decided I wanted to give it."

"Isn't it a little concerning he's so sure he can't resist her without you as backup?" Nadiya digs in.

"Any habit is hard to break." I put my glass in the dishwasher. "I'm here to break his Val addiction."

"Why?" Destiny purses her lips.

While Nadiya is good at picking away at all the things I should be thinking about, Destiny always drives into the middle of my muddled thoughts. It's annoying and also why I love her.

"She treats him like a license to print money, and I hate that she's using him like that. He's actually a really nice guy."

"Oh," Destiny says, realization dawning on her face. "That makes a lot more sense. You've got that protective thing from being so close to the royals. Val is the leech, and you're the salt." She waves me off and heads for her room. "Problem solved."

Once Destiny is gone, Nadiya comes to the island and leans across it. "Is that really all this is? You being the salt? Because I know how long you've been staring longingly at his photos."

"You should see him naked in real life." I fan myself.

"You're really guarded with guys," Nadiya says. "And this doesn't seem like a situation you'd normally involve yourself in. Maybe over the weekend you decided you like him? I just—there's a chance he could end up back with Val —and I don't want to see you get hurt."

"He's not going back to her," I say with conviction. "And no one is getting hurt. We both understand the rules."

Minutes before nine, while I'm waiting outside my lecture hall, the crowd parts, and Brent Faulkner delivers me a latte with an exaggerated flourish.

"Did you want me to find somewhere in here to cash in on the other half of your payment?" he whispers in my ear.

"Oh, Brent. You should never ask about something you're not prepared to deliver." I grab his hand and drag it toward the edge of my skirt.

He steps back like I've lit him on fire, and I laugh.

"You promised me," I say in a voice loud enough to turn heads, "lattes and—"

Before I can get the next word out, Brent drags me into his arms and kisses me. His tongue dips in, and I follow his lead. Class has become the last thing on my mind. The doors to the lecture hall pop open, and my classmates stream around us, and I keep kissing him, molding my body into his, contemplating skipping class.

"Any time you want to shut me up like that," I say, "you can go ahead and do it."

"When are you done with class?" He presses his lips to my forehead.

"Eleven," I say. "Lunch?"

"Come to my place," he says. "I'll cook for you."

For a second, our gazes lock, and a flurry of wings beats in my stomach. If anything should cause a riot, it should have been the kiss, but it's the tenderness in his expression doing it.

"Let me feed you," he says.

"Oh, you can feed it to me." I can't help my wide grin. "I'll take every inch you offer."

His lips quirk up into an almost smile, and he slaps my ass. "Go learn something besides sexual innuendos."

I head into the lecture hall, and when I glance over my shoulder, he's still staring after me. Another rush of flapping assails my stomach.

When I arrive at Brent's apartment, Jaxon isn't home, but Brent is putting together enough food to feed an army. In other words, enough chicken parmesan to feed him with a corner left for me.

"At this point," I say, taking a seat at the small island. "I probably shouldn't be surprised at how much you eat, but are you really going to consume all this?"

Brent grabs a raw carrot from the bag on the counter, runs it through the dip, and bites into it. "Over the course of the day, yeah. When I cook, I cook a lot, and then I just grab and go for the rest of the day."

"Do you need any help?" I ask.

"Nope. You can make yourself at home." He stirs the pasta in the pot.

I rotate on the bar stool to take in the rest of the small apartment. It's sparsely furnished with items that have seen better days. One plus of living with two other women—we actually care what our temporary accommodation looks like.

"We don't spend a lot of time here," Brent says from behind me.

"I can see why. Prison probably has a similar feel," I say.

Brent coughs and then chuckles. "All right, what would you do?"

There's not a lot to work with in the main room. Bare white walls. The furniture could be arranged differently. I lean my elbow on the island and glance at Brent over my shoulder. "Permission to explore everywhere in the apartment for material?"

"And by everywhere, do you really mean everywhere?" Brent winces.

"I won't open a nightstand, look under the mattress, or examine your dirty laundry—literal or figurative." I cross my heart. "I'll stay out of Jaxon's room."

"He's got some stuff in the hall closet that's probably fair game."

"I'm on it." I hop off the stool, and I set to work on rearranging the furniture. Brent watches me with amusement, but he doesn't offer to help. He's lucky the furniture isn't heavy, or he'd be losing fake boyfriend points.

In the hallway, I drag out a thin blanket and some framed photos. At the door to Brent's room, I hesitate. His room is just as sparse as the living room. A box has more character. In his closet, I rummage through and find some gems that'll give the living room more character.

I'm putting the finishing touches on the living space when the front door rattles.

"I haven't had a chance to—"

"Smells good in here," Jaxon says from the doorway without looking up. "I love it when you cook for me." When he glances up, he drops his bag at his feet. "You redecorated? What the fuck?"

"Do you like it?" I ask from behind the couch.

Jaxon's gaze ping-pongs from me to Brent to the redecorated living room. "I have no idea what's going on," he says. "But Posey, if you're here to take me up on my proposition from freshman year, you're a little late, but I'm still game."

"Oddly," I say, "that's not why I'm here. I went to Bermuda with Brent this weekend."

Jaxon rotates on his heel to stare at Brent, and he points at me. "She's Jensen."

"Shocked me too."

"Huh." He looks from me to Brent and back to me. "And now you two are..."

"Fake dating," I say. "To throw Val off the reunion scent."

Jaxon starts laughing, and whatever he's thinking about just makes him laugh harder until he's bracing his hands on his knees in stitches.

"Ignore him." Brent lifts the spoon for the sauce to his lips to taste it. He picks up the pepper and adds more.

Jaxon wipes tears off his cheeks and tips his chin at me. "What do you get out of this?"

I open my mouth, and Brent interjects. "Don't tell him."

"Lattes and orgasms," I say. "As many of both as I want."

"Sounds like my last relationship," Jaxon says. "Not fake, just so we're clear."

"This one is, just so we're clear," I say.

"Your bedroom is that way." Brent points to the hallway.

"Now you're kicking me out of the common space?" Jaxon picks up his bag, but he leans against the wall instead of heading to his room. "Since this is fake and all, my bedroom could use a woman's touch."

"Jax," Brent says.

"Where would you want the woman to touch?" I cock my head.

"Posey," Brent says with a sigh.

The way he says my name, as though he has any right to interfere in this conversation, annoys me. Jaxon is a flirt, and so am I. We agreed to tell our roommates the truth, and so Jaxon is probably the only person it's safe for me to flirt with until Brent and I are publicly and privately done.

"I have all kinds of ideas," Jaxon says. "But I'm not sure what to use for a focal point. The climax, shall we say."

Brent circles the island and ushers Jaxon into the hallway, and his bedroom door closes on the sound of his laughter.

When Brent comes back into the living room, he stares at me for a beat with his hands on his hips. "Can we make a loose rule about flirting with roommates? I promise not to flirt with yours if you don't flirt with mine?"

I cross my arms. "If this is about jealousy—"

"Nope. Not jealous." He holds up his hands. "Jax is one of my closest buddies, but he's got no boundaries. Whatever you want to do once our fake dating is done is up to you. We don't need any complications. It's a couple of weeks."

There is a grain of logic there. No point in muddying the water. "Fine." I'm not convinced his motives are purely practical, but it's not worth an argument since I have no interest in Jaxon Parish anyway. Could have been there and done that in freshman year.

"Food's ready." Brent turns to dish up his plate. "Want me to get yours?"

"I can get my own," I say, and I brush against his arm as I grab a plate.

Once we've both gotten what we want, we sit side by side at the island. There's a weird tension between us that I don't like.

"What do you want to do after this?" Brent asks.

"I have a lot of school work, and since Jaxon is here, he can help run interference with Val, right?" I focus on my food while I speak.

Brent doesn't say anything for a beat. "Yeah." The word sounds heavy, as though coming back to campus has weighed us down in unexpected ways.

We eat in silence, and when we're done, I help him tidy the kitchen before grabbing my bag from the front entranceway. This whole fake relationship thing was probably a mistake. He can't even take me flirting with his roommate.

"Jensen," he says when I'm at the door.

I pause with my back to him, and then he's behind me. A frisson of awareness races up my spine, and the connection I sensed between us in Bermuda is back in full force. *Connection?* Lust. Full-on, undeniable lust.

His large hand grips my biceps, and he rotates me around and presses me against the wall. "Don't leave mad," he says, and then he kisses me.

It's deeply unfair that one brush of his lips against mine causes my panties to dampen with need. My bag hits the floor with a thud, and Brent lifts me up. I wrap my legs around his waist, and he carries me to his room.

His comment about Jaxon was about avoiding complications, nothing more. Sensible, really. The less we intertwine our lives and friends, the easier it'll be to shake hands and move on in a couple weeks.

The only things I want from Brent are orgasms and lattes. When he lowers me onto the bed, I stare into his golden-brown eyes, and I pray I never want anything more.

BRENT

We spend all afternoon in bed, and with a lot of persistence on my part, the deep freeze that sprung up between us when I suggested she shouldn't flirt with Jaxon melted. Definitely made me realize I'd have an uphill battle with her if I wanted to make this relationship legit. Good thing that's not in the plan.

I'm getting ready for my second practice of the day when Jaxon appears at the bathroom door while I'm stuffing dry swim gear into my bag.

"A fake relationship?"

"Val said she was going to convince me to take her back." I shrug and keep packing.

"And you've got so little faith in yourself?"

"Faith you've got? You're the one who told me how it would play out in Bermuda. Honestly, if Posey wasn't there, you'd have been right." My motivation to deny Val's advances was partly my newfound aversion to drama, but it was also a strange loyalty to Posey. I didn't want to let her down.

"If you're sleeping with her, cooking for her, delivering her coffees around campus, you're dating for real. You get that, right? Nothing fake about that shit. You bought her flowers yet?"

Heat creeps across my chest. I picked a single rose on my way back from practice on Sunday because I thought she was annoyed with me. Hardly evidence he's right. "It's temporary. We both know that. Get me over the Val hump."

"Yeah? You weren't jealous when she started flirting back today?"

"That wasn't cool." I glare at him and shove my swimsuit in my bag.

"You two must have had a good weekend together if you're *fake* dating now."

He can be such a smug asshole sometimes. "Just drop it, Jax. She'll be around a lot for the next couple weeks, but that's it. Once we're sure Val's gotten the hint, we'll go our separate ways."

"I'm surprised Posey agreed to it."

"Why?" I sling my bag onto my shoulder and squeeze past him.

"She was very against boyfriends in freshman year."

Makes me wonder if he tried to convince her to date him, and another shot of jealousy surges through me. "She's got her reasons." I grab my keys off the island.

"You've been trading deep, dark secrets too?" He follows me to the door. "Out of the frying pan and into the fire."

"What's that supposed to mean?" I open the door.

"Rebounds are intended to mean less than the relationships that came before them. You're getting it mixed up, man. Good luck to you. That's all I'm saying."

"It'll be fine," I say. "We both understand what we're getting into, and it's not a real relationship."

Jaxon's mocking laughter follows me down the hall to the staircase.

Practice is a good distraction from Jaxon's comments about Posey. While I've never been into strings of casual hookups, I've always been terrible at relationships too. I use up all my energy in the pool or at the gym, and inevitably women get frustrated or furious with my singular focus. Val never minded because her singular focus wasn't on building a relationship either. Her brand. Our brand. The brand.

Brand. What a stupid fucking word.

"Faulkner," Ethan Simpson calls to me from across the locker room. "We're going to Jessica's place for food and a couple beers. You in?"

I had planned to stop by Posey's apartment after practice, and Jessica only lives a couple blocks from her. Although Posey and I agreed we'd spend what free time I have together, Jaxon might have a point about slipping into something serious. Developing real feelings for Posey would be a special kind of hell. A house party is just as good as anything. A buffer between me and Val.

"Sure," I say. "Yeah. I'm in."

Ethan's eyebrows shoot up in surprise. "Seriously? I asked because you're the team captain, but normally you're going home to sleep or something."

Fair point. I could probably count on a couple fingers the number of times I've gone out for a team building event that wasn't mandated by our coach or Northern's alumni. "Just came off vacation," I say. "Not quite back to myself yet."

Ethan is also chasing a spot on the Olympic team. He's one of the few people at Northern who truly understands how much work goes into becoming the best you can be. He also enjoys being the life of the party—the Dennis Rodman of Northern University's swim team, except Ethan is lily-ass white like me.

"Let's hope this version sticks," Ethan says with a grin. "All you do is train, man. It's gotta be fucking boring."

"You train a lot too." I shove my towel into my bag and close my locker. We don't directly compete against each other, since he's a breaststroker and that's my weakness. If you ask me, people who choose that stroke are a whole separate breed. Their brains and their bodies operate on an entirely different wavelength.

"Yeah, but I also have no desire to look back on my twenties and wonder where the hell they went. Being a complete slave to my sport won't keep me warm at night. Women and booze have a place." He winks at me as we exit the locker room with the rest of the guys from the team. "Preaching to the choir, I guess. You've got Valentina." He says her name with a weird accent. "And she is fucking hot."

"Actually, we—"

"Faulkner," Jessica squeals and turns to face me and Ethan. "I just heard you're hanging out with us?" She has her phone up, and she's clearly recording. Another person obsessed with catching every second of her life on video as though it might slip through her fingers.

Her reaction coupled with Ethan's makes me realize our coach and Posey might have a point about my swim-life balance. Most of the time, my lack of a social life doesn't even register on my radar.

"Trying out this whole socializing thing," I say. "I may need Ethan to hold me later."

"I do love to cuddle." Ethan gives Jessica a wicked grin. "Isn't that right, Jess?"

She flushes bright red and closes her phone. "You're a total mood killer."

"Baby, are you embarrassed of me?" Ethan teases.

"Until the end of time," Jessica calls over her shoulder.

"She'll come around," Ethan says to me.

"I didn't realize you and Jess were together." Posey and Coach definitely have a point if I'm not even aware of team gossip that doesn't surprise anyone else.

"We're not. But there's something about her... I doubt she'll ever say yes, but I might die trying." He chuckles. "Some people are worth the effort, even if it'll never go where you want it to."

"She doesn't mind being teased?"

"At the last team social she got drunk and told me she likes the attention but she just doesn't like me."

"Ouch."

"She wants to believe she doesn't like me." Ethan shrugs.

This is getting far more convoluted than I bargained for. No point in digging into that mess. I agreed to socialize, not break my brain. Posey could make sense of this in an instant, but I do not have her people skills.

When we get to Jessica's place, everyone grabs a beer from the fridge and puts five dollars in a jar labelled *Swim Team Beer Fund*. Another thing I didn't realize existed. I pay my toll and grab a beer.

Once I'm settled on the couch, Jess takes the seat beside me. She's a leggy blonde who took a while to even speak to me when she joined the team.

"How was Bermuda?" she asks as she sets up some sort of drinking game with cards and dice on the coffee table. "Who's in?"

"Better weather than here," I say.

"The pictures Val posted looked amazing. It's definitely on my list of places to visit."

After we broke up on Thursday, Val's social media schedule wasn't my problem any more. But I wonder whether she adhered to Trevor's wedding photo ban, or if I went to her profile I'd find a slew of pictures. It would be like her to not only crash the wedding but completely ignore the blackout. If I check, I'll feel like I need to do something about it, and that'll drag me into Val's orbit. Ignorance is bliss.

There's a knock on Jess's front door, and Jess tips up her drink before rising. "That'll be Val, I bet."

"Val?" I clamber off the couch behind Jess. "Val's here?"

"After I posted to my story about you coming here, she messaged for the address." Jess grabs another beer from the fridge. "I didn't think you'd mind." She turns to face me. "But I can tell that you do. Sorry."

I finish my beer and slot it into the empty case beside the fridge. "I'll answer the door. No need to get you involved in this." I squeeze past her into the hallway and narrow foyer. When I draw back the door, Val and I stare at each other through the screened one.

"You don't look happy to see me." A slow smile spreads across Val's face.

"I was just leaving," I say.

"So soon? Jess said everyone would be here a while."

"Jess didn't realize you weren't welcome."

"It's her house. I suppose I'm welcome if she says I am. Are you going to let me in?"

I grab my jacket off the hook in the hall, and I slip it on. My swim bag is on the floor, and I sling it over my shoulder. Guess Posey is getting a visit after all. "Go on in, if you want." With a sweep of my hand, I gesture behind me to where everyone else is gathered. "Thanks, Jess! But I gotta go."

"See you at practice," she says.

"Boo!" Ethan calls from the living room. "Don't be a wimp, Faulkner." He appears at the end of the hallway. "Ah, shit. All right. Whatever. Do what you gotta do. I'll see you at practice."

I squeeze out the front door, and I hold it open for Val. "You going in where you're welcome?"

"I'll walk you home," she says, and she tries to slip her arm through mine.

The one time I socialize with the swim team rather than keeping to my normal schedule and Val pops up. As soon as Jess started taking that video, I should have shut her down. But I don't enjoy being the asshole who's too good for the social media shit, even if that's how I feel sometimes. What I'm doing or not doing isn't anyone's business.

"Nah, I'm good." I remove her hand. "I'm headed to Posey's house. We have plans."

"Oh please. You did not extend your weekend fling." She flicks her hair and tugs her winter jacket tighter around her middle. "It's a smoke screen, and I see through it." She grabs my arm to halt our walk down the street. "If you want a more open relationship, I can agree to that. And if you wanted both of us at the same time, I could arrange that too. I can play nice with others."

My lizard brain goes exactly where she wanted it to go, and for a beat I let my imagination run wild. In every scenario I come up with, Val is out of the picture within minutes, leaving me with Posey. Despite the fantasy she's trying to paint, it's not what I want. At one time, I would have been all for a threesome if she'd offered. She must be getting desperate. The other times we fought or split up, her manicured hand zipping down my fly was enough to overcome whatever I was pissed about.

"Do you need me to call you an Uber? I don't want you walking to the other side of campus alone," I say.

She loops my arm around her waist and presses herself against me. "Walk me home."

I dig my phone out of my pocket, and I order her a car to the closest intersection with one hand while I fend off her advances with the other.

A couple of blocks from here is Posey's place, and I don't want Val anywhere near it. Her persistence is worrying.

While I never expected her to take our breakup well, I didn't anticipate how hard she'd cling either. The only thing being fulfilled by our relationship was her bank account. Guess I didn't realize how important the money was. If she needed the cash to fuel something other than her ego, I'd be more sympathetic, might even agree to play along for a bit.

She's still pressed against me, whispering a torrent of dirty things in my ear, when the car pulls up to the corner I've managed to hobble us toward. The good thing about living near campus is that someone's side hustle, day or night, is as a driver. The wait is never long for a pickup.

When the guy rolls down the passenger window and asks if she's Val, she punches my chest. "You called me a fucking Uber?"

"You're welcome," I say. "I have plans, and you're not in them." I shove my hands in my pockets and haul ass toward Posey's apartment.

Hopefully Val will make the right choice and take the pre-paid ride. If I wait around, she'll never get in, and there's somewhere else I'd much rather be.

Posey

My phone is linked to the buzzer downstairs, and when a notification pops up on my home screen, I go to the door to check the security camera. One of the things we liked most about this building, besides its proximity to campus, is its advanced security measures. No one gets into the building without being caught on camera at least once. Before I let Brent into the foyer, I take a minute to gaze at him in the monitor. When I think about it too much, it's unreal he's my fake boyfriend. That the guy I was drooling over a week ago is outside my apartment building.

Destiny is on the couch, and a mix of male and female basketball players are sprawled across our furniture and on pillows on the floor. Tonight's NBA game is on commercial break, and each of them are shouting opinions about the plays or players as though it's possible to drown each other out.

"Are you going to let him in or just gaze adoringly at the monitor?" Destiny's attention is glued to the TV as the

130

game returns from commercial, but she thinks she's nailed me.

"There's nothing adoring about my gaze." I hit the button to let him in, and a burst of annoyance zings through me. There might be a weird gratitude lodged in the vicinity of my heart, but it's normal to be grateful when good things happen. Amazing sex shouldn't be dismissed. I've had a lot of sub-par sexual experiences, so to have a partner who is already so tuned into me is a gift. I'm in awe that his prowess isn't only in the pool but also in the bedroom.

Something happens on the TV, and the room bursts to life with groans, shouts, and expletives. It's so loud, I would have missed the knock on the door if I wasn't already standing next to it. When I swing it back, Brent peers around me.

"Party on a Tuesday?"

"Party every day, Faulkner," Destiny says from the couch.

"Sounds like you picked the right roommates," he says, and with his hands braced on the door frame, he kisses my temple. "We partying or...?"

He smells like chlorine, which I never would have considered a turn-on before. "I'm partying in my room alone," I say. "Too much jock energy out here." I step aside to let him enter with a bag in his hand. "You packed a bag?"

He glances at me over his shoulder as he heads toward the hallway where the bedrooms are located. "I'm moving in. Fake boyfriend has become fake roommate. Jock energy all over your bedroom."

I shove him in the back, and he turns to loop his arm around my shoulders, drawing me into his side. He plants another kiss on top of my head.

"That's not funny," I say. "I'll break out in commitment hives."

He holds my arm while he examines my pale skin. "Not even one." With raised eyebrows he peers down the hall. "Which room?"

I direct him into the middle bedroom, and he whistles. "What?" I ask.

"Great use of space," he says.

As a challenge, I took the smallest bedroom, and my double bed is raised off the floor high enough for me to get my desk under it. The walls are neutral, but I incorporated dashes of color in the bedding, accessories, and pictures on the wall.

"Kind of beachy," he says as he gazes around.

All right. He's got me. My pops of color tend toward an ocean vibe. "Stop psychoanalyzing me."

He drops his bag by the door. "How was your afternoon?" Without asking for permission, he steps up my wooden boxes and climbs into my bed.

I shut my laptop, and I follow him. He's sprawled out, and I'll have no choice but to cuddle next to him if I want to lie down. Instead of seizing the opportunity, I stare at him with crossed arms. "I don't normally have men in my bed."

He props himself onto one elbow. "No? Where do all these non-romantic trysts happen then?"

"Somewhere else." I crawl across the bed to squeeze in beside him.

"Your day?" he asks again.

"Uneventful. Apart from the lattes and orgasms, of course."

"Of course."

"Your day?" I ask. Sleeping and then swim practice is what he told me earlier when I left his apartment. But he arrived at mine later than I expected. Not that I was watching the clock or anything.

"Eventful. I was offered a threesome."

"Val offered you a threesome, did she? Where'd she find you?" I turn on my side to mirror his pose.

"How'd you know it was Val?"

"The threesome offer is the Hail Mary of sexual plays. It's the last resort." Any of my girlfriends who have offered to either participate in one or organize one didn't do it because they wanted to. They did it to please someone else. Even if Brent doesn't have a fantasy of two women at the same time, Val rolled the dice.

"Have you ever?"

I hold his gaze and consider lying. "Once." Another encounter I'm not keen to repeat. Chris, who was two years older than me, got me really drunk and talked me into it when we were at a house party to 'spice things up.' We were sixteen, and I was way too eager to please. "My personal opinion is that it's not an experience designed to bring two people closer together." In fact, along with my conversation with Julia, it was the final piece in the breakup puzzle. Everything about my relationship with Chris stunted my growth, and I won't make that mistake again either.

"Makes sense," he says, and he traces a pattern on the duvet between us.

"But ruins your fantasy," I tease.

He makes a slow perusal of my stretched-out figure. "No, my fantasy is still firmly intact." When our gazes connect, a delicious electricity zips between us, and he slides his hand into my hair to draw me into a kiss. I scooch closer to him, and he rotates so he partially pins me under him.

"You taste like beer," I murmur. "Were you drinking without me?"

He grins against my lips. "I went to a teammate's place for a beer."

I draw back, and I trace the line of his chiseled jaw with my finger. With our synced schedules, it's easy to see how straightforward his life is, or how he tries to keep it. A lot of his time is devoted to training on land or in the water or going to class. When that's not happening, he has his meal prep laid out in his calendar. That discovery sent me down a nutrition rabbit hole to figure out how many calories he was consuming a day.

"Look at you breaking from routine," I say.

"All over the place. People will start talking."

"Did you have a good time?"

"Wasn't there long enough to be sure. Might have. Val saw Jess's post somewhere about me being there, and she crashed the party."

"Ugh. Val and her threesomes." I bunch my hand into his T-shirt. "Trying to find some balance in your life, and she offers to tip the scales."

A hint of a smile tugs at the edges of his lips. "The good news is that I might have realized the value of socializing with my teammates." He collapses onto his back, and he drags me with him.

I curl into his side. "Oh yeah? Tell me about it."

He relays a story about Ethan and Jessica, and I listen while I play with the hem of his shirt. When he seems baffled by their strange relationship, I give him the inner workings of a playboy like Ethan and a certified good girl like Jessica.

"Why can't people just be straightforward about what they want?" he asks.

"Like you and Val? How'd that work out?"

"Touché, Jensen. Touché." He shoves his palm under his head and tugs me tighter into his side again with his free arm. "You okay if I crash here tonight? I sent Val home in an Uber, but knowing her, she's literally camped outside my apartment door."

An exaggeration, I'm sure, but since he wasn't a bed hog in Bermuda, I could probably share a bed with him again.

"Also, your place is closer to the pool, so I won't have to get up at the asshole of dawn."

"Just the butt crack?"

"Those few inches make a big difference."

"Precious, precious inches," I tease.

"Want to see what else can be measured in inches?"

I kiss his neck, and I slide my hand down the front of his pants. "I'd rather get a feel for them instead."

And just like that, he's on his way to making all my orgasm dreams come true.

The next morning, Brent creeps out of my apartment and promises a latte after his practice. Instead of going back to sleep, I go into the kitchen to grab a glass of water. Nadiya has an early class, and she's making herself breakfast.

"You let him stay over?" She smears peanut butter on her toast.

"Our apartment is closer to the pool." I grab a glass and fill it with water.

"Val posted a shit ton of photos of Bermuda. She even had Brent in one of them. From a distance, but still. She's giving her followers the impression they're still together. She even reposted Brent's teammate's video of him going for a drink with them last night."

My blood runs cold and then hot. Since I met Brent last Thursday night, I haven't checked Val's accounts or his at all. Having the real thing is much better than soaking in something that was never real.

"He broke up with her," I say. "Whatever Val posts or says isn't his responsibility."

"Just be careful," Nadiya says. "This has ugly and messy written all over it."

"A couple weeks," I say. "At some point, Val will understand she's not getting him back." Though last night makes me wonder if it'll take more than a couple weeks to accomplish that feat. There are a few other sexual favors she could dangle in front of him, but I'm open to almost anything, so she doesn't have an advantage there. "Then we shake hands and go our separate ways after a lot of lattes and a massive number of orgasms."

She takes a bite of her toast and eyes me. "I hope she gives up before she decides to come after you."

"There is nothing she can say or do to me that some other jealous girlfriend hasn't done before."

"Sure. Maybe. But those other girlfriends, ex or otherwise, didn't have the platform Val has. She's made a literal living from people believing she and Brent are hashtag couples goals. I'll be watching your back, but you need to be keeping tabs too."

"I follow her, so I'll see anything coming. It won't happen, though. It won't. She'll see their relationship is a lost cause. Brent said he's never put up this much of a fight before about getting back together."

Nadiya chuckles and shakes her head. "Naïve. If that's true, that'll make her desperate. No one wants a desperate Val. That girl already has a mean streak, from what I've heard."

The mean streak is definitely correct, but even hers wasn't the worst I've seen. "I'm not worried."

Brent

Jaxon gathers his wallet and keys off the side table, and he putters around the kitchen checking cupboards for snacks and mixed drinks. "You're sure you're okay with the guys coming here for poker night?"

"Yeah," I say. "I'll even play."

"Huh." Surprise is clear in his voice.

"What?"

"Was starting to think you'd suction cupped yourself to Posey Jensen. What's she doing tonight?"

"Out with her roommates. But she invited me to some house party tomorrow night."

"Deacon's party? One of the basketball guys?" Jaxon pauses with his hand on the door.

"Yeah. I met him the other night at Posey's place. He's dating Destiny."

"You're even double-dating? You and Val never hung out with anyone other than each other."

"It's not—we're not—" It *had* sort of felt like a double date. We'd made dinner. Posey sat practically in my lap on the couch, and Destiny and Deacon had been on the other couch. The conversation between us had been easy, and then we'd watched a movie on Netflix together. If I so much as whispered the words "double date" in Posey's ear, she'd crawl out of her skin and find a new fake boyfriend.

"I'll be back with the beer in a little while. You have practice in the morning?"

"Yeah. Might take a nap while you're gone so I'm not the first one in bed."

"Good plan," he says, opening the door. "Just because you never play doesn't mean I'll go easy on you. Your rent money will be mine."

"I'm a quick study," I say, getting off the couch and heading to my room. My two practices and the weight training along with my reduced sleep after a week of staying at Posey's apartment have taken their toll. At her place I'm closer to the pool, and I could get more sleep in theory, but I stay up later when I'm there than I would at home. The middle-of-the-night, half-asleep sex sessions also have their pluses and minuses. Mostly pluses. There are few things better than cradling a drowsy, turned-on Posey while I ease into her. Just the thought of it makes me fucking hard.

I've only known her a week, and it feels like she's slithered into every aspect of my life. In the morning after my practice, I find her to deliver her latte. We usually end up back in bed before I have class or weight training in the afternoon. Inevitably, I head to her place after my evening practice. Slotting her into my life has been surprisingly easy. Our schedules match well, and she's one of the funniest people I've ever met.

Incredible sex and a lot of laughter. The one-two punch I never realized I needed.

With that thought in my head, I strip down and fall into bed. I've barely dragged the covers across me before sleep pulls me under.

There's a hint of light streaming in from my curtainless bedroom windows, and I stir in the bed. A heaviness in the room niggles at my subconscious, tugging me out of sleep. I crack open an eye, and Val is standing in the corner of my room.

"What the fuck are you doing here?" I say, and I sit up, rubbing my cheeks.

She tucks her phone into her purse and crosses her arms. "The front door wasn't locked. I knocked. Rang the doorbell. You must have been really tired."

"So you just let yourself in?" I gather the covers around my waist. Jaxon is the worst for forgetting to flip the lock when he leaves. We have very little in the apartment worth stealing, but it's still annoying. It's doubly annoying when my ex-girlfriend just spent however long watching me sleep. Suppose that's better than crawling into bed with me.

"We need to talk. This Posey Jensen thing has gone on long enough." She sits beside me on the bed, and I try to shift farther away, but I can't do that without losing my blanket shield.

"We're not getting back together," I say.

"That's not why I'm here." Val stares at me, and there's concern in her dark eyes. "I'm worried about you. There's a lot of gossip around campus about Posey. How well do you know her?"

"It's none of your business." I run a frustrated hand along the top of my head. "We broke up. I can date or do whatever with whoever. That's how breaking up works."

"The list of men she's had casual sex with is—" Val raises her eyebrows "—long. Not very impressive. But long."

"The fact that you're digging into her sexual history in an effort to bother me is sick." My temper will not remain in check if she can't keep a lid on her Posey opinions. Val is the type to spread the rumors she's supposedly uncovering.

"I'm not trying to bother you. I'm informing you about the woman you're sleeping with. She's got at least three guys she sees regularly besides you. You're okay with that?"

An irrational spike of jealousy shoots through my gut. While I'm not sure I believe Val, the idea of it is enough to raise my hackles. Fake relationship or not, we shouldn't be sleeping with other people. A safety concern, that's all. But I can't remember if we agreed on exclusive. I'm tempted to tell Val that Posey's partners are none of my business, but if I do, she'll have confirmation my relationship is a smoke screen designed to keep her away. Not that my plan is having the desired effect.

"The only thing I'm not okay with is you attempting to uncover dirt on her. She's a good person, and she's my girlfriend. That's all you need to know."

"Huh." Val rises off the edge of my bed. "I guess you care about her even less than you cared about me if you don't mind her sleeping around. Do yourself a favor and get checked for STDs when you're done with her. She's bound to have something."

"Get out!" I point to my bedroom door. "Leave before I throw you out." I stand up with the covers gathered around my middle.

The front door clicks open, and Jaxon calls a hello while I follow Val out of my bedroom, the blanket trailing behind me. Jaxon sets drinks and snacks on the island, and his eyebrows almost hit the ceiling as he takes in me in a sheet and Val looking like the cat who caught the canary. Christ. I do not need my fake girlfriend finding out that my ex-girlfriend was in my bedroom while I was taking a naked nap.

Val saunters to the front door, and as soon as it's shut, Jaxon tosses me a beer. I fumble with the covers to keep them secure and grab the beer midair.

"I'm surprised you let her in. Not surprised where it ended up, though. This mean you and Posey are done? I wouldn't mind a second shot at that—or maybe it's a third." He winks at me and cracks his beer.

"I didn't let her in," I say though gritted teeth. "Someone forgot to lock the front door again."

"Ah, shit. Did she break and enter to watch you sleep? I can't decide if that's sweet or creepy." He tips back his beer. "The guys will be here in fifteen. You might want to wear something else for the poker game." He nods at the sheet covering my middle. "It's not a toga or a dick-swinging party."

I crack the beer and chug it, hoping the pause before I speak will give me the distance I need to deal with Jaxon. The empty can is in my hand for a beat before I crush it and send it flying toward the sink. Val's comments about Posey with other guys shouldn't bother me. Whatever she did before we met last Thursday isn't any of my business. But if she's still doing those things, I deserve to know.

"You seem pissed off," Jaxon says, and he tosses me another can.

"Nope," I say, and I open the second beer. "Not a care in the world." I leave the living room to gather my clothes from my room and hit the shower. For the rest of the night, I'm not thinking about Posey or Val or anything other than taking Jaxon's rent money for suggesting he should take a crack at Posey once she and I are done.

Later that night, I'm far too many drinks down but a hell of a lot of money up when my phone pings. It's a voice message, and I stare at the screen for a beat before Jaxon nudges me.

"You in or out?"

"I'll raise." I toss money into the pot in the middle, and I switch off my phone. If Posey is after a booty call, I'm too drunk to go anywhere, and I'm not having her come here with all these drunk assholes. Besides, we've been spending every night together, and neither of us needs to get too comfortable with this arrangement.

"Was that Posey?" Jaxon asks.

"Posey Jensen?" Carl asks from the other side of the island. We've crowded six of us around the space since we don't have a kitchen table.

"They're dating," Jaxon says while he raises the pot.

"That's not—we're not—" I stumble.

"First Valentina Consuelos and now Posey Jensen?" Carl eyes me. "You got a magic dick or something?" He makes a tsking noise while he checks his hand again. "If I had to pick, I'd have no problem being Posey's side piece. To be fair, I'll take your sloppy seconds either way. Get me some of that!"

Underneath the island, I make a fist and release it over and over again. She'd murder me if she was here to witness the jealousy running through me right now. Raw and ugly. Carl doesn't have any chance with her, and inside I'm fuming.

I glance at the clock on the stove. Looks like I will be the first one to turn in. Morning practice waits for no man.

"Don't tease him about Posey," Jaxon says. "He doesn't like it."

Funny, he doesn't have a problem participating in it when it's just the two of us.

My cards are decent, and when it's my turn, I raise the pot enough to make everyone at the table nervous. In quick succession, people fold or call. We turn over our cards, and I win the hand with three of a kind.

"It's been fun," I say while I collect the cash. "But I've got practice in the morning."

In my room, I stare at my phone and consider turning it back on. Instead, I set my bedside clock for the alarm, and I tug the covers over me. I'll deliver her a latte in the morning, but I won't stay. Sleep deprivation made me completely miss an intruder entering the apartment. Jaxon's carelessness could have gotten me murdered, and I'd have slept through the whole thing.

I've never let any woman steer me so far off my sleep schedule. Posey and I are temporary, and if I keep slotting her into every spare moment of my day, she might start to feel entirely too permanent.

Posey

When I get out of the shower, there are two lattes sitting on the island, but no man in my bed. I draw the towel tighter around me and check the counter for a note, but there's nothing. Someone had to let him in.

"Was Brent here?" I call out to no one in particular. Nadiya's and Destiny's doors are both closed.

Deacon opens Destiny's door and peers out. "Dropped off the lattes. Promised to bring me one next time. I gave Destiny hers. You just missed him."

First he ignores my orgasm call last night, and this morning he doesn't stay to fulfill the second part of our deal either. Annoyance zips through me. I showered and brushed my teeth in anticipation of a hot guy who smells like chlorine lounging in my bed. With a huff, I grab my latte and head to my room.

At my desk, I set down my drink and collapse into my chair, letting it spin around while I check social media. Sure enough, Val has posted captions to her photos that reference her boyfriend and things they've been doing without naming him. As I scroll through the comments, her followers are questioning the lack of thirst traps this week.

You won't be getting any more of those, people. My fingers hover over my keyboard, tempted to stir the pot.

There's a knock on my door, and I close my phone. "Come in."

The door creaks open, and Nadiya stands at the entrance cradling her latte. "I mean, it's not an orgasm, but I'll take it."

"Apparently it's all I get this morning too." I hold up my cup in a cheers motion. "How are you doing? I didn't want to ask last night, but I saw West with that other girl on the dance floor."

"It's whatever." Nadiya stares at the lid of her latte. "I broke up with him."

"Does that make it easier?"

Her laugh holds no humor. "It should, shouldn't it?" Her finger circles the rim of her cup, and she glances up. "Did Brent say why he didn't answer the phone last night?"

"He didn't even stay to talk to me." I drum my nails on the desk.

Nadiya tilts her cup up. "You've been attached at the hip up until last night." Her eyes widen. "Unless he's back with Val. Did you read her post this morning?"

"He wouldn't do that—" *To me.* "He doesn't want her back." If she offered him a threesome and he didn't bow down to that mating call, he's probably in the clear. Another week together should cement his certainty and hers that they're done, and then we can go our separate ways. He probably doesn't need me now, but I'm not keen to eliminate my free lattes and an abundance of male-generated orgasms just yet. Both of those are hard to find.

"You're putting a lot of faith in a guy you met just over a week ago."

"As you pointed out, we've spent a lot of time together." I do a slow spin in my chair and grab my latte on the way around.

"Weird he didn't stay this morning," Nadiya says, and she raises her eyebrows in mock innocence over the lid of the to-go cup.

"The beauty of a temporary, fake relationship is that I don't have to care why Brent didn't stay this morning. He gave me part one of the deal, and I'm sure part two will happen later tonight." A knot forms in my stomach despite my breezy declaration. We might have only known each other a week, but he hasn't been one to turn down sex. That's his whole Val issue—he's incapable of thinking with anything other than his dick. It wasn't his dick that steered him out the front door instead of into my bed.

"Yeah," Nadiya says with a rueful smile. "You don't seem bothered at all." She raises her latte and draws my door shut.

The house Deacon shares with the other basketball players is one of the biggest off-campus rentals I've ever seen. It's owned by a basketball alumnus who went pro. To live here players have to be stars on the court and maintain a stellar GPA. The entire main floor is wide open apart from a master bedroom suite and a powder room. The furniture could be rearranged to create more distinct spaces, but the one time I mentioned it to Deacon, he just laughed at me.

Not every guy is opposed to having their furniture rearranged.

Near the front door, I'm deep in conversation with Natalie. It's the first time we've run into each other since the wedding, and I've been filling her in on Val's antics while Sebastian socializes with some of the other elite athletes from Northern's roster. Brent will fit right in whenever he finally arrives.

Destiny approaches on my left with a drink for me. "A Bellerive Blue," she says, passing me the mixed drink. "Chet mixed it for you and asked me to deliver it."

"Is it safe to drink?" I sniff it and narrow my eyes.

"If it's not, Deacon and Chet will be having words." Destiny plucks it from my hand and takes a mouthful.

"He'd roofie your drink?" Nat asks.

"Doubtful," I admit. "But Chet and I had an arrangement for a while, and he proved to be slippery. Not in a good way." I take my drink back from Destiny.

"'Slimy' is a better word. I'm glad he got booted from the house," Destiny says.

"Math and honesty—two things he's not good at," I say.

"I cannot follow this conversation." Nat laughs and shakes her head. "Were you dating him?"

"Posey doesn't date," Destiny says. "Or maybe you do now?" She raises her eyebrows. "Fuckable Faulkner has been making regular appearances."

"Fake dating," I say, "is not the same as real dating."

"And yet it bears an incredible resemblance to the real thing."

"It has to," Nat says, "in order to be credible as real."

"Thank you," I say, and I offer her a fist bump. From the outside, fake and real can look similar, but Brent and I know the difference. I take a sip of the drink Chet mixed me and wince. Much like Chet, the balance isn't quite right. Too much alcohol and not enough fruit juice.

For a while last semester, Chet and I were sleeping together. I'm very open with my sexual positions and my alcoholic beverage choices. Much like the alcohol content in a drink, I like to understand what I'm getting myself into when I sleep with a guy more than once. For safety's sake, I insist on knowing any other ongoing sexual partners. I don't

147

care about exclusive, but I do care about risk assessment. Chet told me there weren't any others, and that was a bold lie.

Sebastian calls Nat's name from the kitchen, and she excuses herself to get the rum swizzle he mixed her. Once she's gone, Destiny eyes me. "You've been tense since we arrived. You waiting for your boyfriend to turn up? What time does his practice end?"

An hour ago. Not that I checked our synced schedules five times or anything. I take a long gulp of the shitty drink Chet mixed. "Nope. He just needs to be here in time to take me home."

"Incoming," Destiny says behind her hand.

I half turn to see Chet swaggering toward us. As the point guard for the Northern Ravens, he's not the tallest guy on the team, but he's still got an impressive build. I've seen better. He has his own Bellerive Blue dangling from his fingers, and I can't help wondering if it tastes as terrible as mine.

"Chet." I raise my glass. "Still shit at mixing drinks, I see. You any better in bed yet?"

There are a few snickers around us, and I hide my smile behind the rim of my glass.

"I think that's my cue to leave," Destiny says. "You've clearly got this covered." She pats Chet's chest on the way past him to see Deacon. "Good luck. You'll need it."

"Luck is for people who don't have skill," he says, and he winks at me.

Gross. I give him a saccharine smile. "What are your skills exactly? None are jumping out at me." Juggling women, perhaps.

"I'm happy to give you a demonstration to remind you." He loops his arm around my waist, and he half carries me to pin me against the wall.

Brent's done a similar move, and it was sexy as hell. This, at a party, when I've made it clear for months that he lost his chance, is repulsive. When my back hits the wall, I glare at him, and then I splash what's left of my shitty drink in his smug face.

His expression turns from amused to pissed off in a flash. Instead of unpinning me, he leans closer and lets the liquid drip off his chin and into my cleavage. "I can lick that off later. Once you apologize for being a bitch."

"The only thing I might apologize for later, and even that's doubtful, is this." Then I raise my knee fast and hard right into his balls.

Chet lets out a deep groan just as the front door opens beside me and someone calls out a greeting to Brent. Chet stumbles back, clutching himself, and when I glance at the entrance, Brent is taking in the scene. His expression goes from confused to angry in a split second.

My stomach flips when our gazes connect. We haven't spoken or even exchanged a single text all day. Since I came out of the shower this morning and discovered he didn't stay, there's been a low-level buzz of anxiety in my gut. While I wasn't sure what to expect from Brent when he arrived, it's clear what's on his mind now.

Murder.

BRENT

People use the expression 'seeing red' for a reason, but I'm not sure why that is. Right now, I'm seeing black spots on the edges of my vision, as though my brain is in danger of short circuiting.

Without waiting for an explanation, I grab Chet by the neck of his shirt and shove him farther away from her.

"What the fuck were you doing?" His soaked shirt, her half-empty drink, and him clutching his balls are three red flags too many.

"Relax, Faulkner," he says. "It's not like you're the only guy to park his Ferrari in her garage."

"Ferrari?" Posey laughs. "In your case it was more like a *Mini* Cooper. Is it in yet? Are you *sure*?"

"Fuck off," Chet says with a sneer.

I shove him again, and Posey grabs my arm and drags me away from him. One more word out of him, and we'd have come to blows. My chest is hot, and as soon as we're out in the cool November air, I suck in deep breaths trying to get whatever this feeling is under control. With Val, I got jealous, but she did it on purpose, and I understood how to play her games. I might not have liked them, but I understood them. The green-eyed monster is familiar to me, but this sensation creeping across my chest and surging through my limbs isn't that. It's a form of anger I've never felt before.

"God, Brent," she says, and her breath forms a cloud in the air. "What is your problem? I was handling it."

"*My* problem? When some asshole makes my girlfriend so uncomfortable she resorts to a sack shot, I'm allowed to care."

She tilts her head at me. Fake girlfriend or not, if I didn't step in to put Chet in his place, one of the other superstar athletes in there should have. The escalation from drink in his face to a kick in the nuts didn't have to happen.

"Why are you staring at me like I'm dense? Are you still sleeping with him? Were you two having a lovers' tiff?" I cross my arms over my bulky winter jacket.

"Are you accusing me of something?" Posey draws herself up to her full height.

"I don't know," I say. "Does that feel like an accusation?"

"Definitely feels like a loaded question."

Two, actually. But they both amount to the same thing. "Are you still sleeping with him?"

She mirrors my crossed-arm pose but she's not wearing a jacket. I wonder how much she's had to drink that her coat of alcohol seems to be protecting her from the late November chill. She works her jaw as though she's considering her answer. "What if I was?"

"I deserve to know," I say. Other students stream into the house from the path a little way from where we're arguing on the grass.

"Do I need to remind you that I'm doing you a favor?"

"You just did." I shove my hands into my pockets. "Are you sleeping with anyone other than me?"

"We never said this was exclusive."

"When I didn't pick up last night, did you call someone else?"

"We're not having this conversation." Posey wags a finger at me. "We're in a *fake* relationship. An exchange of goods and services. I service your dick. You service my pussy, and I get lattes too. That's it." She makes a swirling motion with her hand. "Whatever this is—jealousy or possessiveness— can be stored away for someone else. I don't want it."

"That's not what this is," I say when she tries to walk past me.

"Explain it then." Her glare is defiant.

"I don't know. But it's not that," I say. The other emotions I recognize in myself, but the blind rage I experienced when I realized Chet had made Posey uncomfortable enough she resorted to violence is new. "Look, I'm sorry, okay? It's just that..." *I care.*

"You should really get a handle on those feelings," Posey calls over her shoulder as she heads toward the door. "Or your next girlfriend will be able to manipulate you just like Val did."

A ball lodges itself at the base of my throat at her words. When she goes back into the house, I stand outside debating my options. Go home or go back inside. If Posey wants me to pretend like I don't give a shit about her, I can do that.

Fuck it.

Striding back into the house, I deposit my coat on a chair close to the door, and I head to the kitchen for a beer. When I glance around for some sort of tip jar like the swim team has, Deacon claps me on the back.

"Keep your money. We get one party a year funded by Malcolm Durrant. You're at it."

"Must be nice," I say, and I take a swig.

"Maybe we should be doing shots. Surprised you didn't come back in here after Chet again." Deacon grabs shot glasses from the counter and holds them up to the light.

"Posey can do whatever the fuck she wants," I mutter.

"You're right. Posey will do whatever the fuck she wants." He takes down the tequila from a cabinet above the oversized fridge.

I shake my head and gulp back my beer before setting my empty on the island. The rest of the party is buzzing around us. The house keeps getting fuller, and I'm surprised no one streaming into the house stopped to gawk at my domestic with Posey outside.

"For what it's worth, I was making my way through the crowd to intervene when you showed up."

I wave him off. "I don't even know what the fuck I'm doing. What am I doing, Deacon? What am I doing?"

He slides a shot of tequila across the granite countertop. "Falling in love with Posey Jensen?"

I stare into the clear liquid. Falling in love with Posey Jensen. Seems impossible. It's been a week. Who falls in love in a week? Whatever I felt when I saw the result of Chet pressuring her, it wasn't normal. Val and I were together for over a year, and I never felt anything close to the desperate rage that seized me at the realization he might have hurt her.

"I have two more Olympic runs before I can fall in love with anyone." I hold out my glass for a refill. "You and Destiny can't be serious with her being drafted to the WNBA."

"Not serious? Man, what gave you that impression? This is our last year here, and then I'm following her wherever she goes. We're going to be the power couple of the WNBA. I'm going to run her brand like a champ."

"You sound like Val." I hold out my shot glass for a third. Beer I can handle fine, but hard liquor goes to my head a bit faster. "Brand, brand, the fucking brand."

Deacon chuckles. "Don't hold back." He pours himself some tequila and raises it toward his lips. "You could build an empire off your swimming accomplishments already. Two more appearances and you might be revered as a god."

I roll the shot glass between my hands before sending it sailing toward him across the granite. "To do that, I can't get distracted." I glance over my shoulder to where Posey has gravitated to a group of women and is laughing like we didn't get in a fight outside. "Can't get swept up in unnecessary drama. In six years, I can do whatever I want."

"She's not going to be around in six years. I can guarantee that. She might be a tough nut to crack, but someone is definitely going to think she's worth the effort. No doubt about it." Deacon drops our shot glasses into the cluttered sink.

A tight band twists around my chest, and I stretch my arms toward the ceiling in a bid to dislodge it. Must have pulled a muscle.

He perks up at something happening behind me, and he grins. "Destiny waits for no man." Then he steps around the island, and I turn to see him loop his lanky arm over his girlfriend's shoulders, and she squeezes him tight.

Posey is standing beside her. There's a looseness to how she's standing that tells me the alcohol is getting to her. When our gazes connect, her brown eyes are lit with a familiar desire, as though she could melt into me with very little effort.

Instead of going to her, I head to the chair near the front door that my coat is draped across. She didn't answer my question about any other guys she might still be seeing, and she got irrationally angry with me for defending her.

Drama. It's the last fucking thing I need.

Twice I've turned Val's advances down with Posey nowhere in sight. This fake dating idea is a crutch I no longer need. Cut it off. Cut her out. Someone else can try to crack the tough outer shell she's cultivated to keep men out. I don't have time for that shit.

I open the front door, and I leave the party without looking back.

The next morning, I expect a text or phone message from Posey, but there's nothing. Sundays start with dryland training, and the whole time I'm there, all I can think about is Posey. Though drunk me decided last night that ending this fake relationship was the right course of action—Val isn't a legitimate temptation—sober me is struggling to hold the line. Ever since I woke up, thoughts of Posey circle and swirl.

Either way, I have to see her after practice to deliver her latte. Then I need to man up and tell her I am no longer in need of her services as a fake girlfriend. No matter what Val dangles in front of me, I don't want to be with her, and I'm even more sure of that after this week. Other than her deep aversion to anything resembling real feelings or commitment, Posey has been incredibly easy to be around. Despite what Posey believes and what I let myself buy into with Val, relationships might be better when there's more than desire between two people. Other than good sex, Val and I had very little in common. And I'm not sure Posey and I have more in common, but we're more compatible.

Coach Brown appears at my shoulder when I screw up another set of reps. "You feeling okay today, Faulkner? I've never seen you have so much trouble counting to twenty before."

I do another two biceps curls because I have, in fact, lost count again. My brain isn't functioning on a high level. "I was out last night," I say. "Bit tired today."

"You went out?" Coach's eyebrows rise. "Ethan told me you went to Jessica's for drinks after practice the other night too."

For a guy who enjoys his rebel image, Ethan is also a fan of being in the coach's back pocket with team gossip. I wonder if Coach Brown knows Ethan is salivating over Jessica. I glance over to where Ethan is leaned against a machine while Jessica does chest presses. Now that I know about the attraction between them, it's obvious. Posey's good-girl and bad-boy spin on their attraction also makes sense now. I really have been living in my own bubble for far too long.

I grab a heavy weight for my triceps extensions.

"You know how I feel. All work and zero play makes for a burned-out Brent. We've got six more years for you to hit your goal."

Although that's true, I prefer to take the days one at a time. If I constantly dwelled on how long I'll need to be doing a similar rigorous schedule, I might very well burn out. Instead, if I focus on each day's practices, I don't have to contemplate my life a year or two or six from now.

Nothing I want more than crushing Phelps's records. While Posey and Coach Brown might have a point about giving myself more balance, I won't allow anything or *anyone* to distract me from my bigger goal. Some fake relationship with a girl I met a week ago shouldn't even be registering on my radar.

When I realize I've lost count again, I curse under my breath. I start from one, and this time I count every rep with precision.

A sassy, brown-haired, brown-eyed woman will not get the best of me. Deliver her drink, cancel our fake relationship, and be well rested with a renewed focus for evening practice. Maybe then this tightness across my chest won't bother me so much.

Posey

When Brent shows up on the front door monitor with a tray of lattes an hour after his practice finished, a flurry of butterflies that have been circling all morning flutter frantically in my stomach.

He left the party last night after I gave him my best *come hither* expression. I've never had a guy I'm sleeping with ignore me after that. It's the sex beacon illuminating the sky. The *you're getting laid as soon as I can get your dick out* signal. We were one dark corner away from me serving him my body on a platter. Guys don't turn down sex. Brent definitely doesn't reject sex. He leads with his dick.

Not last night.

Maybe I was too harsh with him after he shoved Chet around. Typically, I don't let anyone fight my battles. My one disastrous relationship turned me into a warrior. The girl with the stone heart. The one who doesn't get attached and never takes anything personally.

Brent leaving without saying a word was very personal. I can't decide whether it was well played, but the message was received.

I even checked his and Val's socials. My theory that he didn't need me because he was getting it somewhere else doesn't appear to be true. Crickets on her account, and I'm sure if she managed to lure him back, she'd be shouting it from the proverbial rooftops. Naked photos galore.

I hesitate for a moment before hitting the button to let him in. Destiny stayed with Deacon last night, and Nadiya went to have coffee with West to see whether they could sort out their issues. We'll be alone in the apartment. Those stupid butterflies lose their shit in my stomach again.

There's a brisk knock on the door, and I jump at the sound. God, why am I like this?

With a deep breath, I open the door. Perched in one hand is the tray of lattes, and the other is shoved in the front pocket of his jeans. I linger over his winter boots and his black winter jacket until I can't avoid eye contact anymore. When our gazes lock, my heart sinks at the expression on his face.

No doubt I went too far last night. He looks as though he's the one I kneed in the balls.

"I hurt your feelings," I say. "I'm sorry." What I said that caused his sadness, I'm not sure. A hairline crack forms in my heart of stone.

His eyebrows lift, and he shakes his head. "I'm not sur—"

Before he can say what I'm pretty sure he's going to say, I rise on my toes and kiss him. He doesn't hesitate to return the embrace, to slant his mouth over mine, deepening it. His free hand splays across my lower back, and he tugs me flush against him. I dig my fingers into his hair, and I can't get close enough.

He walks me backward, and he kicks the door closed with his foot in an impressive display of balance. Once he slides the lattes onto the island, he cups my ass and lifts me against him, carrying me to my room. He sets me on the floor, and we're shedding clothes in a blur of kisses and discarded items.

I turn my back to him to snap the lock in place, and Brent's breath is hot against my ear. A shiver slithers down my spine. One of his hands kneads my breast, pinching the nipple while his other hand finds my clit. He trails openmouthed kisses along my neck and up to my jaw. I lean back into him, and he's hard against me.

Except yesterday, we've been gorging on our desire for each other. He can make me come with very little effort, and any second this flood of sensation is going to drown me. Just before I'm about to go under, Brent withdraws, and I moan.

"No, why?" I turn to find him taking a condom out of my underwear drawer.

He rolls it on, and as he steps toward me, his impressive shaft is in his hand. "Say it."

"Prove it."

"Nah, I've already proved it. I want you to say it."

"Give it to me, and I will."

He smirks, but he lifts me up and braces me against the door. He teases me with the tip, easing in and out with remarkable restraint. "I'm not going to ask again," he says.

"You didn't ask the first time."

Our gazes connect, and I realize I missed this easy banter and gentle teasing yesterday. My whole day was off-kilter from the minute I got out of the bathroom and found him gone.

"You're the best I've ever had," I say, and he plunges into me, eliciting a moan of satisfaction.

"Fuck, Posey," he hisses.

My insides tingle at the raw need in his voice. I graze his ear with my teeth and tighten my legs around him so each thrust hits me in just the right spot.

He establishes a punishing rhythm, as though it's possible for us to fuck away whatever went on between us yesterday. Mutual pleasure as conflict resolution is my favorite. He is so damn good at driving me to the edge. Baring my body to him is easy. I dig my nails into his back, and my muscles shake with the strain of trying to hold my release.

"Oh god." I clutch at his shoulders.

He reads me like his favorite book, and he shifts his hold on my legs ever so slightly. I shoot off the edge of the cliff, and he covers my cries with his kisses. Then he follows me out into the sweet oblivion.

Brent dragged me up to the bed after sex, and he wouldn't even let me get my latte. Those to-go cups don't keep it warm that long. He's underestimating my need for the sugar and caffeine that only a latte can provide.

"So," Brent says. "Last night." His arm is thrown across my middle, preventing me from fleeing this conversation.

"Might actually be all of yesterday." This isn't just me. He was weird yesterday too. I turn in his arms, and I lay my head on his biceps, which is stretched out behind us. His brow is furrowed, and I run my hand along his cheek.

"I brought your latte."

"But you didn't stay, and you didn't even talk to me. Nothing. Complete silence yesterday."

"We've been spending a lot of time together," he says.

"Wasn't that the point of the fake relationship? We spend our time together so you don't spend it elsewhere."

He scans my face, and a muscle tics in his jaw. "Who else are you spending your time with?"

"Seriously, Brent?"

"I deserve to know."

"Last week when we first started sleeping together. Now? You're not asking for the same reason."

"Why won't you just answer the question? You wouldn't answer it last night, and you aren't answering it now."

Jealousy is driving him, and I should find it off putting. My breaking point with any guy in the past has been the first sign of insecurity or instability. But there's vulnerability underneath his question when normally all I can see is anger.

I run my thumb along his bottom lip, and then I place a gentle kiss on his lips. He doesn't return it, and tension radiates off him. "You're the best I've ever had, Faulkner. Anyone else would be a letdown. Why would I do that to myself?"

A hint of a smile tips up the edges of his lips. "You owe me a medal."

"Took you a whole week." I slither my body along his, and he hardens against me.

"To get you to admit it. I bet I hit that finish line before we left Bermuda."

He did. He'll never get me to say that out loud. "I answered your question. Were you jealous of Chet last night?"

"Jealous of a guy who got kneed in the balls?" He chuckles. "Uh, no."

"Obviously not about earning the sack shot."

"Forgive me for giving a shit." He smooths my hair and kisses my forehead. "Next time, I'll remember to be a dickhead in the opposite direction."

"Brent."

"Posey."

"I'm trying to get to the bottom of this jealous streak, so it doesn't happen again."

"Yeah, I got the memo. Jealousy is a big fucking no. I've felt jealousy before—a lot—and that wasn't it."

"Oh please. What was it then?"

He purses his lips and then sighs. "You're still going to give me shit for it."

Jealousy is the only plausible explanation for his behavior last night. He's stalling. I tip my chin at him and wait.

"When I walked in and saw your drink all over him and him clutching his balls, it was pretty obvious what had gone on. I wasn't jealous of him, Posey. I was protective of *you*."

Warmth floods my chest in a rush so strong and so sudden, I'm momentarily overwhelmed. Since that one lengthy episode with my high school boyfriend, I've never needed or wanted anyone else to protect me. The crack that erupted earlier in my stone-cold heart deepens and spiders out. Tears sting my eyes, and I bury my face in the crook of Brent's neck. When that doesn't feel close enough, I wrap my arms around him and breathe in the chlorine that clings to his skin. He reminds me of summer, the sun, and warm days lazing around a pool. All the best things.

"Doesn't feel like you hate what I said." He rubs my back in circular motions.

I let out a strangled laugh, but I can't speak around the lump in my throat. He struck a nerve I didn't even know was buried in me.

"Want to tell me I'm the best you've ever had again?" He nuzzles my ear, and his teeth graze against the sensitive skin.

I draw back and frame his face, and I let my kiss be the answer. The desire that normally springs up between us is coated in something more this time, a new intimacy that I'm not sure I'm comfortable with, but I can't deny its existence. A living, breathing thing between us. He's giving me an easy out from dissecting whatever is developing between us.

I'll give him my body, but there's no way he'll get my heart. Love makes you give up too much of yourself trying to make someone else happy, and I'll never do that again.

BRENT

Considering I arrived on Posey's doorstep determined to deliver her a final latte and break off our fake romance, it's somewhat remarkable I'm still in her bed mid-afternoon. From the minute she apologized and kissed me, there was no way I was leaving. Val and I had a lot of makeup sex, but she never apologized, ever. Her acts of contrition involved a blow job or a hand job or a quick fuck in the shadows of a building. Nothing sincere or real. A means to an end. She emptied my balls but never fed my soul.

Conversations with Posey are a different story. We tiptoe around things, but we're more real than what I had with Val. Anything too revealing is an emotional tightrope. One false step, and I'm tumbling into ex-fake-boyfriend territory. Last night I thought I was okay with that outcome. Even when I arrived, conflicted, I was sure breaking this off was the best thing to do. The need for a fake girlfriend is gone. With my schedule for the foreseeable future, a real girlfriend who wants my time and attention won't work. We'll fizzle and die like every other time I've tried to have a normal relationship.

Except, Posey has been proving my theory wrong from the moment I met her.

Maybe what I've needed is a fiercely independent woman. If I'm busy, she's fine because she's got five hundred other people who'll gladly take my place.

Before she admitted we are, in fact, exclusive, the reality of exactly how many people she could be busy with ate at me, a rot I hadn't allowed to get a hold in me until now. Val dripped the poison about Posey, but I sucked it up. Deep down, I didn't believe Val, but Posey's evasiveness fed my insecurity.

The incident with Chet last night wasn't about jealousy, but my questions around who else she was sleeping with definitely were. Unless I want her to run screaming for the hills, I won't be noting that distinction.

She's sprawled across my chest, and I'm tracing figure eights on her back while she talks about her childhood in Bellerive. It's the one subject sure to keep her talking without too many sexual innuendos. Her love for her country is clear. In theory, I should feel the same about America. I represent my country at one of the world's biggest events, but I've got nothing on her passion for a place.

"Right after graduation," she says, "I'm going back. Tucker and Polidano offered me a junior position in their design office. In a few years, I'll drop a bug in Alex's ear about redecorating a few of the rooms at the palace, and I'll beg him to hire me."

"Alex is..." My Bellerive family tree is still fuzzy at best. Though Posey showed me a few accounts dedicated to the Bellerive royal brothers and Bellerive in general so I'd understand who and what she was talking about. The only one I've been able to remember with any success is Nick because his fractured friendship with her older sister had such an impact on Posey.

"The future king of Bellerive. He's the oldest brother. The prickliest, too, but he likes my sister, so maybe I'll get Jules to ask him."

Listening to her talk about pulling up her Michigan stakes at Northern and returning to her roots in Bellerive shouldn't bother me, but I can't imagine being here without her. Fucked up considering I'm not even sure I'll be able to convince her to stick around beyond next week.

"Do you want to go out for an early dinner?" I ask on impulse. "Maybe catch a movie?"

She peers at me, and I can see the wheels turning. God forbid we do anything that might feel like a *real* date. Dinner and a movie is a radical plan.

"It seemed like you were saying we'd been spending too much time together."

"Did it?" Earlier I was trying to keep from losing my cool over her vague answers. I slide my hand down to rest in the hollow before the curve of her ass. "Might as well enjoy the time we've got, right?"

"Hmm." She taps her bottom lip and then gives a slow nod. "I get to pick where we eat."

"Fine by me. I'll eat anything."

"I'm aware." She chuckles and rolls off me.

I follow her and pin her to the bed. "Might need an appetizer before the main course."

Posey gives me a sly smile and spreads her legs. "I've got one right here."

"Just what I ordered," I say as I trail kisses down her body and then slide my hands under her ass to tip up her pelvis. She digs her fingers into my hair, and when I glance up at her, utter contentment falls over me like a blanket. There's nowhere else I'd rather be than in this bed with her.

"What?" she whispers.

I won't say it, but the realization doesn't send a shot of panic through me either. Deacon said someone would break down Posey's high walls someday, and I'm starting to think I'm up for the challenge.

"You'd better find something to hold on to," I say. "I'm going to make you come so hard you'll be thinking about it for days."

"It's a shame you lack so much confidence." She lets out a throaty chuckle.

"A real mood killer," I say, and with that, I flick my tongue along her slit. She clutches at the bed sheets and rolls her hips.

"More," she says.

She's going to get more. So much more than she bargained for, and I slide my tongue between her slick folds before covering her clit with my lips.

Posey suggests we go to a hole-in-the-wall place on the outskirts of the southern end of campus. Earlier, I went home after practice to work up my nerve to come here and call off our fake relationship, so my car is here. Worked out beautifully.

Pretty sure I've convinced myself I want the real thing instead.

The first heavy snow is supposed to fall sometime tonight. We're still shivering from the cold, and my car hasn't had a chance to warm up by the time we reach the restaurant parking lot. She didn't tell me where we were going, so when I park the car, I stare up at the big blue sign.

"What's Bellerive's obsession with blue?" In bold lettering, the restaurant is simply called Bellerive Cuisine.

Not exactly inventive, but I suppose it gets the point across. Here's hoping the sign isn't reflective of the food quality.

"What's America's obsession with red, white, and blue?"

"Touché, Jensen." I open my door and follow her to the entrance.

The minute we step inside, I'm relieved to see the tacky sign out front bears zero resemblance to the professional gray-and-white décor inside, which relies on splashes of Bellerive's signature blue hue here and there.

"Did you design this place?" I cock my head.

She glances at me over her shoulder, and there's a flush in her cheeks that isn't from the cold. "What gave me away?"

Nothing. And everything. This place *feels* like her.

"Posey!" An older gentleman with salt-and-pepper hair and a graying beard approaches us from the back of the empty restaurant. "You finally brought us a boyfriend?" He extends his hand to me. "She only ever brings her roommates, and my wife and I have the hardest time believing no man has snapped her up."

"She's so slick and slippery, she's hard to snap up." I take his hand, and he chuckles while Posey elbows me.

"He's not my boyfriend. That's what he meant to say." Posey waves me off.

"Oh," the owner says. "She's still playing hard to get. You look very familiar." His gaze narrows on me. "Posey, did you show me photos of your boyfriend once?"

"Um, possibly." Pink appears in her cheeks.

It's not as though I don't know she was obsessed with staring at my half-naked body, but the sheer number of people who are aware of it is surprising. Or maybe it isn't. Posey has no problem oversharing as long as the emotion doesn't hit too close to home. A guy she never thought she'd actually meet is right up her alley.

He shows us to a table near the back, and he gives us menus. Posey sets hers on the edge of the table without opening it.

"How many times have you been here?"

"Drunk or sober?" She takes a sip of the water he placed in front of us. "This is the closest to home I can get in Michigan. I come here whenever I need a taste."

Given how much she loves Bellerive, I'm going to assume that's weekly at the very least. The fact the owners let her have a heavy hand in redecorating the place speaks volumes about her connection with them and this place. Whatever happens over the next week or so, I'll end up here again. Not sure if the food is any good, but the atmosphere is top-notch.

"I'm going to trust you to order for us." I set my menu on top of hers.

"Really?" She grins. "Whatever I want? Can you give me your level of Brent hungriness on a scale of one to ten?"

I rub my belly and consider her question. "A solid eight."

When the owner returns, Posey rattles off rice and fish dishes I've never heard of. She also orders some sort of apple blossom pastry for dessert. While we wait for dinner, we search for movies and times on our phones.

The rest of the evening passes in a blur of food that tastes tropical and European, as though Bellerive has an identity crisis. Not that I'd say that to Posey.

The action film runs long, and when we get back to her apartment, she checks the clock on the dash. "You have practice soon, right?"

I stare at the clock as the number turns over. Technically, I should be at practice in half an hour. If I left now, I'd get there easily. The snow has started to fall, and my car warmed as we drove. There have been a handful of times where diving into a cold pool wasn't remotely appealing, and tonight the only place I want to dive is back under the covers with Posey.

"Practice was cancelled," I say. Coach won't give me shit for missing it since I'll be there again in the morning. He keeps telling me I need more balance, and the girl sitting beside me is the closest to equilibrium I've ever felt. Giving an inch for her doesn't scare me as much as I thought it would.

"Really?" A wide smile spreads across her face. "You're coming up?"

I graze her cheek with my thumb, and I slide my hand around to cup her neck before drawing her into a kiss. She meets it, and her tongue dips and dances with mine. When I draw back, I rest my forehead against hers and I question my sanity.

Instead of ditching the girl and the drama, I'm ditching practice. Not something I ever would have thought myself capable of. No one and nothing has ever come before swimming. But tonight, for the first time ever, I'd rather be in her bed than in the pool.

The last thing she's after is a real relationship, but I'm starting to realize letting her go won't be as easy as I thought. The unattainable has never been so appealing. With swimming, if I work hard enough, the results come. With women, I've learned to set my expectations at a level I can achieve. Brief companionship. A relationship wedged into the cracks of my schedule.

Posey doesn't feel like something I wedge into anything. What I'm starting to feel for her is on par with my drive to win in the pool. A real relationship might be unreachable, but I've always loved a challenge.

When we get out of the car with the snow falling around us, she links her hand with mine and leads me toward her apartment.

In life, timing is everything. Maybe we've met too early. We'll peak too soon. Or never quite get off the ground. But I can't let this chance with her pass me by.

Posey

The library is my least favorite place on campus, but it's sometimes a necessary evil. I have a major project due on Tuesday, and I'm behind. I stretch my arms above my head in the private study room I managed to snag. My phone is off, and I'm ignoring all external distractions.

There's just one tiny internal one that keeps drawing my focus away from my work.

This past week, Brent and I have spent every moment together, when we're not in class or Brent's not in the pool or in the gym. I had no idea I could be with someone so often and not get bored or frustrated or stifled by their company. But the more time I spend with Brent, the more I want. It's the oddest thing.

Val has been nowhere. Her socials have been oddly devoid of boyfriend talk this week, and I'm starting to think she's given up on getting him back. Neither of us has brought up the fact he probably doesn't need a fake girlfriend anymore. I'm getting great sex and lattes, so I can't complain. Although, this weekend, I won't be getting either. Brent has a swim meet in Chicago. Out of state, but only three hours away.

The next few days are a test run of what my life would be like if I called us out for lingering. We don't need each other, and this weekend will prove it. Maybe next week I'll pull the plug on this pseudo-romance. Neither of us needs to risk getting too attached.

Just the thought of telling him we don't need to see each other anymore makes my stomach dip. While he says he's not a relationship guy, he clearly thrives on routine. We've been hanging out for two weeks, and I don't even need to consult our synced calendars anymore to know where he is or what he's likely doing. A creature of habit. I always thought someone predictable would be boring, but I've found that certainty and stability oddly comforting. He means what he says, and he says what he means. We might be in a fake relationship, but he's never once treated me as disposable. Never lied to me or kept something from me. Apart from the one incident at the basketball party, he hasn't tried to put a leash on me either. Seems to enjoy my strong-willed independence.

There's a knock on the study room door, and I get up to open it. Since these things are like sealed boxes for sound and distraction, other students don't always realize when one is occupied. Though the red light above the door should have been a clue.

I crack open the door, and Brent is on the other side. He's got a latte in his hand and a grin on his face. "Destiny told me you were pulling an all-nighter to get some project done. I brought liquid gold reinforcements."

The strangest sensation spiders across my chest and down my arms. Warm and tingly. I take the latte from him with one hand, and I grab the front of his jacket with the other, dragging him into the room with a wide view of the campus out the window. I click a button on the wall, and the blinds come down. I shut and lock the door while Brent stands in the room, an amused expression on his face.

"Jensen, what are you doing?"

Instead of answering, I kiss him. "When does the bus leave?" I murmur against his lips.

"Thirty minutes. My bag is outside the door."

"I hope no one steals it." I unzip his coat and shove it off his shoulders. It falls to the floor in a heap. There's barely enough room in here around the worktable for us to move, but need and desire burn through me. He's on his way to a huge swim meet for the weekend, and he detoured from the athletics complex to bring me a latte.

We're stripping each other in hurried motions, and I grab a condom from my purse. When Brent goes to lift me onto the table, he stares at the mess of my work spread out across it. He rotates me around to the wall, and he presses me against it.

"How soundproof are these rooms?" He trails openmouthed kisses along the sensitive skin of my neck.

"Enough," I say. Not entirely sure how much since we're in the library and people are supposed to be quiet.

"We'll see." He chuckles.

With only half an hour before the bus leaves, I expect him to be in a hurry. But he sets a slow, delicious rhythm that has me striving for the ecstasy I know is just around the corner.

"Faster," I plead.

"Nope," he says against my neck. His teeth graze my ear. "I'm going to enjoy every fucking second of this."

I grip his face, and I kiss him while I hook my legs around him tighter. If he wants to go slow, that's fine, but I'm not giving him a chance to get too far away. The friction is exquisite.

"Cheater," he murmurs.

I squeeze my internal muscles around him, and he hisses in my ear. Drives him wild when I do that. My class time spent strengthening my pelvic floor muscles has not been for nothing.

"That's what cheating feels like," I purr.

His lips seek mine, and as he increases the pace, our mouths barely break apart. The closer I get, the harder it is to breathe. I clutch at his back, and I dig my nails into his shoulders. My legs are trembling, and he pushes up one more time, sending me flying over the edge, and he follows right behind.

I'm still breathing heavily when he eases me to the ground and gives me one last tender kiss.

"You working on your project all weekend?" he asks as he discards the condom and starts retrieving his clothes from the piles on the floor.

"Unfortunately. Too many lattes and orgasms the last two weeks, and I'm behind."

"You should have said." He gives me a peck on the lips. "I didn't have to spend so much time in your bed."

"Yeah, you did." I give him a sly smile. "Trust me, I'm not mad about it."

"The whole weekend in this box." He grabs his jacket off the floor. "Seems counterintuitive for someone like you."

"I'll hate every second," I admit. "You'll send me updates on the meet?"

"If you want me to." A crease mars his forehead.

"Yeah." I slip my shirt over my head. "I'd love to know how you're doing." He's acting like that's shocking. But I've listened to a lot of chatter about his practices and his swimming goals the last two weeks. Why wouldn't I want to know whether any of it is coming to fruition? I'm not an unfeeling monster.

He checks the room to make sure he hasn't dropped anything or left something behind, and then he gives me a quick kiss on my temple. "Good luck with the project. I hope you smash it."

Into oblivion so I can escape this room. "Good luck to you too," I say just before he closes the door behind him.

I snap the lock into place, and I release a deep sigh. The tangy scent of sex lingers, and I'm not sure how I'm going to concentrate on my assignment when I'll remember Brent inside me every time I gaze at the wall across from the desk.

The rest of Friday and most of Saturday pass in a blur of color palettes and window treatments. I went home to sleep, but other than that, I've had my nose to the grindstone. It didn't help that when I did go home, Brent's absence felt palpable. He's slithered his way into my daily routine.

As soon as I was awake and showered, I got out of the apartment and came back to the library this morning. At least when I'm here, I'm not half-expecting Brent to show up with a latte, strip me down, and make me feel all ooey-gooey inside. Even if that's exactly what he did on Friday. Despite my mountain of work as a distraction, I haven't felt like myself since the door clicked shut on Friday.

Life just isn't quite the same without my lattes and orgasms.

When there's a knock on my study room door, I unlock it to find Nadiya on the other side. "Your dedication to your studies is killing me. Are you almost done?"

I turn and make a ta-da motion at my laptop and my notes strewn across my desk. "Probably another three hours of work."

"Excellent," she says, and she produces a bag from behind her back. "You can do those tomorrow, and you can come to the pub with me."

I accept the gym bag from her, and I peer inside to find jeans and a crop top. Not exactly the shirt I would have selected for a pub when it's December, but at least she brought me a change of clothes.

"Why are we going to a pub?" I drop the bag on the floor, and I shove my notes in my messenger bag along with my laptop.

"West is going there with some buddies from the lacrosse team."

"So, are you and West..." She said their talk went okay last week, but the two of them are as different as night and day. They have nothing in common, and I don't even think the sex was that great. Chemistry can't be faked, and I'm not sure either of them truly feel it together.

"I don't know. Maybe? Probably not. I can't seem to let him go." She gives me a helpless shrug.

I throw both bags over my shoulder, and then I put my other arm around her. "Then maybe we shouldn't go to a pub, we should go to a club. And we should get you someone new."

"I don't know if I'm ready." Nadiya bites her lip.

"Won't know until you try. Let's go home and form a better plan."

I've rallied the troops, and in the Uber on the way to the club, I finally get a chance to read the messages Brent sent me earlier today. The idea of reading them while trying to organize a night out didn't sit right with me, so while the car glides through the city streets, I bask in his day. He knew I had my phone off, so he sent me stream-of-consciousness diary entries. Some of them are hilarious.

"What's that smile for?" Nadiya asks. "Faulkner message you? You look like that when he's around."

"Look like what?"

"Happy." She rubs my shoulder.

He and I have spent so much time together that I haven't analyzed or even considered how being around him makes me feel. It's strange to think people see something in me that I hadn't even realized myself. I text him back about my project and going out to a bar.

Within a few minutes, he texts me back a string of shot glasses and then tells me to be careful. Asks me to text him when I get back to the apartment, so he knows I'm safe.

"He's like," I say, "a really good guy."

"Why do you sound so surprised?"

"I've always hung out with assholes before who were marginally good in bed. He's great in bed, and he's also..." I hesitate because this feels dangerous. "He's also great to me."

"Have you told him that you think he's a gem?"

"No, no, no, no, no." I wag my finger. "We're fake. I will not be the one who gets confused about that."

"You keep lying to yourself and you'll find your great guy with his great sex will find someone who appreciates him more."

"I appreciate him. I always thank him for the lattes and the orgasms." Well, the lattes, anyway. If I thanked him for the orgasms that'd be weird.

"Might be worth mentioning to him that he could be your real boyfriend instead of being this fake one."

"I don't want a boyfriend."

"You already have one." Nadiya huffs out a breath. "Denying it doesn't make it untrue. He's your boyfriend. Everything he says and does around you is boyfriend-like. The temple kisses, the top-of-the-head kisses, the way he slings his arm around your shoulders and gazes at you adoringly. I don't know if he's cracked out the L-word, but I bet he's close to unsealing that one. He's going to pop your love cherry."

"Are you trying to freak me out so I get really drunk and don't finish my project in time because I'm too hungover to function?"

"Doesn't sound like something I'd do," Nadiya says.

It's true. That doesn't sound like something she'd do. But if this isn't an elaborate plot to tank my academics then she thinks she's telling the truth. There is no way Brent has those sorts of feelings for me. He's just a really affectionate guy. He went from one relationship straight into a fake one with me. If anything, whatever he's experiencing is a major rebound. He'll bounce right off me and into a relationship with someone else.

A knot forms in my stomach. Flashes of Brent with some other nameless, faceless girls cause my heart to stutter. Maybe we'll see each other around campus and we'll stop to chat, but we'll never again be like we've been the last two weeks. I'll return to staring at his photos, but with a bittersweet tinge. He was mine once for a little while.

God, why does my fucking chest feel so tight? I rub the spot above my heart.

When we get to the bar, I don't even stop to mingle with everyone like normal. I get shots, and then I get more shots. By ten, I'm already a little tipsy, and a freshman basketball player keeps hitting on me. I don't even know how he got into the bar since he's not of age. Elite athlete privileges. Across the bar, I catch Deacon's gaze, and he makes his way over to us.

"Fisher," he says to the giant who is hovering over me. Probably has a clear view down my top. "She's got a boyfriend. Brent Faulkner. You're not making headway. You're just going to piss someone off." He claps his teammate on the shoulder and steers him away.

Nadiya sips her drink beside me. "He said boyfriend, and you didn't correct him, and you didn't break out into hives."

I ignore her, and I take out my phone to find a text from Brent. This past week we've been exchanging memes. He sends me ones about interior design, and I reply with something swimming or sports related. For some reason, the sight of the message causes tears to spring to my eyes, and when I glance at Nadiya, her amusement morphs to concern.

"Oh god. What's wrong?" she asks.

"I think I might really like him. *Like him*, like him."

"Tell him."

I shake my head and stare at my phone. Instead of replying with another athletics-inspired meme, I find one that has a woman with obviously fake muscles who is trying to stay strong over missing someone. Before I can second-guess my drunk decision-making, I send it. His response is immediate.

I'm only three hours away. Come watch me swim.

"Should I go to Chicago?"

"What?" Nadiya laughs. "Go to Chicago?"

I'd tell you to come tonight, but you must be drunk if you sent that meme. And Ethan and I are sharing a hotel room.

Paying for a hotel room is nothing. The real problem is finding a way to Chicago at this late hour. I check the bus times, and I find one is leaving at midnight. Enough time to sober up and be there by three in the morning. I click through the booking process and enter my card details from memory.

"I'm going to Chicago. I gotta go home and pack." I weave on my feet as I tuck my phone into my pocket.

"You're drunk," Nadiya says. "Are you sure this is a good idea?"

"It's probably a bad idea. But I want to see him. And he said I could come. Brent doesn't say things he doesn't mean. He's a good guy."

"Yeah, we established that earlier. I mean...he's home Monday."

"I'll take my computer, and I'll work on my project in the hotel room. Oh shit. I need to book a hotel room."

Nadiya leads me out of the bar and into an Uber. "Are you sure about this?" she asks as she leans into the back seat.

"You said to tell him, and I'm not doing that. But this says something, doesn't it?"

"Yeah." Her expression softens. "It says something. I'll see you when you get back on Monday. Don't forget to turn in your project."

BRENT

It takes a few rings for the piercing sound of my phone to fully penetrate my dreams. On race weekends, I sleep like the dead.

"What the fuck, Faulkner?" Ethan groans. "Who the hell is calling you at three thirty in the morning?"

The time, and the fact Posey was at a bar earlier, register in my brain at the same time, and I'm wide awake. I rub my face and snatch my phone off the nightstand. "Posey? Are you okay?"

"I'm here, and I missed you. And I'm sorry. I've just sobered up enough to realize coming here was probably dumb. You were going to be home on Monday. Why the hell would I take a midnight bus to Chicago?"

"You're here?" I stand up and unlock the door to check the well-lit hallway. "Where?"

"Room 410. I'm sorry. I'll let you go. This is a really important race weekend for you, and I'm totally fucking this up."

"You're in Room 410?" My brain is muddled, and tiredness lays across me like a blanket.

"Yes, but I'll go home first thing in the morning. I shouldn't have come. This was dumb."

"Hold on." I hang up the phone, and I tug on a shirt with my sleep pants. I grab my room card so I can get back in here to gather my swim things in the morning.

In the bright hallway lights, I'm a little more awake. Thankfully warmup is later, so this middle of the night disturbance isn't dire for my performance. If she was anyone else, I'd be pissed at the detour from my routine.

But at Room 410, a surge of elation rushes through me. She missed me, and she took a midnight bus to Chicago. In terms of progress, this is huge. Monumental. Not only does she give a shit about me, but she let herself feel it enough to track me down. I knock on her door, and when it flies open, Posey covers her face with one hand.

She looks fucking phenomenal. Short denim skirt, crop top, hair long and silky around her shoulders. She took a midnight bus looking like she stepped off a modeling runway. Before she can apologize again, because I can sense it coming, I thrust my hands into her hair, and I draw her into a kiss. She sighs into my mouth and molds herself to my body.

The door clicks closed behind us, and I walk us toward the bed. Despite how much I want to bury myself inside her, I'm too aware of what's riding on my shoulders tomorrow. It's my last day of competition here, and it's going to be brutal. My toughest races, and if I make finals, which I should, I'll have to race them more than once.

She's shedding her clothes, and I groan at the sight of her.

"Posey, I really need to sleep. I can't be a zombie in the morning. Too many people are counting on me." Notably, the college relay team where I'm the anchor.

"Oh, right. Yeah. I mean..." She stares at the two queen beds. "We don't even have to sleep in the same bed."

"You came all the way here in the middle of the night." I throw back the covers, and I drag her naked body down with mine. "We're sleeping in the same bed."

Silence settles between us, and I'm wrapped around her and on the cusp of sleep again when she says, "Have I become a stalker?"

I chuckle in her ear. "I appreciate you coming. I'm glad you're here. Don't overthink it. Okay? You brought your computer for your project?"

She rotates in my arms, and she traces the edge of my face down to my lips. "I've never missed anyone before. Well, not a guy, anyway."

"I'm honored to be your first." Tiredness is making this conversation not hit as hard as it should, but tomorrow, I'll be replaying her words. Guaranteed. Just better not be on the starting block. I kiss her forehead, and I snuggle her in tight.

"You're not freaked out by this?"

I go still for a beat and try to figure out the right answer to this question, but I'm too tired and it's too early in the morning for my brain to tiptoe around the landmines. Fuck it. "No." The opposite of freaked out, but if I get into too many details, we'll either have an all-night discussion about our feelings, which I can't do tonight, or she'll run screaming from the room.

"Huh," she says. "I thought you'd be freaked out. I'm kinda freaked out."

No surprise there. "Babe, if I'm garbage in the pool tomorrow, I won't handle it well. I need sleep."

"Okay, right, sure. Yeah. Sleep."

I can feel her staring at me, but I don't care. She can puzzle out her feelings while I keep her close and get enough sleep so I'm not a bear in the morning. As glad as I am that she came, if I don't swim well tomorrow, I'll look back on my decision to come to Room 410 and wonder whether I'm compromising too much. I don't want to regret my choice or her or any of this.

Because right now? I've never been happier.

My alarm goes off just after eight, and I peel myself off Posey as quietly as I can. I scribble a note to her on the pad on the desk, and then I head to my room.

When I get there, Ethan is almost packed. "Where the hell did you go?"

I toss my racing suit and my goggles into my bag before grabbing a dry towel. "My girlfriend is here."

"Val? Don't take this the wrong way, but she seems kinda stalkerish sometimes."

"Val and I broke up weeks ago." The night we went to Jessica's house, I thought I told him that. Maybe I didn't.

"Does she know that? Jessica said Val talks about you all the time on her social media platforms. No one on the team knew you broke up. Jess thought you two *might* be fighting."

"Not fighting. Broken up. Took Val a while to absorb that outcome."

"So who the hell is at the hotel?" Ethan frowns.

"Posey Jensen."

"You're fucking Posey Jensen now? Wow. I think I'm impressed. She's a *really* fun girl."

I'm not touching that comment. Ethan has slept with lots of women—one of the reasons he and Jessica probably aren't together—and while Posey never mentioned she had fallen into his bed, I don't need that mental picture. She came here because she missed me. Whatever happened before us doesn't matter. I can't get hung up on what I can't change.

"I tried to pick her up at a bar once or twice sophomore year. She was *not* interested." Ethan shrugs. "Who wouldn't be interested?" He eyes his muscular body in the mirror.

"Jessica," I say.

"Fuck off." Ethan shoves my shoulder and then he laughs. "She's interested, but she likes to play it cool."

If I believe Posey's logic, Jess will never act on whatever feelings she might have for Ethan. He's too risky for her. It's too early in the morning for a heart-to-heart when I'm so far from an expert. I've got a girl two floors up who won't admit we're actually dating even though she took a midnight bus to Chicago because she missed me.

We're totally dating for real. One hundred percent I am in the most authentic relationship I've ever had, and she doesn't even realize she's right there with me. Cluing her in would scare her off, so I'll have to wait for her to figure it out. I wonder how many years we'll have been dating by the time she admits we're no longer in a temporary, fake relationship.

"Is she coming to watch?" Ethan asks as he shoves a dry towel into his bag.

"Doubtful. I didn't tell her where the pool was, and she's got a big project due on Tuesday."

"She must really love you to take a midnight bus to Chicago when she's drowning in schoolwork." Ethan opens the door to our room and holds it for me to pass through.

Love. Jesus. That's a big word. My heart kicks in my chest. Not even sure I'm ready for that one. It's only been two weeks, and I've never uttered that sentiment to a woman, no matter how much pleasure was being exchanged. There's definitely a strong chance I could mean those words with Posey. A lot of things I once thought impossible don't seem so unfeasible now.

"She's pretty incredible," I say as I slide past him into the hallway, and we walk toward the bus to the pool with our bags slung over our shoulders.

"I'm happy for you, man. Val was hot. Don't get me wrong. Like five-alarm-fire hot. I can see why that'd be attractive. But I never bought what her socials tried to sell about the two of you being deeply in love. You looked great together, but it just felt so superficial. Glossy, but fake."

Glossy, but fake. Probably the truest thing I've ever heard in regard to Val and me. Ethan's insightfulness is stunning. The guy is a workhorse in the pool, but a class-A partier out of it. His whole problem with Jess seems to be that she can't or won't take him seriously. For him to see something in Val and me that I might have felt but didn't acknowledge is sort of amazing.

"Took me a while to see the difference between fake and real. But I get it now." Fake might have suited me then, but that won't be what I'm pursuing again when the real is so much more fulfilling.

Posey

Once I wake up and get over the surprise of having traveled to Chicago on a whim, I buckle down to finish my project. Brent's scribbled note says he has the afternoon off and then he'll likely have to swim in the final races tonight. A quick internet search revealed there are consolation finals and championship finals. I'm assuming Brent will be in the championship ones, but I've never been to a live swim meet before. May have watched him once or twice on YouTube after the fact. It's important to appreciate talent, and when the talent is a work of art, it makes the appreciation even easier. I do like pretty things.

I'm putting the finishing touches on my project when there's a knock on my door just after lunch. Room service has come and gone, so the only person it can be is Brent. My stomach flips, and I close my laptop before going to the door. I'm close enough to finishing that I can worry about the last bit on Monday.

Through the peephole, the sight of him sends a wave of tingles across my skin. Dark-gray sweats and a red Northern

University T-shirt should not skyrocket my heart rate, but it's definitely out of control when I open the door. I used to love just the look of him, but now I'm afraid I've developed a soft spot for the whole package.

Brent takes me in for a beat while leaning into the doorway. "How's the project going?"

"Almost done. How did your races go?" I step back from the door. "Did you want to come in?"

"I actually wanted to see if you were up for a late lunch with some of my teammates. They're going to a buffet." He waggles his brows. "A *buffet*, Jensen."

I laugh at his obvious enthusiasm. Sex and food are Brent's two favorite things. When we've combined them, he's been insatiable.

"You want me to come with you?" I lean against the door.

He smooths my hair and plants a kiss on my forehead. "Very much," he murmurs against my skin. "But if you need to focus on your work, that's totally fine too." He draws me into his chest for a hug, and I sink into him. "I'm just glad you're here."

For a fake boyfriend, he's been affectionate and attentive from our first meeting at the airport. He also happens to give the best hugs, and when he holds me close and I breathe in the familiar scent of chlorinated water, I realize my split-second decision to hop on a bus to Chicago was for *this* moment. I don't just feel wanted; I feel cared for. The best kind of close contact, and one I've been denying myself since Chris tried to turn me into someone I wasn't.

"I'm a sucker for a buffet." *And you.* "I'll grab my stuff."

Instead of making me nervous, the thought doesn't scare me. My resistance is waning. I may be nothing more than a rebound for him, but spending this time together has made me realize there are things about a relationship that aren't so bad. I doubt this fake boyfriend gig would have turned out the same with a different man. Many of the men I've engaged with could be callous or cruel or indifferent. Brent is none of those. Responding to his message in the campus chat might be the biggest risk I've ever taken, but my dream guy has turned out to be pretty dreamy.

In the hallway, Brent slings his arm around my shoulders as we walk toward the bank of elevators. He kisses the top of my head and lets out a deep sigh as we enter the elevator.

"Tired?"

"Gonna need a nap before finals."

"Is that because I showed up at three in the morning and disturbed your sleep?"

"Nah, I usually need one even when a hot girl doesn't show up at my hotel." He winks at me as the doors to the lobby open.

Warmth spreads across my chest, but I let the feeling rise in me instead of trying to tamp it down. He must see something different in my expression because he stops walking toward his teammates and drags me against him before kissing me deeply. It's the kind of kiss that would definitely lead to something more if we were in my hotel room. Instead, we're almost at the lobby, and someone whistles, and another person catcalls us.

"Get a room," Ethan says with a laugh.

"I have one." Brent glances up. "Want me to go use it?"

"The other room," Ethan says, and he points to me.

Brent laces his fingers with mine and takes me over to introduce me to the team. I've seen pictures of some of them before on Brent's socials or on the school website. The team has been successful over the years.

As we walk to the restaurant, Ethan and Jessica walk with us while the rest of the team is spread out around us. Everyone is chattering about the buffet with enthusiasm.

"I didn't know you and Val broke up," Jessica says to Brent from beside me.

Part of me wonders if Jessica is loyal to Val for some reason. Most people don't bring up the ex-girlfriend while the current one is within earshot. As far as I know, nobody here realizes Brent and I aren't the real deal.

"I'm not one to air my laundry," Brent says. "After what happened when I was fourteen, I keep my thoughts and opinions to myself. I don't broadcast my life on social media."

"When exactly did you two break up?" Jessica asks.

"Before I left for Bermuda." Brent squeezes my hand, but this conversation isn't bothering me in the slightest. I have a lot more confidence that he won't slide into old habits.

"But Val..." Jessica's brow furrows, and she glances at Ethan.

"Val can say or do whatever she wants," Brent says. "I could care less. My strategy is the same as any other time someone tries to create drama. Lay low. Keep quiet. It always passes."

His strategy might make sense for him, especially with the media attention and the cyclical nature of the Olympics, but I'm not convinced I could let someone do me dirty and keep my head down. So far, Val hasn't done much other than refuse to admit she and Brent are broken up. Her threesome Hail Mary didn't work, and she's been absent from his life since. In that sense, I can understand not wanting to taunt the tiger.

We get to the restaurant, and I let my outgoing nature lead with his teammates. The best way to get other people to like you is to appear very interested in them and their lives. Easy. On the way back to the hotel, I hear a few people behind us talking about how I'm so different from Val. I don't know if Brent hears them, too, but while he chats to Ethan, he gives my hand a squeeze, and I curl into his side.

While Brent naps, I attempt to finish the final pieces of my interior design project. My concentration is shot with him so close that I can reach out and run my fingers along his naked back. He's so hyper focused on the meet that we haven't even had sex once, which is unheard of. Considering our deal is supposed to be sex and coffee, the break from it should unnerve me.

Over the last two weeks, at every interval where some other guy would have tried to change me or force me to do something I may not be completely comfortable with, Brent has met my issues with understanding. Or at the very least with a *willingness* to understand. Even my middle-of-the-night impulsive decision to travel to Chicago didn't faze him. My relationship record might be next to zero, but I've born witness to enough of them to recognize how rare whatever we're developing is. Considering who I thought I was meeting at the airport, the reality has turned out to be quite different. He has a deep aversion to drama, which I tend to attract, but I think as long as I don't drag him into it, we'll be okay.

My heart speeds up at the realization I'm truly considering whether Brent and I could work beyond our arrangement. He hasn't treated me like a rebound, but that doesn't mean I'm not.

Brent stirs on the bed, and I pretend to be reviewing the final details of my assignment instead of staring at him.

"How's it going?" Brent's voice is deep and husky from sleep.

The sound sends a shot straight to my core. God, I want him. "Pretty much done. What time do you have to leave?"

Brent checks the clock on the bedside table and groans. "I should get going. Warmup is in an hour. We have a team meeting in fifteen minutes in Coach Brown's room." He sits up and rubs his cheeks. "Did you want to come watch? The meet starts at six."

"Yes!"

My enthusiasm seems to surprise him, and he chuckles. "I promise it's not that exciting."

"Do other people come watch? Is there a designated spot where I have to sit if I'm a Ra-Ra-Raven?" I pretend my fists are pom-poms and make a few cheerleading poses.

He tugs me along the bed beside him, and he molds himself around me. "No designated spot in the stands." His hand travels up my inner thigh and between my legs. "Later, I've got a seat reserved for you."

"Oh yeah?" I spread my legs and rub myself against him. "Where's that?"

He nibbles at my ear, and the alarm on his phone sounds for him to wake up. "For the first time in my life, I'd rather race you to the finish than someone else."

"Quickie?" My request is breathless, and I'm already so wet from thinking about him while he slept that it won't take much to get me off.

His phone buzzes again, and he lets out a groan of frustration. "I gotta go, or I'll miss the meeting. Team captain and all that." He tugs on his discarded clothes, but before he leaves, he comes back to the bed for a long, leisurely kiss that promises so much more later.

"Look for me in the stands," I say.

"I'm sure I won't be able to miss you." He kisses my temple.

Once the hotel room door clicks shut, I flop back on the bed and stare at the ceiling. A plan starts to form, and I can't help the slow smile that comes with my idea. He may hate it, but we might as well see whether he can take the full Posey experience before I let myself sink any deeper.

BRENT

My first championship final is the 400 IM. Given that I was the fastest qualifier, I'm in the middle lane, but the margin for error with this race is slim. My breaststroke is weak, so my strategy is not to lose too much ground there and to go hard during the other three strokes. Ethan is also in this final, and while we're in the marshalling area, he lets out a chuckle.

"What?" I ask.

"Posey is here." He nods his head toward the stands.

If I glance in her direction, I'll be distracted. Whatever made him laugh is likely going to have the same effect on me. Can't afford it. Not this race.

"You're not going to look?" Ethan asks while we swing our arms and shake out our limbs.

"This and the relay are my closest events. After the relay, I'll check the stands for her."

"She charmed the pants right off Jess at lunch. I need to learn her skills." Ethan rotates his torso as the heat before us steps onto the blocks.

The final ahead of us makes their turn on the wall, and Ethan goes to his lane while I start stripping off my Northern University Ravens tracksuit, securing my cap, and getting my goggles ready. The person racing in my lane is in the homestretch, and instead of staring at the end of the pool visualizing my race, I sneak a glance at the stands. There, with a sign large enough to block the view of several rows behind her if there'd been more fans, is Posey. I read the sign.

Hey, Faulkner, is your real name the 400 IM? Because you take my breath away.

I grin and shake my head. She's quite possibly the most interesting woman I've ever known. When she sees me looking, she jumps up and down and waves profusely. My heart swells at her adorableness.

The race in the pool finishes, and as we're whistled onto the blocks, I stare down my lane to the end. Normally, I want to win for myself or my school or my country. Tonight, I want to win for her, and there's a fire in my belly at the thought of her watching, being here, cheering me on in the stands. Turns out she's not a distraction. She's added motivation. Not at all what I expected.

As soon as the electronic beep sounds, I'm off the blocks and in the water. My brain switches off, and I race on instinct, letting years of training take over. At the final turn, I catch a glimpse of Don Davidson from Michigan State hot on my heels. Or more like at my shoulder. Too fucking close. I dig deep and pull hard, pushing myself to finish each stroke even though my muscles are on fire.

At the final five meters, I focus on the black line and propel myself toward the finish. My fingertips touch the pad, and I check the race clock on the wall. First by a few hundreds. Don leans over the lane rope and holds out his hand. I take it and congratulate him on his race.

When I glance up at the stands, Posey is jumping up and down with the sign above her head. At some point, she'll show up at a swim meet in a cheerleading outfit, and I'm not going to be mad about it.

I hoist myself out of the pool, and the campus YouTube channel calls me over to chat about my race. While I'm there, Posey turns her sign around. On the back, if it's possible, is something more punny, and I stumble over my words on camera as I read it.

Faulkner, you're one pool guy.

When they're done recording, the interviewer turns to look over her shoulder. "Girlfriend?"

"It's her first time at a swim meet. I think she's confused about the lack of Ra-Ra-Ravens fans."

"Not generally a sport people cheer for."

I laugh. "Not at these sorts of meets. If anyone can change that perception, it'll be her."

We chat for another minute, and then I wander to where my teammates are strewn across the pool deck.

"She's got another one, Faulkner," Ethan says. "Might be my favorite yet."

I turn to read her newest sign, and I shake my head at her audacity. *Faulkner, you dove in hard and came out wet.* Even from a distance, I can see the saucy grin on her face.

"How many of those signs did she make?" Jessica asks.

"If I had to guess?" I turn back to them. "More than I'll want to see." Except, like everything she does, I'm finding her enthusiasm amusing and highly endearing. I've had girls I'm dating come to swim meets before, but they often admit later to being bored. Posey is holding up a generic Go Ravens sign, and she's cheering for one of my teammates in her final. Wherever Posey goes, she unpacks the fun, and she doesn't wait for someone else to deliver it.

"I'm not sure you could have found someone more opposite to Val," Jessica says.

"Funny how life sometimes provides exactly what you need when you're not even looking for it." Saying too much to my teammates, who we'll likely be going out with after, is a tad dangerous. Any of them could replay my comments to Posey, and they could send her running. It's easy enough to explain them as playing along with our fake dating, but I'm wondering if we're reaching the point where even Posey realizes there's more to what's happening between us. Nothing about us feels fake to me anymore.

As finals wear on, Posey drags out more signs riddled with sexual innuendos. If nothing else, she appears to be amusing everyone on the pool deck. Each time one arrives, a burst of laughter somewhere on the deck signals a new opportunity to marvel at her boldness.

The last event of the night is the freestyle relay, and when I glance toward Posey in the stands, she gives me a fake high five, and her sign reads *You really (flip) turn me on.* The whistle blows for the first swimmer to take to the blocks. I'm the anchor, so I don't swim until last. As soon as the beep sounds, I'm focused on the race. By the time I'm on the blocks, we're behind by about a second. Freestyle is my best event, and when I hit the water, I kick and pull as hard as I can to catch Michigan State in the lane beside us. When I hit the turn, I've managed to draw even with their final swimmer, and as I accelerate off the wall, I pass him.

My fingers hit the touchpad, and I check the clock. Not a new team record, but it's a very respectable time for this point in the season. Posey whistles from the stands, and I wave to her from the water. Instead of mentally replaying my race like normal, I stare at her, and I'm astounded that posting on a campus chat server resulted in her.

Outside the locker rooms, the team gathers to decide on where to go for some food. Posey appears in the hallway after I text her to come down to the lower level from the stands. Her other signs appear to be gone, but she's holding one in front of her as she approaches.

Your breaststroke may be weak in the pool, but it's strong in bed.

I grin and loop my arm over her shoulders before tugging her against me and kissing the top of her head. "Nice sign," I say.

"My favorite was about Brent being too sexy for a sport that requires clothes," Ethan says. "'Cause it applies to me too."

"I left them all upstairs by a recycling bin, if you want to retrieve it," Posey says, and she snuggles against me.

"I don't think I've ever seen Brent so relaxed and happy at a swim meet," Jessica says as we stream out of the building into the cold night air. "Normally, he's just like—" She turns her expression into a glaring glower.

"That's called being focused," I say with a laugh. She does have a point, though. At a meet, I'm often in my own head.

"You were still focused enough to win, and you looked like you were having fun. Not sure I've ever seen you smile that much."

When I glance down at Posey, she's beaming. "My signs were pretty punny."

"Pun-tastic," I admit. But I'm having trouble discerning how much I can reveal to my teammates and consequently to Posey before she'll freak out. The swim meet, an event I've been to a thousand times, brimmed with a different energy today. Jessica is right. Having Posey there offered a balance I didn't realize I wanted. I was focused when I needed to be, but I also enjoyed the atmosphere. In the past, I've feared my ability to transition or switch myself into race mode. Whether I've been to enough competitions now or whether it never would have been as hard as I believed, today proved I can switch from grinning at Posey's joke to staring down my lane, ready to kick ass. I can have both. The insight sends a shot of warmth across my chest, and I kiss Posey's temple.

"Thanks for making the meet so much fun," I say to her.

"I'm a fun factory." She squeezes my side.

She is, and my instinct is to press her on why she has been denying herself a relationship for so long. As far as girlfriends go, she's top shelf. The idea that I might get to stay with her if I can keep my cool is a little daunting. At some point, my growing feelings will be painfully obvious to both of us. I'm already wondering whether the warmth in my chest radiates outward, showing her how I feel if she only cared to look. But if she's not there with me, there's no way she'll stick around.

Fake is all she thinks she can offer, and we're already far too real. If coming to Chicago freaked her out, then realizing *why* she wanted to come to Chicago will be one step too far. At least right now. Just keep inching her along until the line she thinks she can't cross is so far behind us, she'll forget it even existed.

Posey

The team's favorite restaurant is an Italian place with all-you-can-eat salad and breadsticks that's within walking distance of the pool but in the opposite direction from the hotel. They're buoyed by their relay-team win and numerous personal successes. From what I can gather at the table, Brent and Ethan are on track for their season goals. The coach makes a speech, after everyone is digging into the food, about striving to be their best and other things that are inspiring for even a non-athlete like me.

Across the table, a couple of Brent's teammates take videos of the food and the plethora of jokes flying around building on the various signs I proudly displayed at the pool today. If no one snaps those up from the recycling, they're missing out.

My favorite part of the dinner is how attentive Brent is. If I were in the market for a boyfriend, I could do a hell of a lot worse than him. From recommending dishes he thought I'd like, to slinging his arm across the back of my chair, to planting random kisses on my temple, I never have any doubt that I've got at least fifty percent of his attention at any given moment.

On the way back to the hotel, he laces our fingers together while he chats to some of his teammates and I talk to some of the girls. Even Jessica, who was reluctant earlier to give me a chance, seems much more open. I haven't figured out exactly what her initial problem with me was, but if she follows Val on her socials, then me with Brent might have been a surprise. As far as I've been able to tell, Val hasn't acknowledged Brent's absence from her feeds, and she's ignored or deleted comments from anyone who dares to ask.

When we get to the hotel, everyone breaks off toward their own rooms on the second floor, and Brent doesn't even hesitate to stay in the elevator with me to go to the fourth floor. His arm is around my shoulders, and I'm pressed against his side, breathing in the scent of chlorine and bodywash. I'm not sure when chlorine became an aphrodisiac, but for the rest of my life, I'm probably going to associate this smell with intense sexual pleasure. Not at all awkward for future me.

"What's up? You're quiet," Brent says when the elevator doors close for our ascent to the fourth floor. "All that cheerleading wear you out?"

"Have I been quiet?"

"You're normally the center of every conversation." He gazes down at me.

There's amusement in his tone, and I squeeze him. If I've been quiet, I haven't even realized it. But ever since I took the bus here, I've been trying to grapple with whatever has developed between us. Tonight's dinner and Brent's acceptance of my outlandish behavior at the pool only increased my confusion. There are very few subjects that are off-limits, but once I say a word to Brent about turning this fake relationship into something real, I'm admitting he's important to me.

He is, obviously. He's great sex and regular lattes.

Deliverer of intense, feel-good affection. Guy who hits home runs off my curveballs.

But boyfriend? Real, legitimate, have-to-care-about-his-feelings, expect-him-to-care-about-mine boyfriend? That's a leap.

The reality is that I *could* be a rebound. Someone to pass the time. The sacrificial vagina, which I found so funny a few weeks ago.

While I dig my room card out of my purse, I decide to wade into foreign waters. "Were you like this with Val?" I ask.

"Like what?" He trails me into the room with his swim bag still slung over his shoulder.

Instead of following me into the main sleeping area, he veers into the bathroom to hang up his wet suit and towel. When I don't answer, he pops his head out of the bathroom and tries to catch my gaze. "Like what?" he asks again.

There's probably no way to ask him without giving myself away. What exactly I'll be giving away, I'm not sure. But the question I have doesn't feel like one a fake girlfriend would bother with.

"So affectionate and attentive?" I keep my voice light, as though it's genuine curiosity driving me and not a burning desire to figure out where we stand without asking the question.

A frown creases his brow, and he disappears into the bathroom without answering me. There's a fluttering in my stomach at his silence, and I stare out the hotel room window at the other high-rise buildings around us. If there was still enough light, I'd be able to see Washington Park.

In the reflection, Brent approaches me from behind without touching me. I long to lean into him. Whenever he's within touching distance, that's what I want to be doing.

"Why are you asking about Val?" he asks.

Our gazes connect in the reflection, and I try to hold my ground. "Call it curiosity."

He places his hands on the glass, framing me in, and his chest brushes against my back. His lips graze my ear, and a shiver slithers down my back. There's no doubt where this is headed, and desire pools in my belly at the remembrance of how good it is to have him tight against me.

"What else could I call it?" He nibbles on my earlobe, and I arch into him before grinding against his erection. He chuckles, and one of his hands slides down to my abdomen and holds me in place.

"Just curiosity," I breathe out.

He spins me around, and my back is pressed against the cold window. "I've never treated another woman the way I treat you."

His words set off an explosion in my chest, and I tug him into a kiss. I drag his shirt over his head, and my fingers find the button on his jeans next. We shed our clothes in a rush, but when we tumble onto the bed, Brent holds himself over me instead of storming ahead.

"Tell me why you really wanted to know," he says, and he brushes my hair off my cheek.

The gesture is tender, and my heart swells in my chest. There's no way I can articulate all the conflicting emotions coursing through me. The *why* feels complicated and dangerous. It *is* curiosity, but he's not wrong. My desire could be labelled something more. "Never?" I whisper instead of giving him a real response.

"Never," he says. "What do you think of that?"

I bite my lip, and I scan his sincere expression. "I don't know." His admission is terrifying and exhilarating—what I imagine parachuting to be like. I'm flying through the air, and I have no idea where I'll land. Soft ground or hard. Would he truly be a good boyfriend or is he just good at pretending?

"You're not running screaming from the room," he says with a smirk. "I'll take my wins where I can get them."

No running, but if we inch any closer to what neither of us is admitting, I might be tempted to flee. Instead, I arch into him, and his gaze heats. "It's my turn to win now, and I'll even scream for you."

"Promise?" He brushes his lips against mine.

"I might even scream your name instead of god's."

He chuckles against my neck as he cups my ass and eases into me, but this time, when he withdraws and our gazes connect, the air hums with something I've never felt before. Warmth floods my body at the tenderness and desire mingling in his expression. I'm not sure if my expression matches his, but his look is how I feel. For years, I've avoided anything that felt even remotely close to this, and now I'm starting to wonder why.

"Slow and steady," he says. "There's no rush."

Instead of answering him, I kiss him deeply and tug him closer. Slow I can do, but I'm not sure about steady. Whatever I'm starting to feel isn't in my control anymore, and I have no idea where it'll lead.

The next morning, I get settled on my Greyhound Bus, which will take me back to Northern University campus, and I scroll through my messages from Destiny and Nadiya. Other than telling them I arrived safely, I haven't said much about my spontaneous trip. Taking a bus on a whim is something I'd normally do, but the reason I got on the bus is out of character.

If Brent and I were just friends, I'd have gone to an important swim meet to support him, without question. That's what friends do. While he's gauging his season's success with each meet, this one wasn't particularly important in the grand scheme of his swimming career, and I still went. I don't need Destiny or Nadiya to tell me I've slipped into unchartered territory.

I *feel* it. There's a change starting in me, and I can't decide if I need to create some distance or embrace the discomfort.

If I dwell on whatever is developing, I'll freak out. It'll be a long three hours lost in my thoughts. I flick through the apps on my phone, and I open the latest social media craze. While I don't use my accounts much, I always claim my name on each of them. When I open it, my notifications are over a thousand despite never having posted content.

My heart kicks, and a slither of dread snakes down my spine. I tap on the icon to view where I'm being tagged.

It's a video compilation from the weekend, and I breathe a sigh of relief. Except as I watch it, I realize Brent and I are the stars of the videos. We're front and center laughing about the signs I've made, walking hand in hand from lunch, staring at each other over dinner, cuddled up together in the hallway outside the locker rooms. Wherever it was possible to catch us looking close and happy, his teammate has done it. Strange to see us as others would have this weekend.

I'm so caught up in watching the clips of us that I haven't fully registered why my account blew up. But once I've viewed it a few times and absorbed the vibe between me and Brent, I check the stats on the post.

Holy shit.

Thousands of shares, reposts, and views. My heart rate picks up at the implication. I've done a lot of dumb things or attention-seeking things, but I've never gone viral before. I click on the comments, and my blood runs cold. Although

I was tagged in the original post, it's Val who is being targeted in the comments.

@valentinaconsuelos Isn't Brent your boyfriend?

@valentinaconsuelos When did you and Brent breakup?

@valentinaconsuelos Holy fuck. Is Faulkner cheating on you?

@valentinaconsuelos Wasn't Brent in Bermuda with you a couple weeks ago? WTF is this?

Bile rises in my throat as I follow a few of the shares and reposts with someone else's commentary attached to them. Very, very few are supportive of me or Brent. Most of the people are in a rage, assuming Brent cheated on Valentina or I somehow lured him away from her. After all, their relationship was #couplesgoals for the last year thanks to her intimate photos and detailed posts. What a crock of shit.

She hasn't responded to anyone's tag, but I can't imagine she hasn't seen this. The original post is a torrent sweeping across the students at Northern University's campus.

I've been in some girl-on-girl disagreements before, but never on this scale. In every other situation, no one has come out a winner. My best hope at an easy resolution is for Val to admit she and Brent broke up weeks ago. Given that she hasn't done that yet, I can't imagine she'll emerge sweet and demure.

No. She's the type to go for the knockout punch, even if her opponent is already on the ground.

At the rate the post is being liked, shared, reposted, and commented on, there's no point in responding. I can't stem the tide. Instead, I'm going to have to learn to ride the wave. I hope I'm a strong enough swimmer.

BRENT

When I wake up from my nap after arriving back to campus, I grab my phone to see whether Posey has texted me yet. She should be back at Northern by now, though her bus left later than mine. There are no texts from Posey, but I have a bunch of messages on my home screen from people asking what's going on with me and Val, and also, what's going on with me and the chick in the video.

Chick in the video?

I throw on some clothes and wander into the living room. Jaxon is sprawled across the couch watching TV and scrolling through his phone since he has an evening class on Mondays.

"Why the fuck are so many people messaging me about a video?" I ask. "Do I have some look-alike in a porno somewhere?"

"Nah. It's you and Posey." Jaxon chuckles and glances up from his phone. "One of your teammates put together a bangin' video, and since very few people realized you and

Val broke up, Northern is in a flutter." The last word is full of mockery.

Jesus. I hope we're not literally banging. We haven't had sex in public, so a leak like that seems unlikely. I rub my face and sink into the armchair across from him before opening some of my social media accounts. Right away, the tsunami that's been unleashed is apparent. Not even after the Olympics did I have this many notifications.

Over a girlfriend.

People are fucking stupid.

Out of curiosity, I click on the video and watch it through. Then I watch it again. God, I could stare at her all day. Makes me think I should definitely be taking more videos of my girlfriend. Or pictures. Or both. When she eventually lands that TV deal, she's going to be dynamite on camera.

"How are you this whipped after a couple weeks?" Jaxon asks.

"What?" I close my phone and stare at him.

"That goofy grin on your face. Some sappy shit. I'm assuming you're watching the two of you all loved up on video?"

A few times, but he's not getting any more out of me in regard to Posey. He loves making me feel like an idiot for becoming obsessed with the girl who was meant to be my rebound. Not my fault that Posey Jensen turned out to be fucking amazing. When you win the lottery, you don't return the winning ticket, even if other people might begrudge you.

In the kitchen, I dump coffee grounds into a filter, fill the machine, and flick it on.

"She took a bus to Chicago to watch you swim?" Jaxon asks, sitting up. "The video is from this weekend, isn't it?"

"She took a *midnight bus* to Chicago on Saturday night." I leave out the part where she was drunk. Laid bare, this version of the truth makes me feel pretty damn good. She missed me so much she took a midnight bus...while drunk. Probably not the safest, now that I think about it.

"Well, I'll be damned." A slow smile spreads across Jaxon's face. "You're not the only one who's whipped. Fucking miracles do happen. You need to buy a lottery ticket, man."

The coffee trickles into the pot behind me. "Don't say a word to Posey about any of this."

"You mean about how the two of you are more whipped than the cream you stole out of the fridge last week when she was over?"

"Did you really want me to put it back after?"

"You owe me. I bought that can for my blow job cocktails."

If Posey was here, she'd have a field day with that comment. Jaxon drinking blow job cocktails, the fact we used the whipped cream for a literal blow job. No question over what the better use was. The coffee finishes dripping into the pot, and I hold it toward him. "Want some?"

"I'm good," he says. "Why can't I tease Posey about being whipped?"

"'Cause I think she'd rather literally be whipped," I say while I stir cream into my coffee. "She's a wild animal. Can't spook her."

"You don't think a viral social media post might have already done that?" Jaxon flops back onto the couch and picks up the remote. "The two of you look *very* comfortable together."

She should have been home hours ago, but she has class this afternoon, and she still had to put the finishing touches on her project. Not hearing from her doesn't mean she's spooked. Making a big deal about this temporary spike in our visibility around campus is unnecessary and likely harmful for both of us. If there's one thing I've learned from all the times I've gotten unwanted attention, it's that if you lay low, people stop caring. At some point, the fervor dies down. Don't fan the flames. Easy.

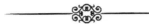

Evening practice is shorter than normal as recovery from the swim meet, and when I still haven't heard from Posey after I leave the locker room, I grab a latte on my way to her apartment. Coffee is always a good excuse to show up uninvited. At least I know she'll let me in the door if I've got a latte in my hand—or at least someone will. I've proven that much in the last few weeks.

After I ring the buzzer for their apartment, I shift on my feet and try not to let Jaxon's words about spooking Posey with a viral social media post get to me. She came to Chicago. She asked whether I'd treated Val the same way I treat her. What I told her was true. I never treated Val the way I've treated Posey—never wanted to.

With Posey, I'm all in. Whether I've never let myself feel this way or I've been waiting for someone like her to wake me up, I've realized Deacon's analogy is correct. I can have more than one glass ball. Swimming is one, but Posey is my other. He was also right that Posey is worth the effort to take down her walls. This past weekend was proof of both those theories.

Now all I have to do is not fuck it up.

Instead of the buzzer sounding to let me up, the receiver on the wall rings. I pick it up, and I frown at the camera on the ceiling.

"Hey, Brent," Posey says. "I'm pretty tired from the weekend. I think I'll get an early night. I can catch up with you tomorrow."

Her tone is too breezy to be real. She never talks like this when she actually means something. Up go the fucking walls. I hold the latte toward the camera. "I brought you a Jack Frost. They just started serving them today." It's my ace in the hole. When I arrived at the coffee shop and saw the latte Posey mentioned last night in bed, it felt like a sign that coming here was the right idea.

"A Jack Frost?"

The hopeful wariness is cute. She wants this latte, even if she doesn't want to let me upstairs. I take a big sniff from the top of the cup. "White chocolate. Vanilla bean. Peppermint. I mean, if you don't want it, I could probably drink it for you." But I won't. Coffee keeps me awake, but Posey can drink one and fall asleep within an hour. It's a sorcery I do not understand.

"Dammit, Brent."

The buzzer sounds, and I do a fist pump into the air before I tug open the unlocked door. If the latte hadn't worked, I would have detailed how I'd score the orgasm of her choice. I'm not afraid to play dirty.

When I reach her door, it's already open, and she's on the couch. Her roommates are nowhere in sight, and I'm not sure if that's a good thing or not. I close the door, shed my coat and boots, and drop into the spot on the couch beside her.

She takes the latte from me, and she smells the top. "Mmm. You weren't lying."

"You thought I was lying? About a latte? Trust me. I know better."

"You're still supposed to be at practice." She gives me a half smile. "You skipping out early for me?"

Not that I wouldn't, but I didn't need to. "Short practice. How was your bus trip back to campus?"

"It was okay," she says, and she takes off the lid of her latte and blows on the hot liquid. "I've been thinking that maybe we should cool things a bit."

Even though I realized her reaction was a possibility and I've prepared for it, my stomach sinks that she's actually saying it. "Is this about the video?"

"You saw it?" Her gaze flies to mine.

I'm probably half of the views on the damn thing. Every time I could sneak a view in around Jaxon today, I did it. "You think there's someone on campus who hasn't?"

Color drains from her face, and I realize that was not the right thing to say. "I've been afraid to look. How many views does it have now? Did you see how many people tagged Val?"

I shake my head. Everyone knows you don't read the comments, no matter how great or terrible a video looks. A cesspool of shitty people. "Good. Maybe now she'll finally admit we're done."

"Brent—"

"It'll die down. People will realize Val and I were done long before you and I got together, and it'll die down." Long before may only be a few hours, but it's long enough. There was no cheating or whatever else people are implying. Checking or responding isn't worth my time.

"What are we doing?" She scans my face.

In every situation I've seen Posey in, she's been bold and brazen. She's neither right now, and it makes me unsure how to answer her. *We're together. You're my girlfriend.* "One more week," I say. "It's almost the holidays. After this week, it'll be clear to everyone Val and I are done for good."

She takes a sip of her drink, and the vulnerability she's showing makes me want to ramble, tell her whatever she wants to hear. But I don't have a clue what the right response is.

"I don't think this is going to go the way you think it is," she says, and she takes a long drink of her latte.

My heart thuds in my chest. The video that I love so much seems to have sliced into the fabric of the easy routine we've developed. The cut is jagged, and I don't know how to sew it back together, make us whole again. A touch of panic lights my chest on fire.

She rises from the couch to go to the kitchen, and I follow her. There's only one thing that's guaranteed to make us close again. A reminder that what she saw in the video, what other people are seeing and dissecting, isn't something either of us can run from. We're not fake, and I'm not sure we ever have been.

She finishes the last of the latte and opens the garbage can to drop it in. When she turns, I'm behind her. I stare down at her as I ease my hand along her hip to the small of her back. She arches into me, and I lean down to nuzzle underneath her ear.

"Everything is going to be fine, I promise." Not a promise I should be making. While I'm sure time will quiet the social media crowd, I have no idea whether she and I will make it beyond next week. I want to. I really, really want to. "Get out of your head, Posey."

"Because you'd rather I wrap myself around yours?" Her fingers dance along my back.

She's not quite herself, but at least that comment hits a familiar note. "Can I stay?"

Her answer isn't verbal, instead she takes my hand, and she leads me toward her bedroom. The sea might be choppy, but I think I can navigate this.

Posey

As long as I travel back and forth to class with my head down and my earphones in, things are indeed fine, as Brent predicted. But without my earbuds in, I hear the muttered comments from my peers. The ones that label me a slut or a boyfriend stealer or easy. Such a stupid label. It's not like sex is hard.

I tug my winter jacket around me tighter and readjust my AirPods.

Brent has said to ignore them, but when I check my socials, a spike of anxiety strikes, and I hate my new reality. The shares haven't stopped, and the mean comments have tripled. Val still hasn't said anything. Her accounts are eerily silent, and I'm not sure what to think. She's not going to take the high road, so it's just a matter of waiting to see how low she goes.

The worst part, though, is that I've never been a social outcast before. I've had people dislike me; that's normal. Not everyone can like everyone. But even people I've been friendly with in the past are avoiding me if they spot me on campus. Somehow by dating my dream guy and having the audacity to appear happy about it, I've become a social pariah.

I've tried to put myself in their shoes. If Brent had suddenly turned up splashed across social media with some other girl out of the blue, what would I have thought? Neither Brent nor Val confirmed a breakup to the world or even to campus. Maybe I would have assumed cheating happened too. A lesson in not jumping to conclusions or putting too much stock in the lives of people I don't know. You can never really know anyone by what they post online.

Val isn't the victim here, but her deep silence, and Brent's insistence on ignoring what's being said, is letting others create the narrative. In most instances, it's that I lured him away and/or he cheated. No one, not a single person, appears to believe Brent was unhappy and he left Val willingly. I'm the mermaid in the ocean singing the sailor into the water to drown. Except, I think I might be the one drowning.

Those stupid photos on Val's account from Bermuda make us look extra guilty. I'm in a few of them—not with Brent—so it appears as though we connected there. The comments on *that* post are out of control. Conspiracy theory central.

When I called Julia, my sister, for advice, she told me that those who matter know the truth, and those who don't aren't important anyway. Easy to say when you're not the one being bombarded with Northern University's warped version of events. Of course, since she's in training to become the king's secretary in Bellerive, she's had to take on the never complain, never explain mentality of the royal family.

As for me? I'm getting tired of pretending to be meek when I'm not normally the one crouched in the corner hoping no one will notice me. The problem, right now, is that I'm not completely sure speaking up will *do* anything. Or at least not anything good.

It's Thursday afternoon, and I fly home for the holidays on Sunday. A few more days, and I'll be out of this environment, and I'll be able to breathe again as long as I keep my phone off. Brent leaves Sunday too. Originally, I was supposed to leave Saturday morning, but I switched my flight to match his. Didn't tell him that part.

His parents have rented a house in Utah for ski season, and that's where he's spending some of his break. With his training schedule, he comes back to campus a few days before me.

Not that any of that matters, because we agreed to only one more week.

Why I'm going through all this vitriol and strife for one more week of lattes and incredible sex is beyond me.

That's not true, at least not anymore. I know exactly why I agreed to another week, and why I'm taking the abuse from my peers on campus. Despite how shitty this situation is, when I'm around Brent, it's like I'm lit from the inside. There's a glow, a warmth, that I've never experienced before, and I can't get enough of it. I want to bask in it constantly.

I tried to shove some distance between us the night we came back from Chicago, but Brent was so tender and sweet with me when we went to bed that my resistance crumbled. My big, sex-crazed, chlorine-smelling jock is hard to resist.

But to what end? I have no idea if he truly wants something beyond this week. The thought of asking terrifies me. He's the one who keeps extending the timeline, so I can't help thinking there's a chance he wants more. Is it normal for someone to go from one relationship right into another?

The whole thing feels messy, and it pisses me off. I want to go back to when we were holed up in my bedroom pretending the rest of the world didn't exist after we came back from Bermuda. Great sex and lattes were my only priorities.

Ugh. Stupid swimmer boys who make me want things I never thought I'd want again. Perfectly happy to become a Victorian spinster and dote on Julia's kids with whoever she eventually marries.

I do not want a boyfriend. I do not want a boyfriend. I do not want a boyfriend.

Up ahead, I catch a glimpse of a familiar black jacket, and Brent is standing in the middle of the path with other students streaming around him. He has a latte in each hand, and my heart kicks at the sight of him. I mentioned this morning how much I hate walking back from class with all the social media bullshit, and here he is. Poseidon come to life—chiseled like a Greek god in a sea of people who do not matter at all to me.

Without a word, he passes me my latte, and he falls into step beside me. I glance at him while I take out my AirPods to slip them into my pocket, and there must be something on my face that gives me away, because he grins.

"Thought you could use some company," he says. "I was in the neighborhood."

Since the entire campus is technically our neighborhood, it's plausible. "I can always use coffee."

"Your addiction to caffeine has no limits."

My addiction to him also appears limitless, and that's far more worrying than the amount of caffeine in my system.

Brent is at practice when Destiny and Nadiya turn up at my bedroom door. They both have their phones in their hands, and I swivel on my desk chair to face them. Their expressions are grave, but I don't touch my device. I turned off my push notifications when it became clear getting them would kill my mental health. Knowing I'm leaving on Sunday for a while is about the only thing holding me together.

"Val just went live," Destiny says. "Blew shit up even more."

Nadiya bites her lip. "She said you and Brent hooked up behind her back at the wedding. Said she and Brent were together at the time."

"She was a fucking mess in the live thing," Destiny says "Crying. Mascara down her cheeks. Said she's been absent from social media because the breakup has *traumatized* her, and she didn't know how to handle it."

"Should I watch it?" No part of me wants to see her dramatic lies, but she's been quiet for weeks. I have no doubt that when she clicked the go live button she knew exactly what she was doing.

"Nope," Nadiya says. "No. But we thought you should know." She glances at Destiny. "We also think you should maybe change your flight and leave earlier."

Leave earlier? Whatever Val said and did in her live stream must be really bad for Nadiya and Destiny to be on the same page. While Nadiya is only confrontational with people she knows well, Destiny has no problem telling everyone exactly what she thinks. Both of them are always straight with me, whether or not it'll bruise my feelings.

"Look," Destiny says. "I get that you like Faulkner, but is he worth all this? He hasn't posted a single thing to deny all the shit takes people have come up with about you." She holds up her phone. "I bet he'll have zero to say about this too."

"He won't have been able to see it," I say. A lame excuse. In her hundreds of thousands of followers, there will be someone who will have recorded it. Right now, it's probably making its way from platform to platform, dragging me so hard I'll have the burn marks for years. "Was any of what she said true?"

"Not a word," Nadiya says. "Not a single fucking word."

"I'm going to respond." I grab my phone off my desk and open it.

"Don't do that," Destiny says. "Absolutely do not do that. You're the other woman. Or at least that's how you've been painted. The only person who can respond is Faulkner, and whatever he does has to be big enough to shut this shit down for good."

I stare at my open phone and replay her words. The one thing Brent has been adamant about since the video of us went viral is that neither of us responds. We let people think whatever they want, and we move on with our lives. But Val has now taken an assumption people were making and declared it the truth.

"Ask him to post his own *this is how it is* video," Destiny says.

He won't. I don't even have to ask him to know. His socials have been almost dead since he changed all his passwords so Val no longer had access. Like me, he considers his accounts a necessary evil, but he doesn't dedicate any time to them or to the people who are interested in him.

"If he won't respond," Nadiya says, "then I think that says a lot about him, don't you? Your reputation is being slaughtered."

"Change your flight," Destiny says. "There's one that leaves in four hours, and I think you should be on it. Campus will be a cesspool of hot takes tomorrow. Whether Brent comes out guns blazing or not—which I doubt, dude needed a fake girlfriend to hold his balls for him—it'll take a while to put out this fire. Better if you're not here to feel the burn."

I bite my lip and catch Nadiya's gaze. She's the more cautious one, less prone to rash choices. "Is that what you think too?"

"I know you like him. That's very clear, but I can't believe he's worth all this." She wiggles her phone at me. "This isn't the kind of attention you like."

No one likes this kind of attention. Public shaming is not for the faint of heart. "I'll change my flight." I've been looking forward to going home, so maybe this isn't all bad. For the next week and a half, I just can't open a single one of my socials.

Since Brent and I agreed to this arrangement, I knew Val would come for me at some point. But I have to admit, she's got patience and impeccable timing. Just as I predicted, she's found a way to kick me when I was already down.

BRENT

When I leave the athletics complex, Posey is waiting for me with a bag at her feet. Her arms are wrapped around her middle, and I zip my coat to my chin as I approach. The rest of my teammates call out goodbyes and say they'll see me at practice tomorrow, but I'm laser focused on my girlfriend. There's something about her posture that's kicked my heart into gear, and a cool sweat has broken out in my armpits. She's never waited for me outside a practice, and her closed-off expression isn't helping my anxiety.

"What's up?" I ask. "I thought I was coming to yours."

"I changed my flight. I'm going home early."

The coolness under my arms migrates through the rest of my body, and I shove my hands in my pockets. "Is everything okay at home?"

"Have you checked your socials?" She tugs her winter hat lower.

"No. I barely used them before you and I went viral. Even less interested now. Why?"

"Val made a video about us. She's telling everyone we cheated and she's devastated."

"Okay." At some point Val was going to say something. I'd hoped it would be the truth, but deep down I knew it wouldn't be. She's clung too hard to let the video of me and Posey go without some sort of response. "She can say whatever she wants. We know the truth."

"But lots of people don't. Her reach is huge."

"Fuck 'em. What do we care what they think?"

"I don't like how she's making me look," Posey says. "But if I respond, people will come after me because I seem like the other woman right now. People believe I'm the reason you and Val broke up."

"I'm not the keeper of other peoples' thoughts and opinions," I say. "This will die down eventually. Just gotta ride it out." The last time I received so much negative attention, I was fourteen, and my parents were right to lay low. It did disappear eventually. Even when the attention has been positive after my Olympic appearances, the intense interest always dies.

"I don't want to ride it out anymore or ignore it or pretend she isn't dragging me through the mud." She takes a deep breath. "I want you to do something."

Do something? Other than telling Val to cut the shit, I'm not sure what she thinks I can do.

"I want you to respond to her or do your own post about all this or something."

"What?" I give a laugh of disbelief. "No. I'm not feeding the trolls and gossips. The more you give, the more they want."

"A consistent diet of Val's lies is currently filling them up." Her tone is sharper than I've ever heard it. "You know what? Fucking forget it." She waves her hand and takes out her phone.

"What are you doing?"

"Ordering an Uber to take me to the airport."

"You don't need an Uber. I can drive you." I step forward to take her bag, and she kicks it behind her without looking up. Somewhat impressive. I would have thought her bag was heavy. The one she took to Bermuda was small but mighty.

She clicks her phone closed, and when her gaze meets mine, the other shoe drops. This wasn't just a conversation about whatever shit Val's been talking. I've missed some subtext here, but I'm still too dense to get it. My gut twists, and it's so fierce, I can feel it in my chest too.

"Am I going to see you after the break?" I ask.

"You mean around campus?" She crosses her arms and checks over her shoulder. Ubers never take long.

My heart dips into my feet like I'm on a rollercoaster. I stare at her, and I search for whatever wording won't scare her off. Each version I prep in my head doesn't quite strike the right note between caring and indifferent. They're all fucking desperate.

"I think our fake relationship has run its course, don't you?" she says. "Something has to stop. I guess it's us."

A black SUV approaches from the end of the parking lot, and it inches along. Whoever is inside is clearly scanning the complex for their pickup.

"Posey," I say, and I try to reach for her just as the car draws flush with the curb.

She jerks her arm out of my reach and opens the rear door to toss her bag in. When she makes eye contact with me, there are tears in her eyes.

There's a vise around my chest, and I don't know what to say to fix whatever I've fucked up.

"This is why I don't do relationships," she says. "One way or another, a guy always lets me down." She ducks into the SUV, and she tugs the door shut behind her before I can get a word out in response.

I throw up my arms at the retreating vehicle, and then I draw them over my head in frustration. She changed her flight, and she came here to break up with me. Wouldn't have mattered what I said. But the idea of just letting her go makes my stomach flip, and I take my phone out of my pocket.

We should talk when you get back. It's not fake for me. Hasn't been for a long time.

I stare at my screen waiting for it to tell me the message has been delivered or read, but there's nothing. The wind kicks up around me, and I let out a sigh.

Fuck. Fuck. Fuck. Fuck. Fuck.

My feelings for her are real, but I'm not sure how much that'll matter. She's convinced herself we won't work, and with an ocean between us, I don't know how I change her mind.

My younger sister bumps my shoulder in the kitchen of our family's chalet in Utah. "At what point do you snap out of this foul mood?"

When Posey reads my fucking text. It's been delivered, but it's sitting unread. *Un-fucking-read.* Her stubborn streak shouldn't be a surprise. She's resisted taking even a whiff of the relationship I was cooking between us.

"Why don't you just call her?" Nicole says.

"She won't even read my text message. She's not going to take a phone call from me."

"What Val did was pretty shitty. You said none of it was true? Have you watched the video yet?" Nicole grabs a glass from one of the cupboards and flicks the switch for the coffee maker.

Although I don't technically have to train for the almost week I'm here with my family, I've been taking the public bus to a local athletics center to swim every day. We're supposed to be skiing, but sticking my face in the water and watching a pace clock is the only thing that seems to soothe this spidering ache that's with me no matter what I'm doing. No other girl has wedged herself so deeply into my conscious and subconscious thoughts. Any time something amusing or interesting happens, I make a mental note to tell Posey, and then I realize I can't tell her. There's a chance I'll never tell her anything ever again.

"There's no point in watching a video filled with lies," I say. "Doesn't make any of it true."

"Want a woman's perspective?" Nicole asks.

"You think I should ask Mom?" I give her a wry smile.

She shoves my shoulder and pours herself a cup of coffee. "Val did your girl dirty. What'd you do in response?"

"Why would I respond?" I get my own cup and pour myself coffee too.

"Was Posey upset about what Val said?" Nicole huffs out a breath.

I stir the sugar and cream into my coffee while I replay all the conversations Posey and I had about Val. To be honest, I knew other people were bothering Posey on campus, but I didn't consider the full impact of that on her.

"I'm going to assume yes," Nicole says. "If my boyfriend didn't defend me after his ex came after me, I'd rip him a new asshole." She shrugs. "I choose violence."

"Rip him a new asshole? Definitely violent. Who raised you?"

Nicole lets out a laugh and then glances toward the bedrooms down the hall. We're the first ones up.

"Posey didn't bother with that. But I'm pretty sure she broke up with me." One hundred percent sure. Remembering the expression on her face when she said I let her down guts me all over again. All the viral posts made it to my sister at her college in California, and even my parents were aware I was involved in "some sort of cheating scandal," but it was easy enough to set them all straight. Conveniently, I left out the part where Posey was originally supposed to be my fake girlfriend. If I can get her back, there'll be nothing fake about it.

"I wish she'd waited until after Christmas so you weren't so miserable. Isn't that relationship etiquette?" Nicole takes a sip of her coffee.

If we were in a relationship Posey acknowledged as real, maybe. I even bought her a present. She has a dangly bracelet she wears that has tiny charms of all her favorite things. I bought her a swimmer for it. Not sure I'd make it on the favorite things list anymore.

"What are you suggesting?" I ask in a huff. "You're telling me I fucked up. I acknowledge that. I'm an idiot when it comes to women. Should I go talk to Val? Tell her to retract all her bullshit?"

"Step one. Watch the damn video. It's everywhere. Not like it's hard to locate. If you don't know what your girlfriend is upset about, how can you possibly fix it?" Nicole holds up a finger. "Step two. Get your ex-girlfriend to back the fuck up. Step three. Grovel. Grovel hard."

A three-step approach to winning Posey back. The first is easy. Unpleasant but easy. Talking to Val is going to take an inhuman amount of patience. As for the groveling, I'm not even sure she'll let me in the door of her apartment for me to start the groveling process.

"You're one of the most driven and focused people I've ever known," Nicole says. "Apply a pinch of that—no need to scare her—and I can't imagine she'll say no. I also saw the video of the two of you. The last time you looked that happy was at the final medal ceremony of the last Olympics. If she can rival *that* feeling, well, that's worth chasing."

She makes it sound simple, but she's never met Posey. Instead of "resistance is futile," her motto appears to be *perseverance* is futile. Though I can't help thinking I made some headway. In our viral video, she's looking at me the same way I'm looking at her. And I *know* how I feel.

"She is one hundred percent worth chasing," I say. Now, I need to figure out how.

POSEY

During the Christmas holidays, the Summerset Royals host one event after another, and tonight we're in the foyer outside the main dining room for cocktails before the staff usher us to our assigned seats at the gigantic dining room table.

The only thing distracting me from my heartbreak is watching Nick and Jules dance around each other with both of them back in the palace. Since Julia worked in California for a few years before returning home, the two of them have barely shared a room, let alone a dinner table.

If my stomach would stop dipping every time Brent crossed my mind, I would be enjoying Nick and Julia's mutual discomfort much more. How is everyone else ignoring the tension? Someone get me a knife. I want to cut it.

A few years ago, when their friendship imploded, I couldn't understand the strangeness between them. Now that I'm older, I can see it for what it is. Sexual tension. The two of them are far, far too aware of each other when they're in the same room. I hope the staff have seated them next to each other at the table. I can't be the only one who's realized what's up.

"Stop staring at him," Julia mutters beside me.

"You won't, so I will," I say, and I snag a glass of champagne off a waiter on his way past. "I think he's gotten hotter, don't you?" At over six feet, Nick is the tallest of the three brothers, and he's done some modeling. His medium-brown hair and hazel eyes coupled with his toned physique made him a regular in the gossip columns, on fashion runways, and on magazine covers. He's quit most of that since he returned from college, but scandals never really leave. Another reason I'm apprehensive about what's happening at Northern University.

"Posey, I'm not debating the hotness level of any of the princes with you."

Her comment reminds me of when I met Monica, which leads me to how she encouraged me to go to Bermuda, which lands me at the doorstep of thoughts of Brent. I down the champagne in one gulp.

"You're not drinking beer, you know. Dom shouldn't be chugged." Julia sips hers, and she turns her back on Nick and the rest of his family to peer at me with her blue-grey eyes through her glasses.

Ah shit. She's giving me that narrow-eyed look that I loathe. Personal questions are headed my way. I'd much rather tease her about her avoidance of Prince Nicholas. She doesn't even call him Nick anymore. Classic case of *thou doth protest too much*. The other two are still Alex and Brice to her.

Julia swipes another glass of champagne when a waiter passes, and she shoves it into my hand. Her lips twitch. "You leave again in two days, and I haven't gotten my gossip."

"Nothing to tell. Met a hot guy. Had a lot of sex. Decided he wasn't for me. Rinse and repeat. Such is my life."

"You've redecorated every room in Mom and Dad's house. Every room. That's a whole new level of avoidance."

"They were very generous with the budget. How could I resist?" I take another gulp of champagne.

"I think you met a boy you actually liked for the first time since Creepy Chris got the boot."

Creepy Chris should have gotten more than my boot to his ass. She's not luring me into discussing Brent. I've avoided lying in bed crying every day by keeping busy. Tonight, I intend to get very, very drunk, and maybe I'll even find someone else to distract me.

Sucks that the thought of being with anyone else turns my stomach. This is why I don't do relationships. Instead of scheming to get under someone, I'm wondering how to get over someone.

I sigh. "I might have liked him a little. The tiniest bit. So small it's hard to even see." I present my thumb and forefinger with barely any space between them.

"You've been obsessed with him for years. Not surprised you came to care a little when your starting position was rampant lust."

I gaze at Nick over her shoulder, and I give her a pointed look. "Uh-huh."

She rolls her eyes. "Yes, he's attractive. He knows he's attractive, but he's not the guy I used to know. He's become the worst kind of manwhore."

After having been sex shamed for the last few days, the whore comment makes me flinch. "I'm with Nick. Sex doesn't have to mean anything." Though I have to admit that I've enjoyed the meaningful sex I've been having with Brent much more.

Why, why, why do I have to think of him every minute of every day?

"Have you read his text yet?" Julia asks.

"No," I say. The first line is visible in the preview—that we should talk when I get back—but if he doesn't understand what I need from him, then there's no need to talk. Destiny is right. If he's not willing to defend me, I don't want him.

Even if I really, really want him.

"He's not the right guy for me," I say, and somehow, I make myself sound far firmer than I really am. Because the truth is that we felt perilously close to having something genuine and real and lasting. But I can't be with someone who believes everything bad will pass easily and with no consequences.

For the rest of the year, whether or not I'm with Brent, everyone will believe I was part of a cheating scandal. Any time my name comes up, that'll be attached to the conversation.

Isn't she the one who slept with Brent Faulkner in Bermuda while he was there with Valentina?

Turns out Brent Faulkner isn't my knight in shining armor. He's just like every other man. A disappointment. More than anything, I wish that thought didn't make my heart constrict in my chest.

That night after dinner and way too many drinks for me, Julia knocks on my bedroom door. While she has her own apartment in the center of Tucker's Town, she's spent quite a few nights at Mom and Dad's house. I think she's worried about me, but there's nothing to worry about.

I've been lying here for the last hour resisting the urge to read Brent's text or to reach out to him. The last time I called him drunk, I ended up in Chicago, and if I called him now, there's a chance I'd book a red-eye flight back to Michigan. The last few weeks, we've filled all our spare time with each other. It's normal to miss a person who wiggled so deeply into your life, and this crushing pressure in my chest is withdrawal, but it doesn't mean we're supposed to be together. If I ever give this boyfriend thing another try, I want someone who is going to listen to me, who'll support me when I need it, and who'll recognize when I'm fading instead of flourishing. Brent seemed like he could be that guy, but I was definitely wrong on all counts.

After hesitating at the doorway, Julia perches on the end of my bed, and she examines the walls, which haven't changed since I left for college four years ago. High school photos litter the room, and my black-and-white color scheme is still classic enough to have endured. It's the only room I didn't touch in my flurry of redecorating since I returned.

"Why didn't you tell me things had gotten so bad online?" she asks.

"Have they gotten bad?" I curl into a ball on the bed and stare at the wall across from me. "I haven't looked."

"You really haven't checked?"

"Not lately. Why would I look? Val spewed a whole bunch of lies about how I lured Brent away from her in Bermuda, and how we've been engaged in a secret affair behind her back for weeks. People ate the details like candy, and now I'm a social pariah on campus. Assholes I've never met think I should *die for having sex*. Not Brent, though. Nope. He's the *man*. Two hot women? All that pussy? Score!"

Julia sucks in a deep breath. "I think it might actually be worse than that?"

"Worse than random strangers wishing I'd die? Doubtful."

"Brent was at her apartment today."

"What?" I sit up, and the room swirls. But I manage to grab her phone. "Show me." The screen is blurry, and I blink to focus. Whatever she's going to show me must be old. He wouldn't get back together with her. He wouldn't do that. Not after what she's trying to do to me. My stomach dips into my toes.

She reaches across me and clicks on an app, and then Brent and Val are on the small screen, standing in the snowy parking lot of her apartment. There isn't just one photo; there are three. Someone from campus must have snapped the pics. No one else would care. In the photos they're talking in the parking lot, walking toward her apartment, disappearing inside.

Like everything else Brent touches lately, these photos have also gone viral with the hashtag *reunion* attached. The assholes have even tagged me as though I've gotten what I deserved.

I toss her phone toward the end of my bed and flop back into the blankets, staring at the ceiling. My brain won't latch onto anything coherent. Instead, my chest feels like it might cave in. Tears prick at the back of my eyes.

Fucking Faulkner.

"She drags me all over campus, and he goes to her apartment? Do you think he's back together with her?" My voice is so thick I don't recognize it. The idea of him with her makes my stomach roll.

"I don't know him," Julia says. "It doesn't *look* good. Maybe he went there to tell her to back off?"

When I asked him to do something, he flat out refused to get involved. Newsflash, he's the reason *I'm* involved. Orgasms and lattes do not make up for a trashed reputation in my last year at Northern. Thankfully, my plan has always been to return to Bellerive, where this mess is a tiny blip in the grand scheme of my life, but if I ever get TV famous, this whole incident will resurface. The internet never forgets.

"Is it possible to hate someone and also feel something so much bigger for them?" I ask.

It takes Julia a moment to answer. "Yeah," she says. "It's possible." She collapses onto the end of my bed. "If you really like him, it might be worth talking to him when you get back in a couple days?"

What would I even say to him? I curl onto my side, and Julia meets my gaze across the expanse of bedding. "He said he felt protective of me." A tear slips down my cheek.

"Then maybe he went to Val to tell her to back off." Julia crawls up the bed and wraps her arms around me. "Don't be like the assholes on the internet and assume things before you talk to him. If you really like him, you should talk to him."

I untangle myself from her, and I grab my phone from the nightstand. The message is still there, and I hover my finger over it. I can read it or delete it without bothering. Even if this doesn't look good, we spent too much time together for me to make assumptions.

After I read it, a tiny spout of hope pops up inside me. Maybe he did go to her apartment to talk to her, to tell her to back off. He hasn't sent me any other messages or tried to reach out to me beyond this one. But what he's sent me isn't nothing either.

I'm at the airport waiting to board my flight back to Michigan when Destiny sends me a text with a screenshot attached. Before I open it, I can already tell it's Brent. I'd recognize him anywhere, even before I knew him so intimately.

I scan the photo, and I realize how starved for him I've been. He's sleeping in his bed, and the dying light must be streaming through the windows in his room. A sheet is artfully draped across his middle. It's a scene I've taken in more than once myself. He looks strong and peaceful...and naked. It's the kind of photo that—the thought draws me up short, and I open the picture to see the entire screenshot.

My blood runs cold.

It's the kind of photo Val would have taken, and it appears she has. This isn't a photo I've ever seen before. Waves of hot and cold are moving through my body as I open the app she's used and click to her profile.

The caption is simple and heartbreaking.

Forgiveness takes many forms. But this one is my favorite.

Forgiveness? What a joke. My heart is spasming in my chest, but instead of letting that feeling take over, I allow the rage to rise in me. If he got back together with her, I will murder him.

I scan through her feed, searching for this same photo elsewhere, but there's nothing. If she'd had this one when they broke up, she'd have posted it to stave off Brent's thirsty fans.

This must be new.

The announcement to board comes over the PA system, and I rise from my seat. My hand shakes as I close my phone and tuck it into my purse. My original plan was to go to Brent and tell him none of this was fake for me either, but it's clear he's slid back into old habits without a second thought.

I've never been good at letting an injustice go, and I'm not about to start today.

BRENT

It doesn't take long for me to realize going to see Val was a miscalculation. Jess is the first one to text me to let me know I'm going viral again because someone posted photos of me and Val entering her apartment. A bunch of other people message me after that wondering if Val and I are back together.

Fan-fucking-tastic.

Here's hoping Posey is still on a social media break. When I called Val from the parking lot, she left her apartment without a coat. I got out to speak to her rather than being in the close confines of the car, but the wind was biting, and I'm not an asshole. She was clearly cold. Which, now that I think about it, the missing coat was likely a ploy on her part to get me into her apartment. There, instead of listening to me and hearing me out about Posey, she tried to get into my pants—quite literally.

I used to lead with my dick, so maybe her assumption would have been reasonable in the past. But I'm not looking for shallow anymore. I'm ready for the deep waters, even if I haven't quite figured out how to navigate them. Right now, I'm drowning in a sea of misinformation.

Jaxon wanders into the kitchen from his bedroom. He returned to campus late last night, and he heads for the coffee maker.

"Man," he says, "your life is like *The Northern Campus Enquirer* come to life. Did you see Val's post this morning? Why is that girl so desperate?"

I rub my forehead and suppress a sigh. The post must be about me, but I've been trying to avoid the swirl of lies. "My chat with her the other night didn't go well."

"No shit. Wouldn't know it from her post this morning. She's running a mile with those photos of you entering her apartment. She's mastered the art of spin."

Reluctantly, I open my phone on the island and click on the app she's likely used. I can feel my jaw harden at the photo of me. "She took that the day you left the apartment door unlocked."

"Hmm." Jaxon pours himself a coffee. "That sucks."

"That's one way to put it." Far too mild for what I'm feeling inside right now. Instead of all this bullshit grinding to a halt, Val is wringing every drop out of it.

"I don't know why you don't make your own post," Jaxon says.

"In my experience, speaking my truth to an unforgiving audience just ends up making me look like an asshole. Best to keep my head down and move on."

"I mean, sure, if you've done something wrong, that's true. But the person who's done something wrong is the one running the ball right now. She's tackled the girl you're actually in love with to the ground, and you're on the sidelines pretending the game isn't even being played. You've been treating Val's version of events as the truth."

"That's not really true. Anyone who matters knows she's lying." Though I can see his point. In the past, I've laid low because I fucked up or the attention was a temporary high from an incredible achievement. There was no need to feed the fire in either direction.

"Do they? I don't know, man. You and Posey have kept a low profile around campus. Could look like hiding to some people. Not a single post on any of your socials about her. None about you on hers."

"I rarely use that shit. Neither does Posey."

"And Val has weaponized your indifference." Jaxon stares at me.

I grit my teeth. *Fuck*. Point taken. To anyone outside my extremely small circle of friends and family, Val would appear more important than Posey. My accounts have photos of me with Val, even if Val is the one who posted them.

"Posey and I have only been together a few weeks," I say. Worse than that is we're technically broken up right now—fake relationship or not. "She doesn't even—she won't even admit this *is* a relationship." Or was. But I'm hoping for is. Our calendars are still attached, so I know exactly what she's been doing the last week since she's been home. Helped ease my absolute panic over her leaving like she did. If she meant to dump me, she'd have scrubbed me from her life. I didn't enter anything into my calendar on the off chance she might reach out, might miss me. No such luck.

"It's your life. You can do whatever you want. I'm just saying, if I didn't live with you, I'd be questioning what the hell went down."

"I don't understand why people care."

"She's made them care. While you were swimming, she fed the world a pack of lies about your *idyllic* relationship. You didn't care, and she benefited from it. A lot of those people probably feel like you broke up with them, cheated on them. Scroll through Val's account and read some of her captions. She tagged you in a lot of them. It's like a cosign when you don't respond or get her to take them down."

I rub my forehead and click on her profile to go through her feed. As much as it pains me, Posey said something similar about Val feeding her followers a steady diet of lies. Perhaps it's time I listened to the music I covered my ears against when we were together.

Three hours later when there's a knock on our apartment door, I'm exhausted from reading every sappy caption Val attached to a photo of me over the year we dated off and on. Even I'm feeling sorry about this version of Brent and Val breaking up—they were epic. It's amazing how easily she dressed up a relationship that was little more than casual sex into a fantasy fit for a romance novel. No wonder people are pissed off. They've already been duped once into believing something that wasn't true. Posey and I have made it easy for her to do it a second time by trying to fly under the radar.

My head is a muddle of thoughts when I open the door to find an irate Posey on the other side. She holds up her phone with the picture of me that Val took when she broke into my apartment a few weeks ago.

"What the hell is this, Faulkner?"

"Looks like a photo of me sleeping," I say, and when her jaw clenches tighter, I realize I've let my frustration leak into the wrong conversation. She doesn't deserve my smart-ass remarks.

"Why did we even bother with a stupid fake relationship if you were going to let your dick run away from you the minute I left the country?"

"A stupid fake relationship?" I step back from the door and sweep my hand to let her in. Jaxon left for his class and won't be back for a few hours. I have practice in half an hour, but we might as well hash this out now. "Come on in. Let's talk about how there was nothing fake about our stupid relationship. I've been wanting to have this conversation for weeks."

"I'm not coming in," she says. "I came to tell you that I faked all those orgasms to match our fake relationship, and I hope you're very happy with Val." She spins on her heel, and I grab her upper arm.

"Posey, wait. I'm in a shitty fucking mood, but obviously you are too. I'm not back with Val. That photo is just another lie."

"So you didn't go to her place the other night?"

I purse my lips. "I did. Again, not what it looked like. You of all people should understand that."

Tears fill her eyes, and her bottom lip trembles. "She's trying to ruin me. Why would you go see her?"

I drag her into my arms. "I thought I could talk some sense into her. Didn't go well."

"Well enough," Posey mutters against my shirt, but she's squeezing me tight. "Everyone thinks you're back together between those photos and the stupid half-naked photo in bed. I used to love those photos. They've been ruined for me forever."

"As long as the real thing hasn't," I say. She came willingly into my arms.

She shoves me away and wipes her eyes. "And I'm crying. I don't cry about stupid shit or stupid boys or any of this."

All right. Not sure what to say to that. She's crying because she cares, but I'm fairly certain pointing that out right now would get me punched. I can't force her to be honest with herself or with me. "I'm not with Val, and I will never be with Val again. I promise. Whether or not you and I can work this out, Val and I are done."

"Work this out? There's nothing to work out."

"Why'd you come here if there wasn't at least a small part of you that thought we were worth a discussion?"

"I was concerned about your mental health."

Somewhat valid. If I was back with Val, I'd be worried about my mental health too. "Tell me you feel absolutely nothing for me."

She sniffs and rubs her cheeks.

"Tell me," I say again.

"I can't, okay? Is that what you want to hear? My stone-cold heart has warmed slightly at your constant proximity. You wore me down."

Not the most romantic thing I've ever heard, but her words make my chest swell nonetheless. That's progress.

She sighs. "But that doesn't matter because I don't want to be with someone who won't defend me when I'm being dragged by their ex-girlfriend or anyone. At Deacon's party, when Chet came on to me, you claimed you felt protective of me." She stares at me for a beat. "Where's that instinct now, Brent, when I actually need it?" She shakes her head, and before I can say anything else, she turns on her heel and races down the side stairs.

"Posey!" I call after her, but I've got no shoes on, and nothing good to say in response anyway. My fuckups in this situation are endless, but none of them are Posey's fault. She met me at an airport and agreed to help me. Look where that's gotten her. Instead of shouting my feelings for her from the rooftops, I've been too afraid to tell her or anyone else how I really feel.

With that small admission she cares, I realize I have a chance. My sister's idea to grovel doesn't seem quite right to me, and maybe I'll fuck this up too.

But I'm not going to grovel.

I'm going to woo.

Posey

The first latte arrives the next morning, but it isn't Brent delivering it. Instead, Jaxon is on my security screen.

"You can tell him it's a lost cause," I say into the speaker system.

"A Jack Frost." Jaxon holds up the latte.

I purse my lips, and I ring the buzzer to let him up. He passes me the cup at the door, and I give him a wan smile. "He's going to have to do a lot better than a latte."

"Oh, he's aware." Jaxon grins.

Once he's left, I realize there's something taped to the side of the cup. I open the slip of paper, and there's just one word: YOU.

Destiny wanders out of her room, and she frowns at the cup in my hand. "I thought we kicked Faulkner to the curb."

"Seems he can take a beating," I say as I stare at the word and try to puzzle out what it means.

Nadiya's door down the hall flies open with a clatter. "Holy shit! Posey are you and Faulkner back together?"

"Technically we were never—" I say.

"He's responding to all the people on Val's posts," Nadiya says, passing me her phone.

I click on his replies, and my lips twitch. Brevity at its finest. On most of the comments, he's simply written "Untrue" in response to whatever rant is there. But at the bottom of Val's post, he's written a longer message saying that Val has deliberately misled people about their relationship prior to Thanksgiving and she's continuing to misrepresent the situation. I'm no sooner done reading it than it disappears.

"The bitch deleted it," I whisper.

"What?" Nadiya takes back her phone, and then she gasps as her feed updates.

I'm almost too afraid to ask, but she turns her phone toward me, and there is a photo of me and Brent. We're in Bermuda at the beach, and we've both got a slice of pizza in our hands. I forgot he snapped that picture. Feels like so long ago.

"That lighting is ace," Destiny says, peering over Nadiya's shoulder. "The two of you are glowing." She points at the caption. "Aww. Look at that."

The caption is simple: *One of my favorites of one of my favorites.*

Warmth sweeps across my body, and I long to stare at the photo and reread the caption a thousand times.

"You cannot melt after one latte, one post, and a bunch of half-assed comment replies," Destiny says. "You gotta milk this till the teats run dry."

"Melting?" I scoff. "No one is melting." Perhaps a slight thawing, but there will be no melting. I snatch my phone off the counter, and I send Brent a text.

Try harder.

Almost immediately, I get a response. *Challenge accepted. The best you've ever had, Jensen. Except now it's not just in bed.*

The trolls will come for you.

Let them try. Val isn't the only one who can craft a love story. 😊

I trace my finger over the word *love* before closing my phone with a decisive click. Destiny is right. One post, a few responses to trolls, and one latte doesn't solve the bigger issue. When I asked him to defend me, he stood by in silence.

For the next week, lattes are delivered to me all over campus, but never by Brent. His roommate, members of the men's and women's basketball teams, swimmers on the team, Sebastian Swan and his girlfriend Natalie, and other people who I've never seen before. It's an endless parade of caffeinated drinks. At least three a day, and sometimes more.

Each latte has a slip of paper attached. Sometimes the slip has a complete message on it, and sometimes it's one to add to the wall of words in my bedroom. *You're the most amazing woman I've ever met. Your punny sense of humor is the best. This is real for me.*

The last one gets me every time I read it—a mantra I was stupid enough to stick to my wall to see every day.

On top of that, he's posted a photo of the two of us to all his accounts each day. The captions are simple, but they are little fires under my frosty heart, warming it an inch at a time.

Destiny stares at the latest post over my shoulder. "I didn't realize these teats had so much milk in them."

"Doesn't change that he didn't do it when I asked." I click my phone closed.

"That's true. I'm so glad you've never made a mistake in your life, and you always do what people ask of you right away. Otherwise, that comment would be embarrassing." Destiny swipes one of my lattes off the island and takes a long sip. "This tea is good."

I can't help the chuckle that escapes. "Have you switched sides? You're supposed to tell your friend when you've crossed over to make yourself some *tea* in the enemy's trenches."

She gives me a helpless look and shrugs. "I cannot deny the boy is working his ass off to get you back."

"He's doing all of it from a distance, though." At the start of the week, that wouldn't have been a complaint. But there's something about being surrounded by Brent-like things that's making me crave him more than if he'd left me completely alone. "Ethan delivered my latte today after swim practice, and he smelled like Brent."

"Like a pool."

"Yes! Like chlorine. Chlorine is not sexy. Why is chlorine sexy? Why?"

"I'm going to say this real slow for your brain cells in the back." She holds her hand up to emphasize each word as she says it. "It's because you like the guy who is attached to that chlorine smell."

I do like the guy attached to the chlorine smell, and there's a chance, however much I don't want it to be true, that I miss him. A lot.

"You think what he's done is enough?" I ask.

"That's not a question I can answer. You're the one he didn't support, the one he hurt. Does it feel like enough to you?"

My home screen flashes with a new notification. Since Brent started posting photos of us everywhere with cute captions, I turned my push notifications back on. At first, I was sure it was a stupid move. Instead, what I've found is Brent on social media like it's his job. As soon as anyone posts a negative comment about me anywhere, he's there defending me or explaining or apologizing for any confusion his initial silence caused. His account must be out of control with notifications, but he's made sure that everything I can possibly see, he's commented on it. I don't even know how he's doing it because he trains a lot and he hadn't missed a single comment.

"Brent can't keep defending me on social media for the next few months while we're still at Northern," I say. "It's not sustainable."

"That sounds like you are contemplating a real relationship." Destiny smirks.

A real relationship still scares the shit out of me, but if I'm honest, Brent and I were pretty much in one before that viral video blew us up. We spent a lot of time together doing things couples would do, and I didn't mind one bit. Would even go so far as to say I enjoyed it.

"He tried to talk to Val, right?" Destiny asks.

"Yeah," I say. "He said it didn't go well, but he didn't elaborate. She obviously used his appearance to spin another narrative instead." I fiddle with my phone, an idea on the edges of my consciousness that I'm not sure I want to follow. "Should I go talk to her?"

Destiny sucks in a sharp breath and gives me a 'yikes' look. "Not alone."

"Should I ask Brent to go with me?"

"Do you think he would?"

I consider everything he's done since I returned to campus and everything he's still doing now on social media, even when he doesn't know I see it. "He would." Whatever corner he needed to turn to see things from my point of view, he's done it.

"Sounds like a threesome in Val's eyes." Destiny winces. "You'd have to meet somewhere very public."

A gross but valid point.

"What are you hoping to get out of talking to her?" Destiny asks. "She clearly doesn't want to play nice. You can't make her do anything she doesn't want to do."

"I don't want the rest of my final year to be constantly on guard and trying to one-up each other. Maybe if I talked to her..." The truth is I'm not sure what I want out of the conversation, but I don't want this battle to go on. Maybe talking to her won't breed anything positive, but I have to try.

"Call your boyfriend." Destiny winks. "See what he says."

I bite my lip, and I stare at the notification on my home screen. When I click into it, Brent has posted another cute photo of us. I had no idea he'd taken so many, although I discovered in Bellerive that I had more of him on my phone than I realized too.

Before I can second-guess myself, I send a text to him.

I think we should try to talk to Val one more time.

We?

You and me somewhere public.

There's a long pause before bubbles appear on my screen. *Can I come over so we can talk in person?*

Destiny is home, and Nadiya will be home in a few minutes. We haven't been alone together in weeks, and I'm not sure I want our first conversation to be with an audience. *Is Jaxon home?*

No. You want to come here?

A kaleidoscope of butterflies takes flight in my stomach at the thought of seeing him. *Be there in 30.*

I click my phone closed, and I yell, "Going to Brent's."

"Atta girl. Go get your man."

BRENT

A dirty apartment and last week's sheets are not how I planned to woo Posey back into my life, so I'm rushing around as though the place is on fire. On top of schoolwork and training, managing my social media notifications has become a part-time job, so keeping this place reasonably tidy has not been a priority.

I've got alerts on her name, alerts on my name, and alerts on the stupid fucking hashtags bitter unknown people created in the wake of Val's lies. To say the experience has been enlightening is an understatement. I'm not sure I ever want to go viral for anything ever again. So much easier to ignore all this shit.

But monitoring the fallout made me realize what Posey faced, and if I ever go through this with her again, I can't ignore what's fired at her. Although I was, according to Val, the one who cheated, Posey was painted as the villain. I had no idea she was receiving so much harassment because, although mine has been a lot, the comments, memes, shitty photos and general bullshit has been much more toxic for her. Some people even posted about how great I must be in bed because I had two hot women after me. I wasn't entirely sure how to feel about that one.

When I talked to my younger sister about it, she called the reaction misogynistic bullshit, and then she sent me a whole bunch of articles to read about how women are often shamed for things men are celebrated for. It's the sort of thing I bet Posey has a lot of opinions on, and after I finished reading all of it, I wished I could call her to talk about it. Maybe someday. Instead, I called Nicole back.

Each time I remember why Posey is coming over, I actually can't believe she's suggested we try to talk to Val. Val's attempts to spin everything I post are exhausting, and she's weaponized her followers, mostly against Posey. Something has to give, but I'm not convinced it'll be Val. On the other hand, I'm not letting whatever cracks be my relationship with Posey either, even if I have to stay vigilant and on guard for the rest of the school year.

Assuming I can get Posey to admit we're in a relationship.

Almost exactly thirty minutes later, there's a knock on my front door. My stomach clenches with anticipation and a hint of dread. We haven't seen each other in person since she stormed away from here and implied I wasn't capable of protecting her in the right way. After a week of notes and latte deliveries, and a crash course in social media PR from Jaxon, I was starting to wonder if I was battling a lost cause. Apart from her *try harder* text, my efforts didn't get much response. If I didn't understand how hard it was for her to admit to *any* kind of feelings for me, I might have backed off or felt defeated.

But I stuck with the full-court press, and if she wants to talk to Val, even if I think that's a terrible idea, she has to be considering something longer-term between us. Otherwise, why bother?

At the door, I take a deep breath, the same one I normally inhale on the starting blocks when I'm staring down a tough race. When I open the door, I scan her long brown hair, her knee-length winter jacket, and the wariness of her expression.

We're not on even ground yet. Good to know before I stick my foot in my mouth or spew out everything I've been thinking for the last couple of weeks.

I move aside to let her in, but nothing between us feels quite right. From that first weekend, I never held back my affection, never questioned the ease between us. But I'm definitely on the back foot now.

She sheds her coat and her boots at the entry, and she takes a seat on the couch. I stand with my back against the island and cross my arms.

"I know I still have some work to do," I say.

"No, it's—" Posey tucks her hair behind her ears. "Thank you for everything you've done so far. It hasn't gone unnoticed."

I hate how stilted and formal we are, as though we didn't spend weeks wrapped around each other. "If we—if you—I'll never ignore something like this again. I promise. I had no idea they were coming after you so hard."

She lets out a low laugh, and the tension in her shoulders seems to vanish. "I pray to god there's never something like this to ignore again." She leaves the couch to stand with her feet between mine. Slowly, she inches her way into my body, and when she wraps her arms around my middle and places her cheek over my heart, we both sigh.

I smooth her hair, and I breathe her in. There's probably something I should say, but I'm so relieved she's here and that she stepped into my arms. Without a negotiation or pleading on my part, she entered my embrace.

"I've missed you," she whispers.

My chest swells, and I draw her tighter against me. "If this is what letting you down is like, I'm not fucking doing it again."

She lets out a little laugh and glances up. "Never? That's a high bar, Faulkner."

"I've got all your favorite lattes and orgasms memorized in case I fuck up again. What's your favorite flower as a backup?"

"Ooh. I do like flowers. Roses. Any color of roses."

"Noted," I say. Part of me feared she'd name some pretty plant that only flowers once every ten years but looks gorgeous in a white room. "Are you sure you want to talk to Val?"

"I want all this to stop, don't you?"

"I want her to stop," I say, "but I don't want *this* to stop. We can ignore Val or confront her, whatever you want, as long as we're on the same page about what comes next."

She doesn't go tense in my arms like I expect. Instead, she gives me a quick squeeze. "Can we figure out you and me after we've called off Val and her dogs?"

It's not a no, so I'll take it, but I'm concerned Val won't call off her pack of wolves, and going to speak to her might just make them bite down harder. Before we go, we need a plan.

We're in the food court of the athletics building, and I'm ninety-nine percent sure meeting with Val is a bad idea. Up ahead, Val is seated at a four-person table, and she's on her phone, so she hasn't seen that I've brought Posey for the conversation.

I can already picture the steam coming out of her ears when she realizes she's been ambushed. My *we need to talk* text was answered immediately, and when she offered her place for the location, I suggested here after my practice. She must think I'm really stupid to get lured into any ploy that puts me in a position to be alone with her a second time.

Val glances up, and she rises from her seat, gathering her purse and phone. She storms toward us. "This isn't happening," she says.

"Hold up," I say. "We just want to talk."

"Talk?" Val huffs out a breath. "Why would I want to talk to either of you?" She eyes our joined hands, and her jaw tightens. "You must have been fucking around behind my back."

"I never cheated on you." I rear back at her comment.

"Bullshit. You can't expect me to believe this is all a giant coincidence. The little interest you showed me disappeared in the final few weeks we were together. You break up with me at the last minute, and Posey appears out of nowhere to attend the wedding with you? Please. I was not born yesterday. Red flags everywhere."

I'm momentarily stunned. She'd been spewing accusations over the holidays, but I never thought she believed them.

"It wasn't out of nowhere. I posted in the campus chat server for a date to the wedding. Posey responded. You can probably search for my post if you don't believe me." For the first time, I don't see her as vindictive but as genuinely hurt.

"I spent a year and a half with you. You never held my hand or posted photos of us or did anything sweet or romantic. A *year and a half.*"

We were on and off the whole time, which to me, answers her question. Why would I want to do anything sweet or romantic when we were often steeped in a battle of wills over something she wanted that I wasn't prepared to do? As a couple, we didn't work, but I was too lazy or too routine oriented to break things off for good. At the time, being with her felt easy, but looking back, now that I know what a real relationship feels like, there was nothing easy about being with Val. We were a bad combination from the start.

"You wanted those things?" I ask. Posey squeezes my hand, but she's been a silent bystander so far.

"What girlfriend wouldn't want those things?" Val scoffs. "And then to see you giving them so freely to her." She tosses her hand in Posey's direction. "After you've known her for five minutes."

A twinge of annoyance rises at her casual dismissal of Posey. "You cannot pretend like you and I had some great love affair. None of the shit you posted was true."

"So that means I couldn't have *wanted* it to be true?" Val crosses her arms, and her purse bangs her thigh.

"But you didn't," I say. "Even you said in Bermuda that we had an arrangement that worked for us. That's not a relationship." I fumble for the right word. "It's a transaction, a business arrangement."

"I couldn't get what I wanted, so I took what I could get," she says.

The food court is starting to get busier, and more people are beginning to take an interest in our conversation. Not a good look for any of us.

"That wasn't the impression you gave me," I say. Sponsorships, branding, follower counts, and the mysteries of the algorithms were the only topics Val ever discussed with me. We had a partnership, but it had nothing to do with romance.

"Desperate isn't a good look on anyone." She gives a pointed stare at where I'm still clinging to Posey's hand.

Whatever. She can think what she wants. But she needs to back the fuck off. "What do you want me to say, Val? Because things either calm the fuck down or Posey and I go low. You're not the only one with photos from Bermuda."

Granted, she's in the background of some of them, but she's clearly pawing at Trev's cousin in a few of them. A lucky find on our part since I didn't include her deliberately. I've got no problem zooming in and posting those with my own detailed assessment of our *relationship*.

Val's jaw works, and for the first time she turns her attention to Posey. "Did he cheat on me?"

"Not with me," Posey says. "I can't imagine him cheating at all. That's not who he is."

Such a simple statement, but it makes me feel a hell of a lot better about where we're headed. She didn't hesitate, even though we've only known each other a few weeks.

Seems unbelievable that Val blew up Posey's life because she thought I cheated on her given her own behavior. Doesn't seem fair.

"We just want you to stop spreading lies," I say. "Let all this die."

"I'm not removing anything or taking anything down." Val shifts her purse onto her shoulder.

"That's not going to work," I say. "I need you to take down the photo that makes it look like I fucked around on Posey. We both know how you got that picture. Your live video you've got saved on your profile also needs to come down."

Posey squeezes my hand.

"That photo makes me look like I went back and forth between you, Val. Is that the impression you want people to have of you? If I post my Bermuda photos, it's going to look even worse. You and Trev's cousin were not subtle." I'm more concerned about the long-term impact on Posey if those lies are lurking out there, and I'll do what's necessary to get them down.

"I'll delete the caption and the comments." She huffs out a breath. "I'll take down the video. I don't know that I believe you weren't cheating, but I don't have any proof either way. I don't understand how you could have gotten so close so fast. Doesn't make any sense to me when you gave me the bare minimum."

The truth is that I gave her what she allowed me to give, and I wonder whether, seeing what I'm capable of, she has regrets over not insisting on more. If she'd pushed, I'd have walked. That was our pattern for a year and a half. She asked for more than I was willing to give, and I called off our arrangement. She lured me back. Rinse and repeat. As Posey pointed out, sex was the only thing we had going for us. Not sure I would have believed I had room for more.

With Posey, it's been the opposite. We started with sex and built something meaningful. I've been the one inching toward a relationship, and she's been the one stubbornly standing still. Not backing off, but not letting herself get too close. I have a clear idea of how a future could work with Posey, and I never saw one with Val. None of that will make Val feel better about where we've ended up, and the truth might freak Posey out. Though, I'm beginning to think she might be almost ready for my honest assessment of us as a couple.

"I'm sorry I was a shit boyfriend to you." It's the best I can do. Val and I were always too different in the wrong ways to succeed. We should have been a brief affair, not a long-term relationship.

"I'm sure you'll slide into old habits," Val says. "And then he'll be ignoring you too." She gives Posey a saccharine smile. "It's not like you're anything special."

I open my mouth to tell her exactly what I think, and Posey covers it with her palm.

"Sure, I'm not special. Your opinion of me really doesn't matter. But if you start spreading rumors again about Brent or if you keep telling people he cheated, we'll be posting those photos of you and Trevor's cousin and going live with our own version of events."

Val rolls her eyes. "Oh, sweetie. You've got a lot to learn. He's only got room in his life for one love, and it isn't you." She fishes into her bag and takes out some gloss to smooth across her lips. "Are we done here? Seeing the two of you together makes me sick."

"Yeah, we're done." She'll either uphold our bargain or Posey and I will be forced to go low. I'd really prefer the train of lies ground to a halt without me having to trash her in the process. Not a good look for any of us, and as Posey noted earlier when we were talking Val strategy, the internet doesn't forget.

Val slings her purse over her shoulder, and she storms through the athletic complex as though she doesn't have a care in the world.

"Do you believe her?" Posey asks.

"About which part?"

She lets out a light laugh. "Any of it, I suppose. She seems like she'd be hard to get to know."

Despite Posey's high walls around a relationship, she's been open with me from the start. Posey's observation about Val is interesting. While Posey told me in Bermuda she wears all kinds of faces, I'm not sure I ever saw Val's real one. Sad, actually. We spent a year and a half together, and we never got to know each other at all.

"You okay?" Posey asks, and she wraps her arms around my middle and gives me a squeeze.

"Yeah." I plant a kiss on top of her head. "I'm just really grateful for you."

She draws away, and she links her hand with mine before raising it to her lips and kissing the back of my hand. She leads me toward the exit. "You know, Faulkner, I think the feeling might be mutual."

A blast of warmth shoots across my body, as though she's just given me the best present. "You gonna let me take you out tomorrow night on a real date?"

"More than lattes and orgasms?" She quirks an eyebrow.

"We'll start with dinner and see whether you can handle it," I say.

"Oh," she says. "I can handle it. I'm an expert handler." She gives me an exaggerated wink.

The words I've been holding back rise into my throat, but I swallow them. Even if she was ready, I wouldn't say them in the middle of a crowded food court.

"Tomorrow night," I say. "I'll pick you up after practice."

At the exit, we part ways. She has class, and I'm behind on my latest assignment thanks to all my social media PR work. With the Val situation resolved, I'm hopeful Posey and I will be able to figure out what even ground looks like for us.

No matter what, I want her in my life.

Posey

I don't know why I'm so nervous, but I've primped and fussed with my hair and makeup for the last hour in anticipation of seeing Brent. We've done so much together the last few weeks, and we've seen each other at our best and worst. Going on a date with him shouldn't be sending the butterflies in my stomach into overdrive.

But tonight feels like the start of something new.

When I emerge from my bedroom in the shortest, tightest dress I own, Destiny lets out a whistle. "That dress is fire! Where's he taking you?"

Nadiya glances up from her phone. "Val took down the video, closed comments on her post of half-naked Brent, and changed the caption to confirm they broke up and she doesn't have any bad feelings toward him." She rolls her eyes. "A day late and a dollar short on all of it, but at least it's done."

With all the fluttering in my stomach, the last person on my mind is Val, but I'm glad my friends have my back. The drama coupled with our return to school from the holidays has meant Brent and I haven't spent much time together the last few weeks. Val isn't our problem as long as she stays out of our lives. My revenge is being happy and enjoying a version of Brent that she, for better or worse, never got to see. He said he was different with me, but part of me figured it was a nice line. Having Val confirm he never treated her the same way he treats me was a real heart-stopping moment.

"You look nervous." Nadiya clicks her phone closed. "You going to tell him that you like him—*like him*, like him?"

Rather than answering her, I lean down to check the straps on my high heels. Completely impractical for winter with the ice and snow on the ground, but I'm hoping I can stick to salted, shoveled paths. Or stick to Brent. If it's slick and slippery, he'll have to lend me a hand or two.

"You're not going to answer her?" Destiny pops her gum. "I think the entire universe knows how he feels about you after his super sappy posts this past week."

"They have not been super sappy." I tug on the strap one last time and face them.

"He just posted another one." Nadiya lets out a sigh. "At this rate, I think *I* might be in love with him."

When I peer over her shoulder, it's a black-and-white photo of just me, and I'm sleeping in his bed. Whether he got lucky or he learned a thing or two about camera angles from his ex, it's a beautiful shot. The caption, like all the others, is simple.

In life there are plastic balls and glass ones. What I have with her is glass, and I'll do everything I can to keep it from cracking.

"Deacon and I are having a chat," Destiny says. "He never does shit like this for me, and we're one-hundred-percent endgame. He needs to step it up."

I'm rereading the caption again, and I'm trying to identify the emotion that's welled up in me. It's so thick my throat feels tight with it.

"Is it too soon to love him? I think I might love him." My hand is over my heart, and I'm so full of emotion I could cry.

"You feel what you feel when you feel it. I knew pretty quick with Deacon," she says.

"I'm still not sure about West." Nadiya shrugs. "Love is unpredictable."

Destiny smacks Nadiya's arm. "That's not a helpful comment. Our girl is dipping her toes in the love fountain. You gotta help ease her in."

"The problem is," I say, "I feel like I might be neck-deep in the water already."

"Oh my god." Destiny clutches her heart. "Our girl is in love."

There's playful mocking in her tone, but I'm too focused on my racing heart. "I can't tell him that, though, right? It's like way, way too early for the L bomb." The thought of saying the words causes sweat to pool under my arms.

Nadiya stares at the post on her phone. "We've all learned social media is not representative of real life, but look at Brent's feed... it's swimming, and it's you. You know how much he loves getting wet."

That elicits a laugh, and the tension eases out of me a pinch. "Do I ever." I give her an exaggerated wink.

"Your sexual innuendoes are wasted on me," Nadiya says.

The downstairs buzzer sounds, and I grab my purse off the island and hustle to check the monitor. Brent is dressed in a suit, and my stomach dips. Forget the date. I want to drag him up here and make up for lost time. A suit? *Hell, yes.*

I snatch my winter jacket off the hook, and I'm out the apartment door before either of my roommates can tease me about how eager I am. When he said he had a night planned for us and to dress nice, I had no idea he'd be wearing a suit too. To most guys, dressing up is a pair of khakis and a polo shirt.

At the front entrance, I open the door, and Brent grins. The pure delight in his expression causes me to drop my purse and coat on the floor, and then I tackle him, wrapping my arms around his neck and my legs around his waist.

He chuckles against my lips, but he doesn't hesitate to kiss me back, to support my legs, and to press me against the cold glass window. When I let out a gasp of surprise, he spins me around to brace me against the mailboxes instead.

I've missed this all-consuming passion, as though we can't get enough of each other. Part of me wonders if I used to fake or inflate my desire with other guys because I've never felt this desperate surge of longing for anyone. We're real in a way I've never experienced with another man.

"If we keep going, we're not going to make dinner," Brent murmurs against my neck.

Our apartment complex is normally busy, and anyone could walk in or out of the door at any moment. I'm also starving since we had to wait to start our date until after his swim practice was over. Earlier, I was too nervous to eat.

"Where are we going?" I ask as he eases my feet to the ground.

"I have plans," he says, "and you don't get to know them."

"You're going to wine and dine—"

"And sixty-nine," he finishes with a smirk.

The urge to blurt out my feelings is so strong I have to turn my back on him to grab my coat and purse from the floor.

"If you could just bend a little lower," Brent says from behind me.

I glance at him over my shoulder, and I do an exaggerated bend. "Like this?" I ask in a mock breathy voice.

"Such a tease." Brent runs his hand along my ass and down my leg.

"Don't worry," I say, and I turn in his arms. "You'd have to really fuck up not to get laid tonight."

"Do not underestimate my ability to fuck up a sure thing."

"Whatever you've got planned will be fun." I slap his chest and grab his hand.

"Should I be worried that I'm not having to heavily medicate you for this date? This is a *real* date."

"I know," I say. "I'm actually kind of surprised you didn't bring me a giant bouquet of I'm-a-dick roses to make up for the hellish couple of weeks I've had."

"I'm-a-dick roses?" His lips twitch as he holds open the door for me to step through.

"It's a thing that I have decided will be our thing." He holds my elbow so I don't fall on the way to his car.

"Would the flowers need to be in the shape of a dick?"

"I would like to hear you order that arrangement," I say as I slide into the car, and when he gets into the driver's seat, I continue, "but I don't need for it to actually exist."

He starts the car and drives out of my parking lot along familiar roads near campus, and it doesn't take me long to figure out where we're headed. We park under the blue sign, but the restaurant looks deserted.

"I think they're closed," I say, checking my watch. "Weekdays they're done at nine."

"Let's go check," he says, and he circles the car to open my door and help me across the icy surface.

The sign is flipped at the entrance, and I shrug. "Closed." There are lots of other places we can eat at, even if I'm touched he chose my favorite spot.

Brent tugs on the door, and he gives me a mischievous smile. "Open." He steps back and waves me in. "Ladies first."

As soon as I'm in the door, I'm struck by how different the place looks. There are fairy lights strung across the ceiling, and there are vases brimming with roses strewn around the main eating area. I press my hand to my chest, and another swell of emotion threatens to overwhelm me.

"Turns out, I already started the tradition of a truckload of I'm-a-dick roses without realizing it was going to be our thing."

My purse and coat hit the floor for a second time as I whirl around and kiss him. He slides his hands into my hair and returns the kiss with the same fiery passion I feel. If I wasn't sure Monty and his wife were lurking somewhere, I'd be trying to convince him that a quicky on or against any surface in this place was the best way to make sure both his heads are in the right places.

The sound of the kitchen door swinging open makes me draw away from Brent, but this time he swipes my coat and purse off the floor for me while I turn to greet Monty.

"Your boyfriend and his teammates came here to decorate for what I gather is a special occasion?" Monty quirks his eyebrows at the two of us.

"Special occasion?" I turn to Brent with a furrowed brow.

"You'll see," he says, and he tips his chin toward the table we sat at the last time we came.

I weave through the empty restaurant to our table, and I slide into my chair. "How did you convince them to let you do this?" I ask.

"Easy," he says. "You're his favorite customer."

Surrounded by my favorite flowers in my favorite restaurant which reminds me of my favorite country on a date with my favorite guy. Sheer perfection.

"Did I nail it?" he asks.

"Bang, bang, bang, baby." I grin.

I'm still staring at Brent in amazement when Monty delivers the first dish. One of my favorite chicken dishes, of course. When Brent gestures for me to dig in first, I don't hesitate.

The food comes and goes while Brent and I chat about our holidays, our family, and what's happening with our classes. It's easy, and the conversation reminds me of how natural it's been from the first weekend for us to open ourselves up to each other. Maybe Destiny is right that everyone feels what they feel when they feel it. With him, it felt different almost right away.

When we met at the airport, I was in love with his outer package. Tall, fit, smoldering. As the weeks wore on, and we peeled away layers of each other with our clothes, the outer package was matched by an equal love for his mind and soul. There's no part of him that I don't love.

That thought would have terrified me when we met, and it still causes my heart to race to verbalize it. But I definitely feel it.

We're lingering over dessert when Brent takes a small velvet box out of his suit pocket and slides it across the table. It's the exact shape and size of a ring box, and I raise my startled gaze to his.

He wouldn't, would he?

"No need to look like a deer about to get hit by a Mac truck. I'm not skipping from fake dating to getting married."

I press a hand to my chest and breathe a sigh of relief. Dating is one thing, but marriage is something else entirely.

"It was supposed to be a Christmas present for you, but that didn't quite go to plan. Instead, it's an anniversary present."

"Anniversary?" I laugh.

"Happy day zero," he says, and he pushes the box closer with his index finger. "You and I have been real for a while, a long while, but I want it to be official."

I crack open the box, and inside is a swimmer charm for the dangly bracelet I wear almost every day. My parents bought it for me when I left Bellerive, and I've been very selective about the charms I put on it. They have to mean something.

"Posey Jensen, will you be my girlfriend?"

I slip the charm out and hold it in my palm. Everything sings in me at the realization that we're embarking on a real relationship. Tears prick at my eyes, and when I look at him, I'm all watery inside.

"Yes," I say. "It's a definite yes."

He rises from the table, and he comes around to draw me into a hug. I cling onto him with the charm clenched in my hand.

"This might get complicated, though," I say. "I'm in my last year of college, but you've got more of your MA, and I want to go home, and—"

"We can figure it out. We're both independent people. That's one of the things I love. We can have our own things, and we can have each other too."

That sounds great in theory—really, really great—but I've never missed anyone the way I've missed him when we're not together. I can't imagine having him in my life full-time until college ends and then getting on a plane out of here, not being sure if we'll work out.

Brent

It's been weeks since Val removed or locked her content smearing me and Posey, and since she stopped putting us on broadcast, our socials have quieted. Maybe other people would have wanted revenge, but Posey and I just wanted it to stop. Keeping on top of the mean comments isn't a part-time job anymore, and I'm grateful for that.

Slipping into a familiar routine with Posey has been easy. On nights when I have early-morning practice the next day, I sleep at hers. Others, when I have dryland training in the morning, we sleep at mine. In between classes, coursework, and practices, we squeeze out every moment of time we can together. I've never craved another person's company like I do hers.

Despite my bravado over the long-distance relationship looming ahead of us, I have no idea how I'm going to cope. I've already contacted the head coach of the biggest swim team in Bellerive to see whether it's possible for me to train there sporadically whenever I need a Posey fix. From what I've been able to determine online, the island has decent facilities, and my coach has encouraged me to have a life beyond swimming. We can make this work. I just have to keep telling myself that.

The final year before the Olympics, my flexibility will change as my training ramps up. At this point, I don't know what I'd do if I had to choose between keeping Posey and going after my swimming goals.

We haven't exchanged the L-word, but it's getting harder and harder to hold it in when we're together. Every time I lay eyes on her, the torrent of emotion takes me by surprise, and I have to consciously watch what I say. We've both danced around the truth. Instead of saying we love each other, we'll talk about qualities we love in one another or things we love about us as a couple. Baby steps. Inching her toward the magical reveal.

Surprise! You don't just love all those things. You actually love me too.

I've never been in love with someone before, so I get how easy it is to freak out about how big this feels. She'll be ready to admit it when she's ready.

There's a knock on my apartment door, and I open it to find Posey with two pizza boxes, a six-pack of beer, and a huge smile.

"One Netflix-and-chill session at your request. Emphasis on the chill." She waggles her brows, and she slides the pizzas onto the island.

I take the beer from her hand, and I deposit it into the fridge. "What are you making me watch tonight?"

She gets a plate out of the cupboard for herself. A plate is pointless for me. I'll eat a whole pizza myself and probably steal some of hers. I give her a kiss on the temple before grabbing my box to take a seat on the couch.

She plops down beside me and snags the remote off the coffee table. Lately we've been on a *Veronica Mars* binge. Prickly, sarcastic heroine who fears love. Seems about right.

"More teen angst," I say as she clicks through to the newest episode.

"Don't pretend like you don't love it," she says.

"I might love it a little bit." She turns to look at me, and our gazes catch.

"Just a bit?"

The air grows thick around us, and I'm surprised she's the one inching us further tonight. Normally, I'm the one prodding her forward, but there's something in her brown eyes that makes me think I can take a chance. When we've danced around the L-word before, she's laughed off any tension, but she's riding it tonight. Not a single flutter of hesitation in her expression or posture. A cool sweat breaks out under my arms.

"What if I said a lot?" I watch her carefully. "Would that freak you out?"

She bites her lip. "No...because I think I might love it a lot too."

I slide the pizza box onto the coffee table, and I take her plate and set it on top. Then I thread my fingers through her hair, and I kiss her. In a minute, I'm going to take a bigger risk, but I have to get her primed first. As I lay her back into the couch cushions, I cradle her, and her hands are already tugging at my shirt.

"Babe," I murmur against her lips. "Can I tell you something?"

She scans my expression, and she grazes my cheek with her thumb. "Anything."

My heart is hammering in my chest, and I'm pretty sure I've never been so nervous in my life. "I love you."

She frames my face, and she swallows. "That's big."

"Yeah, it's—if you're not—"

"I love you too. Really, really love you. The scary kind of love."

"There's a non-scary kind of love?" I ask. "Should have ordered that one." But her words have filled me up in a way I never thought possible. Energy courses through me.

"You're the best I've ever had, in every way," she says.

I ease onto my side beside her on the couch, and I give a fist pump of victory. "Finally, you admit it without me having to tie you down."

"You didn't tie me down to get me to admit it before."

"You're right. That was just for fun." I plant a quick kiss on her lips.

She releases a deep sigh, and a tiny frisson of unease snakes down my spine. She doesn't sound like how I feel.

"Aren't you worried about what happens when this semester is over?" she asks.

Deathly afraid, but not about whether we'll work. More about what I'm willing to give up to keep her. "Lots of people do long-distance."

"It's at least six years of distance, and would you even want to live in Bellerive? I don't want to live anywhere else."

"I know where your head and heart are at. That's not a problem for me. My de facto citizenship will finally come in handy." The next part might surprise her since I didn't discuss it with her earlier. "My coach and the head coach of Bellerive's national team agreed to work together to train me. I'll be able to flip back and forth between the two programs pretty seamlessly, or so they assure me."

"I don't understand what that means?"

"It means that if you need me, I'll be able to be there. Or if I miss you, I can spend a week in Bellerive to train and hang out with you. Whatever job you have will have holidays too. Long weekends."

"You've really thought about this."

"Obsessively," I say with a chuckle. "I'm not looking forward to it, and I think it's going to be hard, but if there's anyone worth trying this with, it's you. There's no one else."

She rolls onto her side and throws one leg over my waist. "I might need a demonstration of what it'll be like when I haven't seen you for weeks. For research purposes."

"Well, if it's for science." I slide my hand along her ass and tug her tighter against me.

"Very scientific."

I feather kisses along her neck, and she arches her back into me. "Does this mean you're up for giving long-distance a try?" I ask.

"With the way I feel about you," she says, "I don't think I've got a choice. You aren't someone I can let slip away." Her lips twitch. "I'd rather you slipped somewhere else."

Abandoning the pizza, I lift her into my arms, and I carry her into my bedroom. If she wants a demonstration of the depth of love and desire I have for her, who am I to deny her?

As I lay her down on the bed and follow her down, a surge of happiness races through me. We both understand that what's between us isn't fleeting, and I can't wait to see what the future holds for us.

"Come on, big boy," Posey says with a wink. "Show me what you've got."

BRENT

Since Posey's negotiation skills are top notch, she managed to convince the interior design company to hold off her orientation and starting date until after summer was over. She and I spent the rest of her final semester at Northern and the entire summer vacation idiot proofing our relationship. As much as it's possible for any couple to be prepared for long-distance, Posey and I are. We have examined the situation from every angle. Neither of us wants this to fail.

Given that she's not prone to crying, we established that tears equal getting on a plane right away. So, two weeks after she left Northern to return to Bellerive, I'm stepping off a plane onto the airy tarmac and walking toward customs and immigration. The wind kicks up, and I shield my face from the dirt and dust swirling around me and my fellow departing passengers. My swim bag on my shoulder slips, and I hoist it back into position. In my other hand is my carry-on bag with enough clothes to last me two weeks.

She tried to play off her tears yesterday as the stress of moving and establishing a new routine, but that's not how we work. We don't go the distance by trying to tough it out alone when we don't have to. I can train in Bellerive for short stints without compromising my spot on any of the elite US teams I've been chosen for. If that means I do a lot of flying back and forth while Posey gets settled here again, then that's what I'll do. I opted to take my first semester courses for my master's program online. Flexibility is key.

I didn't tell her I was coming, and she's at work right now. My frequent flyer miles will be racked up and promptly used. Her first year with the company, her vacation is limited, and so a lot of the back and forth will fall on my shoulders. Between international swim meets, finishing my degree, and the rest of my training, the next six years aren't going to be easy. But I know she's worth every flight, every middle-of-the-night phone call, every other sacrifice that'll come my way.

In the arrivals terminal, a guy with light-brown hair and a cocky grin is standing with a huge sign with my name scrawled on it. Has to be Brice. Posey said they have a similar sense of humor, and I could envision her doing exactly this. Nothing subtle.

Last night I called Julia and asked whether she could arrange to get me into Posey's apartment on the sly. She said she'd come up with something, and it looks like the youngest Bellerive Royal is the answer.

"Brent Faulkner?" he asks when I get close. There's a man in a lightweight suit beside him. A humid breeze blows in the open doors behind them.

"You must be Prince Brice." I extend my hand.

"Just Brice," he says. "No need to stand on formalities when you're practically family. Never thought I'd see the day when Posey gave a shit about a guy. The apocalypse has to be coming." He gestures to the exit. "I've got a car. Jag here," he nods to the guy on my right, "will drive us to Posey's apartment. Julia gave me the spare key."

"Sorry to take you away from whatever you're supposed to be doing to play chauffer." I hitch my bag onto my shoulder again.

"Just finished college this spring. Giving me things to do is a bit of a low priority for the Bellerive Royal brand. Chauffer fit my mood today."

He leads the way toward the waiting car, which is parked in a slot that clearly indicates No Parking. Being above the rules must be nice.

Jag takes my bags and pops them into the trunk before Brice and I slide into the rear of the Rolls Royce.

"How long are you here for?" Brice asks as the car pulls away from the curb.

"Two weeks." I peer out the window, and I marvel at how green everything is. The airport is on the tip of the island. As the plane was descending, it felt like we'd land on the cliff. There wasn't much room for error to hit the runway.

"If there's no fog today, take West Shore Road," Brice says to Jag, and then he turns to me. "You've never been here before, right?"

"No, I haven't. My mother was born here, but we've never been back."

"Shame." He grins. "I have a feeling you'll fall in love with more than just Posey once you've been here a while. No better place in the world."

We turn onto a road that feels balanced on the edge of the cliff. It reminds me of California State Route 1—spectacular views as long as you're okay with extreme heights. That drop would be deadly.

"This is incredible." The ocean stretches out beside us, and a sports car zooms past, going far faster than I'd think safe on a road like this.

"A lot of dare devils take this road," Brice says when I turn to follow the sports car that's disappeared behind us.

We turn to the right at the edge of the cliff and go through a tunnel. As we emerge, I'm struck by the old-world feel of the town ahead of us. All the buildings are limestone, brick, stucco, or what looks like the black rocks from the cliff face.

"Welcome to Tucker's Town," Brice says. "Capital city, and named after the Tucker Family. Way, way, way back this was their farmland."

He must have missed a *way* in his description of time because it feels like I've stepped back in history. The car slows on the river rocks that take the place of the smooth asphalt.

"The whole city is like this?" I ask.

"Just the center. You can sort of tell from the architecture of each subdivision and business area when it was built. We only allow teardowns in exceptional circumstances. The exterior of a building has to remain mostly unchanged, but we allow interiors to be heavily modified. Coolest place on earth. Outside looks like the 1500s, but inside is a modern beauty."

Another reason Posey probably loves this place. The blend of history and modern interior design. Sounds like exactly the sort of challenge she'd love.

The car glides up to the outside of a four-story brick building, and Jag comes around to retrieve my bags.

"What are you doing while Posey works?" Brice asks when I open my door.

"Training," I say. "Two practices a day plus dryland."

"If you can squeeze in a lunch or dinner while you're here, send me a message." He passes me a slip of paper with his number on it along with a set of keys to Posey's fourth-floor apartment. "I'll give you the grand tour of the royal estate in between shots of Patron."

"Tequila drinker?"

"It's the truth teller." He grins.

"Thanks for the ride," I say as I slide out.

"Any time," Brice says. "Posey has a giant heart. Glad she found someone to show it to."

Jag closes the rear door behind me and stands in front of it while I pick up my bags and use one of the keys to unlock the front door. As soon as I'm inside, Jag circles the car, and the horn honks as they pull away from the curb.

As an introduction to the royal family, that was a lot more relaxed than I expected. Of course, Posey told me Brice was chill like her, but I didn't expect him to be quite so down-to-earth.

After taking the elevator, I slot the key into Posey's apartment door, and when the door swings back, it feels like I've come home. The décor is exactly like I'd expect—white and grey with some splashes of color here and there. It's the pictures on the wall that are a surprise.

Warmth spreads across my chest. There's a whole wall of artfully displayed black-and-white photos of me and Posey from the last few months. In the center is one color photo, the first one I ever took of us. We're sitting on the beach in Bermuda with pizza in our hands and grins on our faces. She is pure perfection. The thought of her putting this together causes my throat to tighten.

I swam this morning before hopping on a plane, so it's close to dinner now. She should be arriving home from work within the hour. As we drove up, I noticed a flower shop on the corner, and I drop my bags before heading back out. While I'm pretty confident I'll be enough to put a smile on her face, flowers never hurt.

I relocked Posey's front door so she wouldn't be freaking out about a break-in, and when I hear a key in the lock, I ready myself. Dinner waiting on the counter from the deli she loves down the road. Check. Freshly showered. Check. Flowers in my hand. Check.

The door swings open, but she's got her head down, rooting around in her purse. When she glances up and sees me in the center of her living room, she drops everything and lets out a shriek of surprise.

"Oh my god," she cries. "You came?" Her voice cracks on the last word, and then she bursts into tears.

Shit. Did I read this wrong?

"Babe." I set the flowers on a side table and circle the couch to draw her into my arms. She clings onto me and cries against my shirt.

"I hate how much I've missed you." The thickness in her voice is muffled by my chest.

I chuckle. "You don't have to miss me at all for the next two weeks, so there's that."

"Two weeks?" She wraps her arms around my neck and hops into my arms.

I hold her steady while I shut the front door with my foot and then press her against it, but she won't take her head out of my neck to look at me.

"Babe," I say again. "Come on. Look at me."

"You came," she whispers against my neck.

"Every time," I say against her ear. "I'll show up for you *every* time."

"How is it possible to love someone this much?" She frames my face with her hands, and her tear-stained cheeks are flushed.

"I don't know," I say. "But I'm right there with you, Posey Jensen. Nothing in the world I wouldn't do for you."

"You got me flowers?"

"I did."

"And you didn't even do anything wrong."

"Hopefully something very right by coming here." I give her a half-smile.

"Yeah," she says, and she runs her fingers through my hair. "Yeah, you nailed it."

"Bang, bang, bang, baby." I nuzzle my nose with hers, and then she's kissing me, and the familiar fullness returns. When I'm not with her, there's a noticeable absence, and I can't wait until the day when I don't have to leave her or she doesn't have to leave me. But for now, this is where we're at, and I've got no regrets.

"I have no food in the house," Posey says when we break the kiss.

"You know, food isn't the only thing I think about," I say. "But I already grabbed us dinner from the deli you like. It's on the counter."

"I'm not hungry for food right now." She runs her nails along the nape of my neck, and I shiver at the contact. "Do you think this will get easier?"

"I don't know," I admit. "Feels pretty fucking hard right now."

"Yes, yes, it does." She cocks an eyebrow and wiggles against me.

"There's my girl." I give her a quick peck. "Might not get easier, but I think we'll get used to it, if that makes sense. Like a bunch of hard swim practices. When I'm doing it, I hate it. But afterward, it feels totally worth it. Right now, here with you, *worth*—" I kiss her "—*it*."

"Do you have to train tonight?" she asks.

I shake my head. "I'll all yours until the morning. A bit of a Frankenstein schedule since I arranged everything last minute, but I'm here."

She searches my face for a beat. "I fucking love you, Faulkner."

"I love you too." I slide my hand into her hair and trail a line of kisses down her neck.

"A demonstration," she says, kissing me deeply. "In the bedroom." Her teeth graze my earlobe. "Now."

I spin us around, and Posey laughs as I stride toward the two bedrooms off the main living room. She points to the right, and when I lay her down on the white bedspread, I stare at her for a minute.

"Whatever it takes," I say. "It's you and me."

"Whatever it takes," she agrees, and then her lips twist into a naughty grin. "It's going to take an orgasm right now."

I reach for the hem of her shirt. "I'll get you a latte afterward."

"That's a good man," she murmurs.

For her, I aim to be the best man for the rest of our lives. Then her lips meet mine, and we're wrapped around each other again, just like we've always been meant to be.

Pre-order Book 2 - Nick and Julia's story - here: **https://www.amazon.com/dp/B09PKGW1P7**
Read Nat and Sebastian's story here: **https://books2read.com/u/4DRPGg**
Read my Hollywood second chance romance here: **https://books2read.com/u/bQVPx6**
Join my newsletter for bonus chapters and the most up to date series information here: **https://wendymillion.com/**

Acknowledgments

Thank you to my husband for his unending support, to my children for their patience when I'm "doing my computer work", and to my dad who loves spending time with his granddaughters. They are the biggest reasons I'm able to pursue my writing dreams, and I'm so grateful for their love and support.

Thank you to all of my first readers on Wattpad who get me through a first draft. Your enthusiasm for my writing and my characters keeps me writing there and encourages me to finish what I start.

I'm fortunate enough to be part of a few writer communities that are incredibly supportive. To my fellow Wattpad Stars, Nottpad Community, and WritersConnX members, thank you for your guidance and cheerleading throughout the writing and promotion process.

I'm also eternally grateful to those people who have consistently read and reviewed my work. In particular to Karen, Michelle, Liana, Camilla, Phyllis, and Misty who read and review with enthusiasm.

Thanks to Nancy for having another read of the story to find some special moments between Brent and Posey.

Lastly, thank you to Avery and Cole who've been my sounding boards with covers, blurbs, and the writing process. I appreciate all your help.

About W. Million

W. Million is a Watty Award winner whose contemporary romances about strong women and troubled men have captivated her loyal readers. She is the author of the romantic suspense series *The Donaghey Brothers,* the NA sports romance *Saving Us,* and the contemporary second chance romance, *When Stars Fall.*

When not writing, Wendy enjoys spending time in or around the water. She lives in Ontario, Canada with two beautiful daughters, two cute pooches, and one handsome husband (who is grateful she doesn't need two of those).

Also By

Wendy Million/W.Million

The Donaghey Brothers Series (Romantic Suspense)

Retribution

Resurrection

Redemption

Northern University Series (NA Sports Romance)

Saving Us

With Wattpad Books (Second Chance Romance)

When Stars Fall

Novella (free with newsletter signup)

First Date Challenge

Made in the USA
Columbia, SC
20 May 2023

16406867R00174